IMPETUS

IMPETUS

R. E. SCHELL

authorHOUSE®

AuthorHouse™ LLC
1663 Liberty Drive
Bloomington, IN 47403
www.authorhouse.com
Phone: 1-800-839-8640

Published by AuthorHouse 08/26/2014

ISBN: 978-1-4969-3580-9 (sc)
ISBN: 978-1-4969-3607-3 (e)

Library of Congress Control Number: 2014915478

Any people depicted in stock imagery provided by Thinkstock are models,
and such images are being used for illustrative purposes only.
Certain stock imagery © Thinkstock.

This book is printed on acid-free paper.

Because of the dynamic nature of the Internet, any web addresses or
links contained in this book may have changed since publication and
may no longer be valid. The views expressed in this work are solely those
of the author and do not necessarily reflect the views of the publisher,
and the publisher hereby disclaims any responsibility for them.

For Trinity, Bevin, and Mikayla, and
Ms. Steuben, for always caring.

ONE

It was autumn, the first weeks of September. The winds were getting colder and the mead was getting warmer, the cloaks heavier and the people tighter. In the North Empire, everything seemed to be seasonal, like events were placed on a spinning wheel and came about once in the annual cycle. When the wheel spun wrongly, it was the talk of the town. That day, there had been a tiny fluffy outside, and, though no snow had stuck to the ground, people were worried about the last of their crops freezing over. I was a barmaid in the Riverdell Inn, in the town of Wittman's Creek, a community of mostly-farmers, so I knew how anxious everyone was.

Perhaps that was why we were so busy that. As Eorlund, my friend and owner of the Inn, always insisted, people drank more when there was more to drink about. It was true. Every time there was something odd about the weather in the few months I'd been there, people crowded the tavern to drink. Eorlund Winter-Born had lived here all his life, and had run this Inn for nigh on fifty years. He knew. He always knew.

I sighed and looked down at my hands as they poured a mug of beer. The palms were red from washing dishes and carrying firewood. But they had seen worse, and a bit of pre-winter chapping wouldn't hurt them. I scanned my eyes over the scars on my hands, remembering each stroke of a blade, each fall onto stones and marble which I had braced against. The long one on the back of my left hand, from a red-hot poker. Yes, these old hands had seen much worse than dishes.

"Talia, dear," Eorlund called from the kitchen.

"What is it?" I replied, turning around and wiping my hands on my apron. He poked his head around the corner looking confused.

"Where did I put my oven gloves, Talia?" I smiled. He was always forgetting something. It came with the age I suppose. He was, after all, a few winters over seventy by now.

"They are next to the oven, Eorlund. Next to the kettle." He gave me a rumpled look.

"Now, Talia, I think I would have seen them if they were in such a place! Watch, I will look right now, and they will not be there." He turned his head towards the oven, ducking back inside the door frame. When he reappeared, he was embarrassed. "It, err... Seems to be that they are, indeed, right there." I laughed and turned back to my customers. The door opened and a blast of chilly air hit us. People grumbled and looked up at the newcomer.

He was tall, dressed all in black, with a cloak that hung over him like death and made him seem like a living shadow. His cowl covered his face, making his figure all the more eerie. Everyone in the room thought the same thing; "*Weird.*"

And I heard them, all the thoughts. Ever since I could remember, I could hear what people didn't speak, only chewed over in their heads. Every sullen remark, every dirty comment, and every passing inkling. Nothing escaped me, nothing ever had.

I had been out on the road since I was seventeen, nearly eleven years. I wandered, I taught, I did jobs for people, some of them less than legal. I had been inside the heads of thousands of people. Humans, Elves, Dwarves, and everyone in between. I dived into a brain, looked around, got what I needed, and left, all in a few seconds, and all without leaving a trace. I was the world's most efficient blackmailer, ever since

3

the age of four, when I would extort candies from neighbor children by threatening to tell their parents about broken toys and hidden pets. Really, when I thought about it, the only thing that changed in those years was the value of both the broken toy and the candy I received in return.

Of course, I didn't *just* blackmail people. It was simply a handy capability. No, mostly I dug around inside heads because it was interesting. Through harmless looking I had lived a thousand lives, done nearly everything there was in the world to do. The name my parents gave to me was Talia, and the surname I gave myself Storm-Cloud. But so many names have passed through my head that sometimes I forgot which was which.

A customer spilled his drink and swore loudly. I looked up, snapping back into reality. I noticed the stranger with the cloak had not moved from his table near the door.

"Hey mister," I called at him. "Come have a drink! This is a tavern, not a convent." Drunken guffaws erupted around me and I smiled. I saw a frown form under his dark cowl. I frowned too, wondering what made a man come into a tavern, if not to drink away his coin. I decided to try and hear what he wasn't saying. I tuned out the men around me and reached my mind out to his, looking for a way in.

"Should'a left my wife home..."

"One more drink..."

"Damn! Coin's out..."

4

Everything faded and became a faint collection of white noise. The tendrils of my mind grew out towards the stranger, getting closer and closer until...

I felt myself gasp.

Nothing.

His mind was completely blank. Or, at least made to seem that way. My mind recoiled at the barrier that blocked my path. Cool, hard to the touch, like glass on a winter's morning. The longer I touched it the more I wanted to pull away. But I refused, instead pushing and prodding, looking for a weak spot desperately. It felt like hours as I searched his mind's peculiar surface, pressing my subconscious against his until I felt woozy. I sighed dejectedly and retreated, snapping back into my own body. I had to grab the edge of the bar to steady myself. Eorlund slipped past me to give out the free bread that came with dinner.

A wariness grew in me. Never in my years had I ever encountered a man with such power over me. Every now and then there happens to be a wizard or warlock with a bit of psychic training. Those kinds of simple mind tricks are easy to break. I think of them as a wall made out of straw; there are gaps which can be slipped through if one knows where to look. But to completely block me out? Who was this stranger? I looked with a furrowed brow at the frightening being and took my leave into the kitchen.

There was still a lingering chill in my bones from his odd, freezing blockade. I shivered, feeling the heat leech from my flesh. I stood before the oven and let it warm my body. It seeped into my skin and relaxed me. My nerves settled and my mind became a little clearer. Perhaps there was nothing very odd about him after all. Maybe he was simply another magick user that was more advanced than those I'd seen before. Or, could it be that he was another telepath like me? Maybe that was what my mind looked like to him, too. Hell, there had to be more psychics than just me running about. I knew that the Elves had a bit of knowledge of physics, and just because I'd never seen one didn't mean that there were none to be seen.

Yes. That was the answer. Another telepath had wandered into the Riverdell Inn by chance. With my head clearer on my shoulders I stepped back out into the dining room, further convincing myself that this was the case. Still, I thought, he frightened me. Something about him told me he was no good. I scolded myself and looked back at the place he was sitting.

But he wasn't there anymore.

My stomach did a flip and I frantically looked around for him. I nearly vomited as I saw him placing a few coins into Eurrie's hand and going upstairs. I took Eorlund by the arm and led him to a deserted corner.

"Eurrie," I whispered frantically, "who is that man?"

"Oh the quiet one who just rented room eight? He said he's from the capital. Name's... Jorgen, I think." I twisted my apron in my hands.

"Eurrie, we can't let him stay here."

"Talia," he began sternly, "you'd best have a good reason to turn away a paying customer."

"He scares me, Eorlund. I can't hear him. There's... There's a *wall*, of sorts. It's wrapped around his mind so I can't hear him." Now he looked a bit worried.

"That's impossible," he murmured. "You hear everything. How can someone keep you out?"

"I've never seen it before, Eurrie. Maybe he's like me. But I don't need to hear him to be able to tell you that he's no good. Please, Eorlund. Don't let him stay."

"Well, if he has the same gift as you, he's damn good at hiding it. I... I suppose that I'll speak to him." Eurrie patted me on the arm and gave a half-hearted smile.

"Please be careful," I said. "He could be dangerous."

"I'll be okay, Talia." He touched my shoulder and kissed my forehead. "Hold down the fort, would you?" He winked through the nerves and left to go after the strange man. I waited at the bar, nervously tapping my nails on the wooden surface. I couldn't hear the thoughts from upstairs, they were just out of range. It felt like I was going to crazy as I waited for Eorlund to come back. I only grew more nervous as the minutes ticked by. Someone asked for a drink and I absentmindedly tipped the pitcher of mead into his flagon.

There was a sudden scream from the upstairs. My stomach lurched, and, before I could think, the pitcher had clattered onto the floor, spilling the mead everywhere, and I was already halfway up the stairs. I tore down the hall and flung open the only closed door I found. Inside I found Eorlund lying on the floor in a pool of blood, a knife lying next to him and blood gushing from a hole in his stomach. He was sputtering and gasping for breath, and his wound spurted more blood every time his heart would beat.

"Call the doctor!" I shrieked, nearly falling as I made my way over to him. I knelt beside him and tore a strip off my dress to press it on the wound, holding with one hand and ripping more and more strips of cloth off of my dress. One by one all of the cloths turned to blood in my hands. Eorlund was gasping and trying to talk to me.

"No, please Eorlund, you mustn't speak," I scolded, hands and voice shaking. "Don't talk, you'll be okay! You'll be okay. Okay. Okay." I murmured my mantra over and over, ripping and pressing and soaking up more and more of his blood.

Finally the doctor rushed into the room, carrying a leather case. He shoved me out of the way and started to try to stop the bleeding, using a more proper set of sterilized rags. I crawled to a corner and sat there numbly, watching the man press more sterile cloth into the wound. His name came to me; Hjond. Hjond Raskun.

My mind seemed to be going three dozen directions at once. I couldn't tell if what I was seeing was real. My chest hurt and my head spun around faster than I could keep up. I looked at my bloody hands, my bloody skirt, my bloody knees, and I cried.

TWO

The next few hours passed as nothing more than a blur. I remembered pieces of the time in the days that passed after the attack, but nothing more than flashes, and none of it made sense. The next clear moment I had was being next to Eorlund, and seeing him lying in his bed with a corset of bandages around his abdomen. I was sitting in a chair next to him with a small glass bottle in my hand. There was a note from Hjond on the nightstand instructing me when to administer the medicine in the bottle I clutched.

People came to visit me, brought food for me, and offered their sympathy. The guards were saying that the attacker *must* have fled out the window in the seconds it took me to get there. Or, perhaps, said a few people, he'd slipped out the back exit while everyone was rushing around. I didn't care much for theories, myself. All I knew was that my friend was mortally wounded, and hadn't been able to speak yet. He laid silently, save for occasional groans and whimpers. I gave him his medicine diligently, even attempting to learn a healing spell. It failed, though, and nothing changed. Days passed and he grew paler, and his wound began to fester with putrid infection.

Hjond came back four days after the incident and declared that the blade must have been poisoned, and that the infection had spread to the blood. He told me sadly, with a stony face, that Eurrie was going to die.

"Please, Hjond," I pleaded. "There must be a way to save him. We... We'll go to the temple up north in Silmen, and get the wound blessed. The priests will save him!" He shook his head wearily.

"You know as well as I that he will not make the journey, Talia." I did know, but I refused to believe.

"I cannot sit here and watch him die, Hjond! It's only thirty miles to the temple; we can get a wagon, fill it with straw, pillows... Please, Hjond. I've saved my wages for two months!" I knew I was getting hysterical, but I couldn't calm myself down. My eyes were filling with tears, my heart was pounding, and my hands shook.

"Talia." Hjond took me by the shoulders and looked into my eyes. "We can't do anything now except make sure he isn't in pain. The poison is pumping through him as we speak. I'm sorry, lass. He's gone."

I fell to my knees at his bedside and cried. Hjond thought of pity for me and my sorrow. I cried harder.

Two days later, Eorlund died. The official cause on his death certificate was written as complications from the stab wound. It was six days after the stranger had come. After the burial, I sat in the kitchen of the Riverdell Inn, surrounded by baskets of cookies, trays of bread and cakes, wheels of cheese, and a few meat pies. I sat with my hair curled (by the neighbor, in hopes it would cheer me up), my makeup done (by the herbalist down the road), and new clothes (a gift from the tailor). I put food into my mouth absentmindedly, barely caring what it was, and wondered what in hell I was going to do. There was a knock at the door.

"Yes?" I called hoarsely. Hjond's face appeared in the doorway.

"How do you feel, lass?" he asked softly, pulling a chair in with him and sitting across from me. I forced a small smile.

"I'm... All right," I sighed. "Food helps. So does this," I raised a bottle of a curiously-spiced distillate from a company called Ash Barrel Brewers. The local trader had snuck me the bottle during the wake. Hjond shook his head.

"Poor lass," he thought, *"I won't feel right if I leave her alone."*

I popped out the cork and looked around for a glass. I couldn't see one, so I shrugged and tipped it down my throat. The burn felt good, and after the fire it tasted like honey and all-spice and molasses.

"Be careful with that stuff, lass. Strong as all hell. Knocked me on my ass two decades or so back, right after I got my license from the Physician's College. A few friends of mine bought a bottle or two and we all woke up a day and a half later in a completely different province with the Smajen guards on our asses and a goat that didn't belong to any of us."

"That's why you're here, Hjond," I said, chuckling. "To make sure I don't steal any goats." I took another drink. He smiled softly.

"Talia," he began, "Eorlund left you the inn in his will, you know... And I hate to ask at a time like this, but only the Divines know what time will be a good one... So, what will you do with the Inn now? Will you stay here, in Wittman's Creek?" I sighed.

"I don't know, Hjond. I'm not exactly the type to settle down."

"Ahh, I understand, lass... I heard the Meadery is looking for another inn to expand their franchise." He didn't have to say which one. He meant the Gold-Flower

13

Meadery. Three brothers bearing the same surname ran it out of Silmen, the capital city of Adaima, to the north. They'd already made deals with two innkeepers to take over their businesses, and were apparently looking to spread their wings even more.

"I might sell to them," I conceded. Hjond imagined a Gold-Flower Inn in the middle of town, and thought about the money it would bring to the town. He decided it would be good business, but then thought about the injuries that it would bring to him, and made the smallest bit of a frown. Burns from the hot mead, broken limbs from falling off ladders, honey bee stings. He sighed. I took another drink, and sucked in a breath through my teeth when it went down.

"Didn't think you could drink like that, lass," Hjond commented.

"Please," I huffed. "You think I traveled around the entire continent without some drinking contests? I've out-drunk Dwarves, Nords, Elves and giants alike."

"You've drank with a giant?" he asked, astonished.

"You bet. His name was Skaldjur, and his tribe was roaming The Neck while I was on my way to Highland two summers ago. I stumbled across their camp and offered them half of a deer I had shot earlier that day. Long story short, I'm now a *Glukshul* to their tribe."

"What in hell is *that*?"

"It means 'wise one' in the giants' tongue. Well, that's the closest it gets in translation. It really means 'one who is worthy to tell the word,' or something like that. It's kind of like an elder in their tribe, one they can come to for advice and wisdom."

"So... You're a wise woman to a tribe of giants?"

"Yup." Hjond just shook his head.

"I thought, being a doctor, I'd heard everything. That was, until I met you, lass." I was struck with a sudden sadness. Eorlund used to say that, too, when we'd stay up until the wee hours of the morning and I would drink and tell him about the things I'd done and places I'd gone. I took a long drink to fight the tears.

"I guess you have more adventures to go and have, though," he said quietly.

"I suppose. I might... Do some errands first," I said, flashes of blood running through my head. Hjond furrowed his brow.

"If you think I'm going to let you go after that treacherous bastard alone --"

"It's not like that Hjond," I said, even though it was exactly like that. "He must be found. He was... A lot different than anyone else I've ever seen in my travels. Too odd to be left alone."

"Well anyone who murders an innkeeper is odd in my book," he replied vehemently. I ignored him.

"There was something that unnerved me about him when I first laid eyes on him. I need to know. I need peace."

"I understand, lass. But shouldn't the province guards handle this?"

"Hjond, you know as well as I do that the province guards are as useless as a three-legged pack horse. Remember when someone stole your good marble mortar and pestle? It took them a week to think of looking in the trader's store. You're both lucky it was still there!" He sighed.

"You're right. At least... At least let me help you get ready to leave. Clean up the inn, pack your things, settle the deal with the Meadery?"

"Of course. Thank you, Hjond." He smiled and the answer in his head was good enough for me. I stood and staggered a little bit, then made my way up the stairs to my room. Hjond was behind me making sure I didn't fall. I plopped into the chair in the corner, bottle in hand and now almost half empty. My head had been buzzing for a while, and I took another drink. The room was swimming soon, but it didn't bother me much.

"Can... Can you get the... the bags out?" I slurred, pointing under the bed. He did, placing my three saddle bags on the bed. More drink and I motioned to the dresser when he asked where my things were. He packed my clothes neatly into one bag. I just kept drinking. Hjond wondered if I was going to pass out, and suddenly I was very sad again. I started to cry, plunging my bedroom further into blurriness. I missed Eorlund so much. In the six months I'd been in town, I'd grown so close to him, and he'd taught me so much. He showed me how to do finance and how to bake, how to make a bed properly, how to run an inn. I'd never stayed in one place for so long, with so many friends. I'd gotten to know all the villagers and shopkeepers in Wittman's Creek, and my heart was shattered. I knew I couldn't remain here. Too many memories, even for me.

Hjond moved my things to the floor, took the bottle from my hands, scooped me up in his arms, and carried me to my bed. He tucked the blanket over me and dug around in the satchel he always wore across his barrel chest. He pulled out a small vial and handed it to me. I carelessly poured its contents down my throat. Almost immediately, a deep sleepiness overcame me, and I closed my tear-soaked eyes.

THREE

The next day I woke up with a pounding headache. I moaned in pain as the sunlight struck my eyes and sent a stinging pain through my skull. I pulled the blanket over my eyes and suddenly felt nauseous. I laid very still and hoped it would pass. When it did, I gathered my strength and sat up. I felt hardened streaks of kohl on my cheeks, having ran because I had been crying. There was a note on the dresser reminding me that he'd given me a sleeping draught, in case I couldn't remember, and that there were some things in the night table drawer for my headache. It also said he'd packed my bags for me -- one full of clothing, one full of food, and one with a frying pan, a water skin, my "feminine things" (as he put it), rope, a few iron bars, a hammer, a blanket, and both my sewing and fishing kits inside.

I smiled at the thought of him. Hjond Raskun thought of everything. I opened the drawer and found a bottle of something dark red and foul smelling. The label instructed me to drink it and allow a quarter of an hour for it to work. I held my nose and chugged the rancid stuff, trying not to gag, and then laid back on the bed and waited, marveling at the wonders of medicine. When the draught kicked in, the pain melted and I was able to fully take stock of my room.

My bags were piled neatly in the corner of the room by the door. On the dresser were my bedroll and my travel clothes. Still foggy, I started to straighten my skirt before realized I couldn't ride a horse very well in a dress, and made a resolution to take a bath and change. I dragged the washtub out of the closet and then went downstairs to get the water heating. An hour of heating and pouring later, I had a hot bath. My dress fell to the floor and I rubbed the cold bumps on my skin. I ran a hand over my chest and stomach to keep from shivering in the unusually-brisk morning. Quickly I dipped myself into the tub, sighing as I submerged.

I wet my hair and ran my fingers through its golden length. The curls from yesterday had long since tumbled out and replaced themselves with the sighs of waves. I picked up a jar of scented oil that I'd gotten out of my bag (filed under "feminine things" by Hjond), uncapped it, and poured a little bit into the water. The soft, sweet, almost-cloying scent of rose petals wafted through the air. I relaxed for the first time in several days. Apparently I nodded off for a bit, because the water was lukewarm when I opened my eyes again. I yawned and dipped my air-hardened tresses into the water, rinsing out the grime and oils that hair likes to collect. I groped for my towel and wrapped it around my hair, rubbing furiously to dry it. Then I stood and wrapped the same towel around my body. I then laid the towel down on the floor and stepped onto it, standing nude in the middle of my room.

I looked in the polished-metal mirror and observed myself. I ran my hands over the light pink marks on my hips, breasts, and inner thighs, marking where I had grown quickly as a teenager. My hair flowed over my chest and grazed my navel lightly, but I braided it and threw it over my shoulder. I stretched my back and shoulders, watching the corded muscle of my arms and upper back flex. That's what using a bow does to you, I mused. I realized I should get dressed, and looked at my armor sitting on the dresser. I sighed. Having to put clothes on after being so wonderfully naked was always such a killjoy.

I wrapped my chest in a linen cloth, put on my tight-sleeved tunic, and my tight-fitting, dark green tights.

Then I strapped on my armor. The chest-plate was made of leather and steel, and had chain mail attached to protect my neck and shoulders. I strapped on my pauldron for my right shoulder, the one I didn't have to see over when shooting my bow, and my bracers, then heavy woolen socks that came to my knee. Finally I laced up my soft, cured-leather boots, which came about an inch under my sock and had a protective knee-plate attached.

Then I added the finishing touch. I strapped my quiver to my back, stuffed full of arrows of mixed origins, then added my prized possession -- a beautiful, gleaming Elven bow. That bow meant more to me than anything in the world, and I went to extreme lengths to make sure it was never damaged in battle. I strapped a belt around my hips, added two daggers, one on a strap around my left thigh and one in my left shoe, and then pulled on my worn black cloak. It fell to my ankle, so it didn't drag on the ground, but still protected my entire body from any sort of weather. I took one last look at myself, then picked up my bags and left the room.

When I walked into the main room of the inn, I was surprised to see Hjond, Leila the herbalist, and Alvir the tailor sitting at the bar waiting for me.

"What are you three doing here?" I asked, setting my bags down on the bar. Hjond smiled.

"We thought we could offer you our services one last time before you left," he said. I tried to protest, citing

21

how much they'd done for me already, but they wouldn't have it.

"We're not taking no for an answer, lass," said Alvir in his reedy, accented voice. I was trying quite hard to ignore the images of gifts they were giving me. If I couldn't tell them no, I at least wanted to be surprised.

"You've been good to us, good to the town, and we cannot let you leave without some things to remember us by," Leila added. As if I could forget. I fought back a sigh.

"All right," I said. "I suppose I won't be able to get out of this, huh?" They smiled at me, and Hjond and Leila looked at Alvir, telling him with their eyes to go first. He pulled out a package wrapped in paper and handed it to me. I unwrapped it and found a tunic with slim sleeves, just like the one I was wearing, but newer, and made of cotton instead of wool.

"Hjond said you favored the tight sleeves, since you use a bow," Alvir explained. "I figured you might need a new one."

"Thank you, Alvir. They're lovely," I said sincerely. I kissed him on the cheek and he turned pink.

"Welcome, Miss Talia," he said shyly. Leila was next. She pulled out a bottle of dark-colored liquid.

"Hjond said you were going after that maniac, so I made you something."

"By the Five, Hjond, does everyone know where I'm going?" I exclaimed. Hjond flushed.

"Not everyone." I raised an eyebrow as a list of names and faces flooded my head.

"In any event," interjected Leila, "it's made of something called Doll's Eye. Nasty stuff, makes your heart lock up and stop. You can dip your arrows or your blades in it, put it in food. Anything you want, dear," she said cheerily.

"Thank you, Leila, I'm sure it'll come in handy eventually." I put it in my miscellaneous bag and kissed her on the cheek, too. Hjond cleared his throat and pulled out a leather sheath with a dagger in it. I took it from him and pulled out the blade carefully, mindful not to cut myself with it, because once a blade has tasted one's blood, it will always find a way to taste it again. I sucked in a breath as I looked at the blade. It was polished steel, smooth and hard, carved with ancient Nordic symbols on the flat sides.

"Hjond, you shouldn't have," I murmured.

"It was my grandfather's," he said. "He fought in the White War. For eight years he fought with nothing but that dagger and a bow. He was an archer in the White Hand, the elite group that fought in the battles where the future-Emperor was present. I thought, since I haven't touched it in years, and my wife is always telling me to sell the old thing, it would be of better use to you than some stranger." I removed the dagger from my belt and put it in my bags, then strapped on the new one on in its place.

"Thank you. Thank all of you. You've shown me such kindness, I..." I started to tear up. Leila hugged me tight to her.

"Oh, you're welcome, dear," she said just as tearfully. "Now, I promised myself I wouldn't say anything, but I feel like I have to. Since Eorlund's wife passed -- and that was thirteen winters past, mind you -- he'd been so sad. Sometimes he'd turn to drinking, and someone would have to help him run the Inn for a bit. But then you came, and you were like a breath of fresh air for him. You made him so happy. Happiest anyone had seen him since his dear Elfrid passed. So, for making our friend feel good in what ended up being his twilight days, we have to thank you." I smiled sadly, letting a few tears fall. Eorlund never mentioned his wife, but sometimes, late at night, when he thought I was asleep, he would think about her, and I could hear him crying.

"I'll carry these things in his memory," I vowed. "And that monster who took him from me -- from all of us -- will soon know the fury and the sorrow we feel." They all nodded solemnly. I kissed each of their cheeks one more time, picked up my things, and made my way to the door.

"You'll see me again," I said, and then walked out of the inn with a newfound fire in my heart.

FOUR

My horse, a grey mare named Rosemary, was already saddled, probably the work of Hjond. She was a good horse, quiet and easy-going unless something was seriously wrong. I'd won her in a game of darts almost seven years prior, when she was just two years old. Since then, we'd been inseparable.

I strapped my bags onto her saddle, untied her ropes from the side of the stable, and lead her out into the open. I patted her muzzle and smiled into her deep chocolate eyes. I couldn't hear the thoughts of animals, something I'd known since I was small and tried to talk to the garden rabbits. It was nice, in a way, to have a bit of silence every once in a while, and to know at least my horse could surprise me. She lipped at my hand and I chuckled. I kissed her right in the middle of her long face and pulled over a stool to help me mount her. I swung my leg over her back and settled into the saddle easily. She huffed excitedly. I smiled.

"You know we're going somewhere different, huh, Rosemary?" She whinnied. I laughed and nudged her with my heel. She walked out onto the main road and I faced her to the north. Together we took off at a canter, increasing to a gallop at the edge of town. People and houses became smaller and thoughts became dimmer until both were gone. Countryside appeared around me, with the autumnal colors of trees decorating the road. Working in one place was all right, but I was made to do this. I didn't need anything else. To be free in such a wide, beautiful world was enough for me.

After about a mile, Rosemary slowed on her own and we cantered. We were headed towards Silmen, the capital. I had spent a good bit of time there before I travelled to Wittman's Creek, and I had contacts there who I had been meticulous about staying in touch with. They held positions where they could observe things and tell me about what happened inside the city. One of them owned a tavern, and I knew that if the man who killed Eorlund had passed through Silmen, she would know about it.

It was, in my opinion, a rule that only two types of people knew a city as it really was -- those who serve the alcohol, and those who watch the drunks. Those people were sometimes, but not always, one in the same.

It had been a while since I'd ridden Rosemary on a long trip, so I took it easy on her, and we went slower than usual. As the day grew too dark to travel, I dismounted my horse and lead her to a little clearing about twenty feet off of the road. It was surrounded by shade-bearing trees, and had enough low-lying foliage that one couldn't see very much from the road. I looked around. There was a small stream that ran on the eastern side of the clearing, babbling and singing in the quiet evening. Rosemary trotted over to it and took a long drink. I rolled out my bedroll on a patch of soft grass under a tall oak tree, looking up at the sky when I finished. The pinks, purples, and oranges of the setting sun reminded me of the blue and green lights that danced above the Imperial City of Highland, nearly a thousand miles to the northwest. Huge, spiraling, twirling lights, spinning like a ballet of snakes in the night sky.

Eventually, the colors faded and I built a small fire in the middle of the clearing using some dried twigs and leaves from the ground. This was, after all, the season of turning leaves, so there was an abundance of kindling. I ate some of the salted meat Hjond had packed me and wrapped myself in my cloak to watch the fire crackle and spark. I listened to the sound of the night birds, leaning back against the tree under which I'd made my camp. The sparrow song, the muffled breathing of a dozing horse, the bull frog banter, and the smell of burning wood all intoxicated me, and I began to close my eyes. I was slipping into subconsciousness when all of the sudden...

SNAP!

A twig crunched under someone's foot. My eyes shot open and I froze, and the hand that had already been near my hip was fingering the handle of Hjond's dagger in my thigh strap. I didn't hear any thoughts, but since the murderer came, I couldn't rely on that to mean an absence of danger. Rosemary had apparently heard the noise too, because she hoofed the ground and whinnied nervously.

SNAP!

The noise wasn't as distant this time. My breathing grew more ragged, adrenaline pumping through my veins. My muscles tensed like a cat's as it is about to pounce on a fly. Rosemary shuffled, getting anxious. I bit my lip, squeezing the handle of the dagger. I tried to stay still, even though my heart felt like it was about to leap from my chest.

CRACK!

Gods, it was coming even closer. I struggled to remain quiet. Crashes and cracks kept coming, eventually becoming so close I could hear the sounds of rapid, hysterical gasping coming along with them. Now I knew the thing was human, and I could tell by the pitch of the voice that it was a female. I heard the frantic, shaky breaths as she stepped into the clearing. Rosemary huffed and shuffled her feet, and I dared to peek beyond my hood.

She was thin, almost skeletally so. Her dress hung off of her body like a ragged curtain and her dark hair was matted terribly. Her inky body seemed to shimmer with beads of sweat, or maybe something more sinister. She was trying with fumbling, shaking hands to unlatch my saddlebags. I hoped she was looking for food and not a weapon, but Gods knew if that was the case. I slowly stood up, making no noise that would overpower her own stammering and sobbing. I snuck up behind her, pulling out my dagger very slowly. When I got within arm's length, I quickly wrapped my hand around her mouth and pulled her close, putting the dagger at her neck. She screamed through my hand, chest heaving with fright, and I could feel tears falling on my skin. No matter how hard I tried, I couldn't hear her thoughts.

"Who are you and what are you doing here?" I asked quietly, moving my hand away from her mouth so she could answer.

"P-Please help me," she whimpered. "Th-They're after me, they'll kill me!" I loosened my grip on her.

"Who is after you?"

"The Blackhawks! Pl-please, they're going to kill me," she repeated, sobbing. The terror in her voice was enough for me. I removed my dagger from her neck and sheathed it. She turned and faced me, but refused to make eye contact. I could see now that her dress was splattered in blood.

"Where are they?" I demanded.

"I-I don't know, I... I ran so long..."

"Do you know where you are?" She shook her head. I thought for a minute, then stomped out my fire and packed my bedroll onto Rosemary. The girl just stood there, sobbing and clutching herself. I mounted my horse and pulled the girl up onto the saddle behind me. She buried her face into my cloak and I urged Rosemary onto the main road. Once we were there, I pressed my heels into her sides, let out a yell, and we galloped off into the darkness, towards Silmen and towards safety.

We reached the city in the wee hours of the morning, when the stars were just starting to fade, and the faintest hint of grey lurked on the horizon. The girl had fallen asleep on me and I still couldn't hear her. I found the first inn I could find that would let me check in before dawn, and got us a room. I carried the girl upstairs and laid her down on the mattress. She didn't wake up through the motion, just snored softly and moaned a little as I laid her down. I sat in a chair in the corner, observing my new companion.

I finally could get a good look at her face, and in this new light I could now tell she was an Emïlan, someone of mixed Elven and human decent. She had slightly pointed ears, high cheekbones and nicely arched eyebrows, all characteristic of Elves. But her mouth was full and her hair was a dark brown and looked curly in the way of the human natives of Middle Vale, a dry, arid place home to the nomadic tribes. Her nose was flat and slightly wide, with a splattering of freckles across the bridge and along her cheeks. Her skin was a rich, earthy brown, similar to cocoa powder. I watched the rise and fall of her ribs, wondering who she was and how she'd found her way to the clearing. I also pondered how she could be so terribly thin and still have run so far through a forest in the dead of night.

I knew some people were naturally thin, that was simply a fact of nature. But this girl had been deprived of food for months. I could count her vertebrae and her ribs, see the hipbones through her thin dress. Her hands looked as though there was only a layer of skin between the air and the bone. Even her neck looked thin. Were the mysterious Blackhawks responsible for starving her? Why couldn't I hear her? Did she have any connection to the man who killed Eorlund? Questions spun in my head, but

I knew she was nearly dead from exhaustion, so I stewed in my thoughts until she woke up.

Around ten or eleven in the morning, she began to whine and toss in her sleep. She was dreaming of something. A nightmare, actually, based on the furrowing of her brow and the tear that leaked from her tightened eye.

"No..." she moaned quietly. She turned over, like she was avoiding someone's touch, then stopped suddenly and yelped. Then, quick as a bolt of lightning, she sat up with wide, fearful eyes. I jumped in surprise, almost falling from my chair, and she looked around with a panicked look as though she couldn't remember where she was. Then she saw me and her face softened into one of ashamed shyness. She flushed and pulled her knees to her chin.

"Are you okay?" I asked cautiously. She nodded. "Can I sit closer?" She nodded again, this time a bit hesitantly. I pulled the chair over closer to the bed but was careful not to touch her. "Can you tell me your name?" There was a pause.

"Reida," she croaked. I smiled softly, then offered her my waterskin.

"Small sips, all right? Don't want to shock your stomach." She sipped. "I saw you're an Emïlan," I offered. Reida nodded a bit, and sipped again. "I'm Talia, Nord. From The Basin."

"My mother was an Elf," she said, seeming to be a few seconds behind me. She had a slight Elvish accent. She spoke like a river, her words flowing and ebbing with the tide of the sentence.

"How did you end up in Adaima?" There was a pause.

"I was... just travelling. I heard the Head Counselor of Adaima was looking for a court alchemist. I'm... I'm good at brewing potions... I was hoping to get the job, to get a good spot in the court. But then... the Blackhawks came," she said, choking back tears. She took a few breaths and then continued, still teary-eyed. "They found me in a tavern in a town in the south of Adaima, they wore dark cloaks and didn't say much. I kept wondering... Why I couldn't hear them, but I didn't know what to think of it.

"And... and they put something in my drink... I didn't even see them do it... And it made me trust them, and I don't remember how I got to the cave, but I woke up and I was in a cave. I woke up and I knew, I *knew*, they hurt me... and I could still feel it..." she was sobbing now. "And I was there for so long. They left my cage unlocked after they'd... And I got out and ran. I ran." She collapsed in on herself, crying and shaking.

Unconsciously, I opened my arms to her. She looked at me like I had offended her, but she broke down and moved into them, hiding herself in my chest. I closed my arms around her and held her to me. I stroked her back and held her to me, a mixture of disbelief and heartbreak filling my insides. If there was any doubt about staying and protecting Reida, it was gone now. I felt hot anger seep into me, as well, lighting my very bones ablaze in the inferno. The tiny, broken sobs from the girl in my arms sealed the deal.

This wasn't just about Eorlund anymore.

FIVE

Reida had fallen asleep in my arms, so I tucked her in and left her a note saying that I was coming back with some food for her when I was done talking with some friends of mine. "Make sure you drink small sips of water while I'm gone," I wrote. "I'm bringing juice and soup, to build back your strength."

I left the inn and walked to the library. It wasn't a long trip, and the building was hard to miss. The Silmen Athenaeum was a large, glittering marble tower in the middle of the city with tall gold-trimmed windows and a large gold-plated door. It was older than the Empire was, having stood in that spot for centuries, while the Empire was only eighty-five years old. It had been the center of learning in Adaima for as long as it stood, and people made long journeys to read rare books stored there. I'd heard that some of the rarest books -- those with only one or two copies left -- had a waiting list of those who wanted to read them, and it could only be done on the Athenaeum's property, with permission from the librarian. You were searched when you walked in and when you walked out, to prevent smuggling of destructive substances and the theft of books.

I walked inside and was stopped by two men. They searched me and asked my business. I told them the truth; that I was there to speak to the librarian. They eyed me curiously, but allowed me to enter. I walked up the narrow spiral staircase that ran all the way up the middle of the tower. It took me quite some time to reach the top, and when I got there my thighs were burning. It was fifteen storeys up, taller than even the Grand Palace in Highland, and was the second-tallest building on the entire continent. I took a moment to breathe, then turned to face the large golden door that separated me from the librarian. I knocked on the door.

"Go away, I'm busy!" came a voice from the other side of the door.

"Can't you make time for an old friend, Azark?" I asked, smiling to myself.

"Talia? Is that you, dear? Hold on, let me get the door." I heard locks and bolts sliding and clicking, then the door swung inwards. The wrinkled, brown face of my friend Azark-El Manot from Middle Vale appeared in the door. He smiled and opened his arms to me. I hugged him and he kissed both my cheeks.

"Talia! So good to see you," he said. "It has been far too long!"

"It has," I agreed. "Sorry that I didn't write to tell you I was coming. It was short notice, and I would have beaten the letter here. Something came up. I hoped you wouldn't mind doing a bit of digging for me."

"Of course, Talia," he said, turning so I could come into his chambers. I walked inside. "What seems to be the trouble?" Azark shut the door behind me.

"It would be easier to show you, friend." He nodded and sat in the chair in front of his writing desk. He motioned for me to do the same, and I obliged. "Ready?" He nodded.

I closed my eyes and reached my mind out to his. He was used to this, for we had traded information many a time before this. I touched his mind and he did not squirm. I sent him copies of every memory I had since Eorlund died. It flashed before his eyes quickly, like the blur of wheel spokes turning -- one can tell what they are looking at, but explicit details are not seen. The Riverdell Inn, the man, Eurrie on the floor, the death, then we skipped to the part where Reida ran into the clearing, and finished with the moment I left to come here. When the show was over I retreated back into my own mind and we opened our eyes. Azark was stone-faced.

"I see what you need me to do," he said grimly. "And I will tell you want I know." His thoughts flashed violence.

"You seem as if you have seen mention of these people before, Azark."

"It's because I have." He sighed and his face seemed to age before my eyes. "I am old, Talia. I'm nearing my eightieth year. I have seen much of this world, good and bad times. The Blackhawks hold a place in the bad times. They have plagued us for many generations. They change their purpose every so often, and at first they held a noble cause. The Blackhawks were, at their beginning, an organization for the extermination of black magick. Necromancy and the like, that is. Then they became vampire hunters, and then they hunted those who created potions they thought were unnatural -- love potions, elixirs of life and such. And every time they switched focuses, it was for another abomination. Or, I should say, things they believed to be abominations. They were quite *violent* in their methods of business, as well.

"Then, about twenty-five years ago, they vanished. There were no reports of activity, no sightings, no murders or kidnappings. Their stronghold was abandoned, and there were no records inside of it detailing where they'd gone. It was as though everyone had just stopped what they were doing and left. Food was left cooking, pens were set down in the middle of a word. Prisoners, poor souls, were left chained to the walls, wailing and crying for someone to hear them. Every single Blackhawk was gone."

"But they're back now. Why?" I asked, rubbing my temples. "What are they hunting this time? And why have I never heard of them, if they have been around for hundreds of years?"

"You were only two when they disappeared, Talia, and for generations it has been thought to be a sort of bad luck to speak of them aloud. As for the timing of their return, I haven't a clue. They've always been a secretive bunch, only revealing their motives when it was good business. As for who they've decided to target this time, I'm afraid there is only one answer. You."

My heart sank.

"And, by 'you'... You mean everyone like me, right? And, like Reida?" He nodded. "So, they're after an entire group of telepaths with no number that we know for sure? To torture and kill!?" He had no reply, but his thoughts confirmed. I stood and kicked over my chair, anger clouding my vision.

"Talia," Azark began.

"How am I supposed to fight this?" I yelled. "There could be hundreds of people out there about to be kidnapped! Reida's barely alive, it will take weeks to get her into fighting condition. If she even *wants* to fight!" I was almost spitting with fury.

"Talia. Listen to me, friend. People will die; it is a truth of life. But it is up to you to decide *who* will die. The Blackhawks, or you and Reida?" I sucked in a breath and I was calmed. I picked up my chair and set it right on the floor, then went over and hugged Azark. I kissed him on the head and started for the door. Before I opened it, I turned around and looked back at my friend. His kind eyes looked worried. I bowed my head and turned the handle of the door.

"I choose the Blackhawks." I walked out and down the spiral stairs.

SIX

I left the tower having been cleared once more by the guards. The sun was just leaving its peak position in the sky. It must have been about one in the afternoon. I headed towards a different location, and a different contact. Well, more than a contact. She lived and worked at The Silver Flagon, the most popular inn in town. Travelers made up most of her clientele, so she learned a lot about who was in town and why. Gossip passed through that tavern like mead through a Nord, and she never missed a beat. She was the cause of my rule about who knows the city, because she both served the alcohol and watched the drunks, and she knew everything about everyone.

It took me an hour to reach my destination, but only because the market place was in full swing, and people were packed into the streets like fish in barrels. I ducked into the inn and threw back my hood. My contact, a Nord woman named Majka, was sweeping the floor in front of the bar. I took a moment to look at her before she saw me.

Majka was just a handful of years older than me, maybe thirty-five or thirty-six. Her hair was red-brown and straight as a pin. She wore the sides pulled back from her face but still hanging down her back, showing off her bright face. She had the faintest traces of laugh lines like parentheses about her mouth, but no worry-lines, because she hadn't many worries. Her dress was very nicely cut, drawing attention to her full chest and slim hips, just as she liked it. She looked up and saw me, then smiled warmly and set down the broom. Majka wiped her hands on her dress and leaned on the bar.

"Well, well," she cooed in her heavy accent. "If it isn't my little songbird." I smiled and walked over to her.

"Hello, Majka. Nice to see you again."

"Oh, don't bore me with pleasantries, Talia. Come here and kiss me." In a heartbeat I was in her arms. She kissed me hard on the mouth and I tasted wine on her lips. I pulled my head back a bit and smiled. "I've missed you these months, my songbird."

"As I you, my phoenix." She kissed me again and then took my hand and led me to her room. With deft hands she threw off my cloak and unfastened my armor. With Majka, it was always sex first and business later. Not that I minded. She set my things down on the floor and then pulled off my shirt. I unlaced my boots as she sat down on her mattress, unpinning her hair and giving me a look that said 'hurry.'

I pressed her down on her stomach and started to undo the lacing on her dress. I slipped it off gently and kissed her shoulder. She made a throaty purring noise and her thoughts were full of ecstasy. I nipped at her neck and she giggled like a young girl. My hands trailed through her hair and over her soft skin, smelling the soft scent of her perfume and tasting the excitement she expelled, I smiled to myself and thought back to all the times before that she had been more than a contact.

Sometime later we were lying next to each other with our hands and legs intertwined, her chest on my back. Majka was running her hands through my hair, which she had unbraided at some point, and planting the occasional peck on the back of my neck.

"So, songbird," she murmured, "what brings you to my inn?"

"Besides this?" I teased. She chuckled and buried her face into the crook of my neck, biting softly. I shivered and my legs twitched on their own accord. "I need information about the Blackhawks." I could feel Majka's heart flutter.

"Whoever told you about them?" she asked.

"I sort of... found of on my own." She ran a hand over the curve that lead to my hip and bit her lip, thinking of how to answer me.

"Well. No proclaimed Blackhawks have been through here since my father owned the place. I was only ten or eleven then, but I remember the terror on my parents' faces when he walked in. Although... There was an odd man about a month or so ago who came through and asked if anyone had seen a woman who looked like you. He called himself Jorgen, but that was a name faker than the people in a wax museum, and I could tell he didn't mean well for you, so I sent him on his way without telling him anything. It was like he'd been tracking you, songbird." She paused. "He... He found you anyway, didn't he?" I sighed and rolled over to face her.

"Yes, Majka. He found me. He killed my friend and fled. The plan was probably to drug me, kidnap me, and take me wherever he and his friends had set up. He was a Blackhawk. They've resurfaced and have started hunting again. In any case, the plan failed, my friend got in the way and he was killed." Majka ran a hand through my hair, looking sad.

"I'm so sorry, songbird. How do you know they're taking prisoners?" I knew she didn't like me going into her head, so I refrained from sending her any images.

"I was on my way here when a girl ran into my camp. Her name is Reida. She's skin and bones, I swear. They nearly starved her to death, raped her and beat her, just for information she didn't have. But Majka, that's not the worst of it. She's a psychic, too. They're hunting *all* psychics." A sick sense of understanding broke over her.

"Oh Gods," she breathed. "How many of you are there?"

"I don't know. I don't think there *is* any way to know. But I have to try. I have to find them." I sat up and started to get dressed again.

"Why don't you stay a little longer, songbird?"

"I am sorry, my phoenix. Reida is waiting for me. I told her I'd be back before dark. She's still a bit... Well, she's sort of damaged from her ordeal." I paused and pictured her. "Gods, you should see how thin she is, how scared she was when she ran into that clearing. They almost killed her, Majka." She sat up and put a hand on my hip.

"Talia... The Blackhawks have always been violent and cruel. They're monsters disguised as lambs, veiled by good intentions with holes in the screen, punched by murders and arson and unhesitant cruelty. Maybe once,

45

a long time ago, their motives were pure. But that has not been so for many, many generations... Go get 'em, baby. I know you can." I smiled and turned around. I'd finished dressing and kissed her softly before I brushed a finger along her cheek.

"I'll slit a throat or two for you, phoenix."

And with that I turned and left my more-than-a-contact sitting nude on her bed.

At the market place, which was nearly empty now, I bought a bit of sugar (figuring it would help Reida gain back some weight), a stone container full of soup, and fresh bread a few different stands. I got back to the inn just as the sun was starting to set. I knocked on the door to our room.

"Reida? It's me. I have food." A few seconds later the lock clicked and a golden-green eye peeked out at me. The door opened farther and Reida stood in front of me, a good three or four inches shorter than I was. She looked longingly at the food in my hands. "Come on, you must be hungry." I closed the door behind me and Reida took up residence on the bed. I pulled the tiny writing desk from the corner of the room and laid my cloak on it like a makeshift tablecloth. Then I looked around and realized that it was remarkably clean. Reida had bathed and brushed her hair, and thrown on a large, worn tunic from my bag.

"You look like you're feeling better," I observed happily. She twitched out a smile and less-than-cautiously dived into the food, sitting on the floor. I smiled softly and sat on the edge of the bed, eating the portion I'd saved for myself. I watched her devour the food I'd given her, wondering how long it had been since she'd been given a decent meal. I remembered then that I'd once seen a starved dog eat so much, and so fast, that his stomach had turned inside of him, and he vomited everything up and died. I frowned.

"Eat slowly, Reida," I said. "Else it will just come back up." I left out the bit about her stomach turning. She looked at me, then at the bread in her hand. Reida set it down slowly and came over to sit at my feet. I was startled, but the way she laid her head on my knee made me refrain from pulling away. Her softly-perfumed hair billowed over my lap. I stroked it a bit. Reida reminded me of a small, frightened animal.

"I didn't think you'd really come back," she said in her small, sing-song voice.

"Why did you think that?" I asked quietly.

"I... I didn't honestly think you cared enough to protect me."

"Well... I promise I care. And I promise I'm not going to leave. I'll take care of you." There was a pause. "How old are you, Reida?"

47

"Oh, uhm... What month is it?"

"September. It's the twentieth."

"I am sixty-two." It took the information a moment to reach my brain, and for me to remember how slowly Elves and Emïlan age. I had been imagining her to be twenty-four or twenty-five, such was her appearance, and forgetting that she wasn't completely human.

"I'm twenty-seven. My birthday is the fourth of January. What is yours?"

"The twenty-fourth of August. It was six days before my birthday when they took me. I was there for thirty-two days." I stroked her hair, looking down at her sadly.

"Tell me about your family." She toyed with my shoelace while thinking about what to say.

"I grew up in Glïnéa, the Elvish province, with my mother. She was a healer and enchantress. That's why I'm good at alchemy and potion making. She always used to let me help, and she never had to yell for what she needed because I could hear her. It was good for customers who needed discretion, as well. We ran her apothecary shop together in the city, Amèni. People came and bought herbs, had their possessions enchanted to ward off diseases and poisons, their weapons to burn the target and drain their life. It was a good life. I remember, I always had silly little pets. Mice, caterpillars, cats. I even tried to bring home an abandoned horse once." Reida smiled, and I wished the memories could play for me as they did for her. I was so unused to all the silence.

"I left home after my mother died. She was five-hundred and one. Old even for an Elf. That was almost seven months ago. Now I'm here." She smiled softly, but there was pain in her eyes.

"Can I ask about the Blackhawks? Will that bother you?"

"No," she whispered. "I'm all right."

"You know they're looking for more of us, right?" She nodded.

"They talked about strategy all the time. It was obvious to me that they didn't plan on letting me go, because they talked about their plans even when they knew I was awake and could hear them. I guess that's why I sort of gave up on myself. I know everything they know, now, though."

"What were their ranks?" I asked gently.

"They called themselves by the same ranks as your military. Two were therms. There was one drene and the other four were thralls. I think, by listening to their conversations, that they were one of at least five small groups scouting for us. After I'd been there for a while, they were talking about another man they had found out about and had started tracking him. They were talking about springing an ambush on him when I escaped."

49

"If they were planning it then, they might have already made their move. Especially after losing you. Do you have any idea where you were, Reida?"

"I ran to the northeast, I think. It was a cave, I remember that part very well. It was surrounded by flowers, and I tripped over a log on my way out." She looked like she was going to cry again. I hesitated.

"Reida, what did they do to you?" She looked up at me tearfully. I helped her to her feet, gingerly, and let her sit on the bed with me.

"After they took me, the first thing I remember is *pain*. Pain between my hips, pain on my neck, pain in my back and my legs and... Just everywhere. I was on a cot in a tiny stone room with a cage door on it. I had a collar around my neck and it was chained to a steel hoop on the wall. I didn't have any of my things. My dresses, my knapsack, my dagger and even the enchanted necklace my mother had made me. It really scared me. Because I was in a ragged dress, because they'd taken off my clothes and they'd seen me and I was bruised and sore so I knew they'd done things to me. I sat and cried for a long time before they heard me and came to my cell. It was dark, so I tried to hide in the corner, but they had a lantern. They barked questions at me like I was an animal. 'Can you read my mind?' and, 'Do you understand me, bitch?' They called me such horrible names. I was crying too hard to answer, and they hit me.

"I never knew when they would come to question me. Sometimes I didn't see them for what felt like days. Other times it felt like I was never alone. Time blurred together and I began to function like a wild beast -- sleeping when I could, eating and drinking whatever they gave me to eat and drink, even vile things a person shouldn't have to eat, like a savage. When I did see them, it was nothing more than a choppy interrogation. They asked me if I'd ever met people who were like me. I said no. They gave me names I'd never heard and demanded to know if I recognized them. And, I found out why we can't hear them."

"Really? How?"

"I heard them talking one night, after they'd beaten me and thought I was unconscious. Turns out the years they spent in hiding were really spent training. They've learned how to raise shells around their mind and maintain them without exerting any energy. They've built an immunity to the probes we can send out. I think a magical source is strengthening their abilities, making it work in the background instead of the barrier being their main focus. The way they spoke of it, it sounded like their leader was in control of the source."

"What, so... Like a beacon?" I asked.

"It did seem to be a physical object," she replied, calmer now. I got the impression that talking about magick was quite a bit easier for her. She understood magick, she could use it, and it made her feel more in control. I made an effort to remember that.

"So, we find where it is, we smash it, and we destroy them from the inside," I reasoned. A few moments after it had left my mouth I realized just how absurdly simple it sounded. Reida did too. She sat up and scowled.

"Yes, but where in the hell is it? They never said where the place was, only called it by name. Blackhawk Hall." I sighed and racked my brain looking for anything I'd learned in my travels to help me.

"When they first took you, do you remember any weird smells?"

"Uhm... one of the therms smelled like honey for the first few days. Like pure, dripping honey, straight from the hive. It was on his boots, I think."

"What about rashes? Did they itch at any part of their body?" She rubbed her temple and sighed.

"I... I think. It's so hard to remember."

"I know it is. But that's a good bit of information. Have you ever been to the Neck?"

"No. Do you think that's where they are?"

"Oh, yes. The central region of the Neck are groves of poisonous hag's grass and hives of lightning wasps hanging from the trees. Lightning wasps are the only kind of wasp that make honey, and when they do they make tons of it. The combs drip out of the hive and litter the ground under the hives. The Blackhawk therm must have stepped on a honeycomb, and they all must have passed through a grove of hag's grass." She looked at me and smiled.

"You're amazing," she said quietly.

"No," I said. "I've just been travelling for ten years." She laid down next to me.

"We need to get you a dress, don't we?" I said, eying her mostly-naked body, and how frail she looked. Reida blushed and her eyes wandered over to the blood-stained rag she'd left in the corner of the room.

"I'd offer to pay you back, but they took all the coin I had, and they've no doubt spent it already." She looked embarrassed.

"Pfft. It's a dress, Reida. It's not like I'm buying you a horse."

"Well... all right," she relented. "But when we get to the cave to get the other psychic, I'm raiding the chest inside for my things. I know just where it is." I smiled at the tenacity in her eyes. She was slowly becoming a different girl than the one I'd found in the forest. She seemed happy, at least right now. I wondered if it would last.

"All right. But after they're dead, okay?" Reida nodded and snuggled up into my side.

"Have you slept since we've been here?" she asked. I realized that I hadn't.

"No," I said, somewhat surprised. She motioned me down onto the pillow.

"Then do so." I laughed.

"Can I get out of my armor first?" I asked. I stood up and stripped it off, leaving only my breeches and my tunic on. I un-braided my hair and turned to see that Reida had already settled down into her place, curled up under two layers of blankets. I started to get into bed myself when I realized I should ask first.

"Is... Is it okay if I sleep next to you?" There was a second where nothing moved, and I started to pull my foot back out from underneath the cover. But then Reida nodded her consent and I got in. She rolled to face me and her bony chest pressed against mine. I moved her hair to the side and she hid her face in my shoulder.

"You're warm," she said quietly. "I'm so used to the cold." I held her closer and unconsciously kissed her forehead. A moment of worry struck me but she didn't seem to mind. "The cave was cold and damp," she continued. "I got sick once. They gave me weak medicines, just enough to keep me alive. I asked to make my own but they didn't trust me. I guess they only cared when they thought they were going to lose me."

"Well," I said, "I care about you even when you're clinging to my knees like you're never going to let me go." She smiled and played with a strand of my hair. Slowly she began to slip off into sleep. I breathed deeply and slowly, knowing that loud noises would wake her up and scare her. When I was sure she was asleep, I dared a small cough. Reida flinched, rolled over, and snored. I smiled and drifted off to sleep myself.

SEVEN

I was woken up in the early hours of the morning by Reida slipping out of bed. I cracked open my eyes and winced at the bright grey morning light. I rolled over and saw her standing naked in the middle of the room with her back toward me, having taken off my tunic and laid it on the side of the bed. She was stretching with her hands over her head. My eyes trailed over her broad hips and shallow curvature, to the large space between her thin thighs. It was caused by starvation, I knew, because when one goes without food for a long while, the body begins to eat away at itself to keep running. Reida's knees and ankles were affected, too, for they looked almost too frail to support her weight.

I could count the notches on her spine between her shoulder blades.

In the pale morning light, I could see a large purple bruise on her rib cage, one that I hadn't seen before. It looked as though someone had wrapped their arm around her waist and squeezed. It was a wonder that she didn't have any ribs broken from the action, which looked to be around the right color for it to have happened the night she escaped, or maybe a day before. Reida turned, saw me looking, and looked embarrassed.

"Good morning," she said quietly.

"Good morning, Reida," I replied, sitting up and yawning. "Why are you up so early?"

"Still getting used to sleeping at night," she said, putting on the tunic and coming over to sit on my lap. I hugged her. "Did you sleep well?"

"Fairly. And you?" I ran a hand through her sleep-warmed hair.

"I woke up once because of a nightmare, but I rolled over and saw you, and I fell back asleep." I was touched. I kissed her forehead.

"Well, I'm here, and you're safe. What do you say I run out and send a message to the seamstress, and she can measure you and get you a new dress? I know someone who can get it to you before dinner tomorrow night." Reida smiled.

"All right." I smiled, moved her onto the mattress, and stood. I drew my cloak on and went downstairs. A messenger was sitting at the bar taking his breakfast. I caught his eye and approached him, getting waves of nervousness from him.

"I need a message sent," I said flatly.

"To whom?" he asked, pulling on his collar. It was only his first week as a courier and had already seen plenty of shady deals. He'd even transported a vial of poison to one of the nobles around town who was looking to finish off a business partner.

"Don't worry," I assured him. "I'm not looking for an accessory to murder. I just need a message sent to the seamstress in the High District. Tell her a very thin woman needs a dress. Send her here, to room eleven." I handed him some coins and he stood.

"How did you...?" he began. I smiled.

"The question is really, 'When don't I?' isn't it?"

An hour or so later, he and the seamstress arrived at the inn. She was a stout, plump woman with grey hair and fleshy jowls that quivered when she talked.

"Damn girl, waking me up so early to dress some twig of a woman," she thought, dripping venom from her tone. Reida heard her thought as well, for she let out a whimper of cowardice and shame. I looked back at her, still dressed

in my tunic, and gripped her hand tightly. I turned my attention to the seamstress.

"I am not paying you to complain, nor to thrown insults. You are here to dress my companion and nothing more, and I suggest you begin to act like it." She scowled and pulled a piece of cord with tic marks on it out of her bag.

"Strip and stand before me, girl," she ordered. Reida looked at me, hesitant. I nodded encouragement and she pulled off my tunic and stepped into the view of the seamstress. I narrowed my eyes at the old woman, making it clear I wanted no comments.

"Well, well. Never dressed a skeleton *before."* Reida's eyes began to water, and she wrung her hands in shame, trying to hide her bruises. The seamstress, however, continued to bark orders at her and shout abuses inside her head.

"Raise your arms. No, too high. Higher. Spread your legs. Tilt your head. Close your mouth!" Reida obeyed quietly, fighting tears the whole time. The woman was revolted by the measurements she took, and I could tell Reida was starting to be revolted, too. She shifted uncomfortably, and when the woman was writing down her numbers, she ran her hands over her chest and grimaced. Finally the seamstress finished and packed away her things.

"I've finished measuring your... *companion*," she said distastefully. I took a shivering Reida into my arms. I felt my shirt begin to dampen and felt her body begin to quiver. It took a lot of my resolve not to slap the seamstress across the face.

"I'll pay extra to have it done overnight. I'm not looking for grandeur, she just needs something to ride on the back of a horse with." She scoffed at me.

"To think! *My* work, put on a time limit. You'll have your dress, whelp. But expect a hefty price tag." She waddled out of the room repugnantly. I rubbed Reida's back and kissed the top of her head. She let out a sob.

"Don't pay her any mind, dear. She's a nasty old woman. But you'll have a dress, and I'll get my money back in two days." She was not contented, though, and continued to cry into my chest for a long while afterward.

The day passed quickly. We took our meals in the room, talking about things that didn't matter. Before we knew it, the sky was dark and we were lit by starlight and the oily glow from the lantern on the bedside table. Reida had spent most of the day wrapped in a sheet with my tunic on, but now she was naked and was laying on the mattress reading a book I'd given her. She was scantily-covered by the sheet, hand under her chin. I was sitting on the chair using my sharpening-stone on my daggers and arrows.

"Talia?" came her tiny voice.

"Yes?"

"Do you think she was right?" I set down my stone and the arrow I was working on.

"Who?"

"The dressmaker. Do you think I'm disgusting?" I paused a moment, then shoved the arrow into my quiver.

"No, sweetheart. You're thin. 'Thin' and 'disgusting' are not the same thing. You didn't have substantial food for a long time. You lost weight because your body tried to eat itself to keep you alive. You're a victim. And even if you were not a victim, and just thin by nature, anyone who says you are wrong for being what you are is disgusting themselves, and they should be silenced. There is no wrong way to look, only wrong ways to act." She nodded thoughtfully.

"I've already put on a bit of weight, you know. My legs aren't as weak as before. I'm not constantly cold." I smiled, standing and walking over to her. Reida sat up and let the sheet slip off of her breasts. She leaned into my stomach, which was covered by nothing more than a tunic. I smiled and kissed her on the top of her head. I felt a curious sensation in my heart.

"Why don't you go to sleep, Reida?" I suggested. "You're tired." She nodded after a moment and laid down, pulling the sheet up around her. I sat back down and began to sharpen my arrows again. From my angle all I saw of her was her shock of hair poking out from under the blankets. I sharpened and watched until the light grew too dim to continue, and then I slipped in next to her and blew the lantern out.

EIGHT

Around nine in the morning there was a knock at the door. I answered it, and almost immediately regretted that decision. It was the seamstress, looking up at me. She thrusted a small parcel wrapped in paper into my arms. Then I received a scolding from breast-level.

"You insolent people! Making me, an old woman, stay up to all hours of the night to finish a dress that wouldn't even fit on my *thigh*! You better have an extra forty coins laying around, you overdeveloped harlot!"

"Here! Now shut your mouth and leave!" I yelled, shoving a bag of coins into her face and slamming the door. I heard her grumbling and screeching and her footsteps down the hallway towards the stairs.

"What an *ealslün*," Reida mumbled. I turned and nearly dropped the package for my laughter. I gasped for air and Reida blushed and giggled as well.

'Ealslün' is the Elvish equivalent of 'bitch.' But it's worse than that. The direct translation is something like 'family bitch.' It means that you ashamed your entire clan by your attitude, and that they shun you for your bitchiness. I was nearly in tears when I flopped onto the mattress and handed the parcel to Reida.

"Open it," I said, smiling and wiping the tears away from my eyes.

"Alright," she laughed. She tore the paper off the package and pulled out a mass of sky-blue cotton and wool. She stood and slipped it on over her head. The white-trimmed skirt tumbled down to her ankles. The sleeves were loosely cut and came to her wrists, and the waist of the bodice came to just above her hips. The bodice itself was corseted, so I tightened it up for her. It was clear the seamstress had made it just a little too big, probably out of spite, but it fit our purposes of getting her weight back up quite nicely. I chuckled to myself and looked her over.

"At least her work is good," Reida admitted.

"She dresses the court here, so it must be... Now. We'll buy you a cloak and we'll be on our way back to the cave. Are you sure you're ready?"

"I'm sure."

Within the hour we checked out of the inn and gone shopping. Reida had picked out a forest-green cloak with an ebony button. By eleven we had exited the city walls, heading south. We decided to go back to the clearing where she'd run into me, and then she would lead the way back to the cave. She said she could remember, and I believed her. The journey wasn't long, but it was tedious and boring. The scenery was similar for the entire ten-mile stretch, save for the occasional bear and curious deer.

Finally, about one in the afternoon, we reached the clearing. The wind was blowing softly, but sometimes puffed up in leaf-rattling gusts. I knew it would make good cover for our footsteps through the trees. I tied Rosemary to a tree and let her drink from the stream. I filled my waterskin we ate a fast meal. Reida looked distant, as though she had something pressing on her mind. Afterwards I drew my bow and Reida her gifted dagger. Rosemary saw the weaponry and shifted nervously, huffing. Reida put away her blade and patted my horse on the muzzle.

"Shh, *maéle*," she said soothingly. She continued, speaking Elvish. Animals understood Elvish better than other languages, simply because it was older and Elves are a part of nature more so than humans. I knew some of the words she said, but the language had never been my strong suit. I heard *"zül,"* meaning "peace," and *"anaata,"* which meant "return." Rosemary flicked her ears and listened, calming down. She started to graze on the wind-blown grass.

Reida drew her blade again and started into the forest. I followed her.

"If I remember correctly," she said after we'd walked a while, "it's about a mile to the cave. There are two guards that stand outside, both ranked as thralls. One carries a mace, the other a bow."

"I'll take out the one with the bow first," I said thoughtfully. "He'll be more dangerous. Then, I'll get the guy with the mace and we'll sneak inside."

"Sounds simple enough," she replied. We walked softly until I spotted a wall of light ahead of us. I pointed it out to Reida and she nodded silently. We tread more carefully over the ground now. Reida nearly glided over the ground, her thin figure and Elven dexterity making her feet nearly noiseless. I felt clumsy and wobbly next to her, even though I made nearly no sound as well. I watched her. Her hand was shaking. But she floated ever forward. When we neared the edge of the light, I looked out and observed.

It was just as Reida had said. Clearing full of flowers, log near the entrance to the cave, which was a hole in the side of the cliff on the eastern side of the field. One of the guards, the one with the mace, sat on the long, and the other one stood with his bow in his hand. I slid closer to the grass, looking for a good shot. He was only about one hundred and thirty feet away, but the wind was getting a little stronger. I pulled back the string with three fingers, my corded arms tightening with the tension of the bow. I shut my left eye and aimed, then adjusted for the wind. I sucked in a breath and then --

TWANG!

A soft buzzing noise, and then my arrow was soaring through the air. A fraction of a second later I heard a sickening *thunk* and the archer sputtered. He fell backward with an arrow buried in his chest and took his last breath. Meanwhile, his friend had begun to stand and pull out his weapon. Quickly I nocked another arrow and took aim. He came charging in my direction, mace readied. Before he took ten paces I'd released another arrow and it had hurdled into his heart. He fell to the ground, there was a wet, gurgling noise, and then he was dead.

I lowered my bow and realized I'd been holding my breath. I exhaled heavily and looked back at Reida. There was tension in her eyes and her knuckles were white as she clutched the dagger tightly. I took her hand.

"Are you all right?" I asked quietly. She hesitated.

"I... I don't know. I know I said I could do this... I thought I could... But I don't know." She seemed to be on the verge of tears.

"You don't have to come in, Reida."

"I want to, I just --"

"Here," I stopped her. "Why don't you stay in the tree line and I'll go in? You can stand guard." She nodded a little.

"O-Okay. Please be careful." I squeezed her hand and then stepped out of the trees. It took me just about one minute to cross the field, crouching a bit, and reach the entrance to the field. It wasn't incredibly large -- only about four feet wide and seven tall. With one last look back in Reida's direction, I slipped inside.

It took a few seconds for my eyes to adjust to the dim lighting. The walls were made of stone and there were a few torches scattered around on them. I went deeper into the cave, following a sort of narrow hallway until I saw a turn ahead of me and a light emanating from beyond it. I snuck up quietly, nocking another arrow, and I heard two men talking. Peeking around the corner, I saw them to be standing at a table with papers sprawled across it.

"He said he knew of no others," grunted a tall, brutish man. By the pompous black, purple, and silver uniform and the cape he wore, I inferred he was one of the therms.

"They've all never met each other, Sir," said the man standing across from him. He wore the same uniform as those outside, and must have been a thrall.

"Yes, yes. A bit odd, don't you think, Thrall?"

"Quite, Sir."

"Perhaps we will try and freshen his memory," the therm said, pulling a steel dagger from his belt. "A few less fingers should do the trick."

I'd seen enough. I pulled back my arrow and fired at the thrall, shooting him through the bicep. He screamed and fell back onto the floor. The therm whirled around and drew his sword, looking for me in the darkness. I shot another arrow before he got the chance to find me. He cried out and fell backwards, dropping his sword. It clattered on the stone floor and slid across its uneven surface to the far wall. He was sitting on the floor grunting in pain when I stepped out of the shadows with my bow in hand. They looked up and groaned.

"Alright boys, there's been a change in command," I said, pinning the therm to the floor with my boot on the shoulder I'd shot. He howled. "Oh hush now, Therm. I'm Talia Storm-Cloud and I'm in charge now. If you, Thrall, so much as move a single toe while I am speaking to your friend here, I will fire an arrow through your jugular, got it?" He whimpered. "Good. Now, we can do this very easily, or not so easily. I have two daggers, and you each have ten fingers. Answer my questions nicely, and you'll keep them. If not, then the number of total fingers shall decrease.

"So, first question. Why are you people so suddenly interested in my kind?" It was an ambiguous question, directed at no one.

"You-You people are monsters!" the thrall shouted. "Thoughts should be left inside one's own head!" I clucked my tongue.

"Now, now, soldier. Didn't your mother ever teach you not to speak to a woman that way? Well, apparently, she didn't teach you not to kidnap and rape one either!" I hissed, taking a step and kicking him in the ribs. He let out a yelp and tried to scoot away from me, dragging his bleeding arm. "What did I say about moving, Thrall?" I nocked an arrow. He gulped and stopped. I smiled and set my bow down on the table.

"The boy didn't touch her," the therm spat from under my boot. "He wasn't man enough. But I took her and I fucked her while she was out, and she cried like a little fucking *bitch*!" Rage pooled up inside me and I stomped down on his shoulder. I heard something crack and he screamed. I stomped harder. He was in tears as he screamed. I leaned down near his face.

"How does it feel, Therm?" I asked quietly. "Would you consider this crying like a 'little fucking *bitch*,' or should I stomp harder?" He let out a sob. "That woman is my friend. She has a name. It's Reida. And you had better show some damn respect about it."

"You're crazy!" yelled the thrall. "You and your freak friends!" I straightened myself up and removed my foot from the therm's shoulder. He curled up in a ball, still crying. I got close to the thrall.

"Maybe. Maybe I am. If I could hear your thoughts, I would twist them and drive you mad. But only because you disgust me. Does that make me crazy? Possibly... I didn't ask for this ability, you know. I won no favors, pulled no tricks, and bedded no men to get like this. I was made this way. So hunt me and my 'freak friends' all you want, soldier. But remember that you hold nothing over me, and that I *will* destroy you." I pulled out my dagger and showed it to him, then traced a line on his neck with the tip.

"You think me a monster? A freak? Well, until you came and fucked up my life, I wasn't. You created this war, Thrall. You, your therms, drenes, and everyone else in your fucked up little band of heroes. You decided the way I was born is unnatural. And as always, those who wage war will be met by those they wage it on." I slit his neck and his blood spurted onto the wall. He fell to the side, the red liquid pouring from his throat and splashing onto the sole of my boot. I turned back to the therm.

"Now, more questions." He looked up at me, face pale with fear and blood loss. "I know you have a man here as a captive. I'll need the key to his cell."

"Never," he said weakly. "Another one of you people will not slip through my fingers!" I grinned to myself.

"Speaking of fingers..." I bent down, right knee bracing his left elbow and my left foot on his other wrist. I hacked at his pinky, and he screamed and thrashed something awful. My grip was iron, though, and within a few seconds it was off. I pressed the blade down on his ring finger.

"What about now?" I asked, slowly increasing the pressure.

"Stop! Okay! There are three more of us down in the lower chamber. They're working on the prisoner now." I smiled at him.

"Thank you for cooperating, Therm. Although, I don't think it really makes up for anything, huh?" I slit his throat too. He gurgled on his own blood and then died. I wiped my dagger on the edge of his cape and then stood. I grabbed my bow, readied an arrow, and continued out the doorway that lead down another narrow hall.

The cave seemed to go on forever. I was beginning to think I'd missed a turn when I came across a set of three cages that sat back into a little hole in the wall. There was no one in them, but there was blood on the straw that lined the bottom of one cell. It was fresh, no more than a half hour old, judging by the color. I knew I was going in the right direction. I continued, and got no more than another ten feet when I heard a booming laugh echo through the cave. I froze, then snaked my way along the wall until I came to another opening.

I snuck along the wall and observed. This chamber was much bigger, almost ten times the size of the previous one. The walls were lined with racks of weapons, tables of instruments, and a few cages scattered around the edges, bathed in shadow. There was a table in the middle of the room that held a young man, barely more than a teenager, strapped onto the metal with leather bonds. By his skin and frame I judged him to be a Nord. His hair was black and damp with sweat. He was grimacing and hissing with pain. There were inflamed-looking whip marks across his torso, and the second therm was standing to the right of the table holding the weapon responsible. The drene was standing to the left. As I drew closer, something felt wrong.

Then it hit me. The therm had said there were three guards. But I counted only two. Where was the other thrall? My heart began to race and I tried not to panic. I looked around quickly, but the shadow I stood in was too dark for me to see very far.

Then a hand wrapped itself around my mouth and another took my wrist. I screamed and dropped my bow. It clattered onto the ground and everyone in the room looked towards me. The hand moved away from my mouth and grabbed my other wrist, and I was dragged into the light by the second thrall. The men standing by the table sneered as I was made to kneel. I thrashed and jerked, but the grip was too hard. The therm walked over slowly, observing me.

"Now, now. What do we have here? A little girl come to rescue the little boy?" he cooed, his voice dripped cloying honey and an intent for blood.

"Let him go and I'll let you live," I snarled. He smiled.

"And let the beast roam free, spreading his abnormalities throughout the entire continent? Plus, you don't look like much to handle."

"He's just a boy, what harm could he do? Though... A skinny Emïlan woman fell out of your grasp, so maybe you *should* be worried about him." His sneer faltered and his eyes seemed to cloud over with rage. He raised his hand to strike me but I didn't flinch.

"The bitch isn't worth it," he decided, and coolly lowered his hand. I smiled slyly.

"Won't you hit me?" I asked, almost laughing. "You had no issue hitting Reida, or the boy." Something in his face twitched, and instead of smug he looked nervous. "Oh, I get it! You're afraid now! Never had someone stand up to you before, Therm? It's nerve racking, isn't it? When someone tells you they can see through the little show you put on." They were all listening to me, watching their leader falter, and I didn't have to hear them to feel the illusion slipping. The grip on my wrists loosened ever so slightly. But it was enough. I swung my hands over my head, using my legs to push with them, and the thrall came along. He flipped over my back and onto the ground. I pulled the dagger from my belt and kicked the fallen thrall across the face.

The drene came charging at me, drawing his sword. Before it was all the way out I ducked under his arm and swung behind me, plunging the dagger into his back. He screamed and fell, dropping his sword. The therm had retreated to the other side of the table that the young telepath was strapped to. I picked up the drene's sword and pointed it at him.

"Coward!" I snapped. "Draw your weapon and face me like a soldier!" With fumbling fingers he raised his sword. "What is your name, Therm? And your fellow officers' names? I want names to put to faces."

"I am Green-Wind," he said. "The other therm is... *was* Emaery. The thrall with him was Redgrass, the drene was Sven and the thrall Drathis."

"Very good. Now, I'm going to disarm you and you're going to unstrap the young man here. Got it?" I motioned to the man on the table. Green-Wind swung his sword angrily at me. I blocked it with my borrowed blade and with a flick of my wrist I tore it from his shaking hands.

"Ah, but you have forgotten the first rule of combat, friend. Anger leads to miscalculation with your blade." He cowered in defeat and freed his prisoner. There was a pause while the buckles were undone.

"What should I do with you, Green-Wind? Should I kill you, or leave you in one of those pretty cages to starve to death?" He trembled, getting frightened. "There is fear in you, Therm. Like a cornered animal, ready to bolt. I wonder, now that you know how it feels to be trapped... Do you regret it?"

"W-What do you mean?"

"Do you regret imprisoning my friend, or this boy, or anyone else you may have trapped?" There was a sudden change in character from the therm. He finished the last strap and glared at me.

"No," he spat. I smiled and cut his throat.

NINE

It took a few minutes for the man to fully wake up. By that time I'd dragged the drene, thrall, and therm into three side-by-side cages. I found my bow in the darkness and strapped it back onto my back. When he came to, he tried to sit up, but he grimaced in pain and cried out, leaning back onto his elbow. I caught his back.

"Easy, friend," I said quietly, easing him up and guiding his feet to the floor.

"Who... Who are you?" he muttered.

"No time now. Come on, let's get you out of here. Can you walk?" He nodded and I took his arm over my shoulder, helping to steady him. Together we made our way to the exit. It took us ten minutes, because he had to stop every now and then because the pain was too much. When we got outside, Reida was sitting on the log near the entrance. Her face was tear-stained and she looked relieved to see me walk out.

"Oh, Talia! I thought you had surely died," she cried.

"I'm all right, but he isn't. Come, help me lay him down onto the grass." Together we got him down onto the ground. He was delirious with pain. I wiped his brow on the hem of my cloak.

"I'm going back in to get your things and look for things to help us learn about the Blackhawks," I told Reida. "I'll be right back."

"The chest is under the shelf in the first room," she told me. I nodded and went back inside. Sure enough, it was right where she had said. I broke the lock instead of wasting time looking for the key. Inside were two knapsacks, an apothecary's satchel, and an empty mailbag. I took all three, filling the mailbag with papers from the table and food from a nearby barrel. When I came back outside Reida was kneeling next to the young man, murmuring half in Elvish to him.

"Oh you found my satchel!" she exclaimed. I gave it to her and she opened it up. "They've used some of it but it looks like I have enough to treat these wounds." She pulled out a small wooden jar.

"What is that?" I asked her.

"An Elvish flower. I don't know your word for it, but we call it *vielänea*. It heals flesh wounds, burns, and animal bites. I don't have enough to treat him completely, but it should keep it from getting infected until I can get something else." She pulled out a mortar and pestle, ground the small, purple flowers into a paste, and pressed it onto his torso using a leaf. He moaned at the touch of it. Reida said that she didn't have enough to layer it, because she wanted to apply it later, but this would have to do. I touched the man's face.

"Wake up, friend. You're safe now." He groaned and tried to sit up again. "No, no, lay back." His eyes opened all the way.

"Who are you?" he asked again.

"Talia Storm-Cloud."

"And I am Reida of the clan Bollaïne. We're here to help you." His eyes welled up with tears and he began to cry.

"Thank the Five," he exclaimed. "I thought I was going to die." He took hold of my cloak. "Thank you."

"You mustn't upset yourself like that, friend. What is your name?" I asked. He took a deep breath.

"Erak Birchdal. Of Hell's Creek, in The Basin."

"I am from The Basin as well," I said. He was still weeping, his chest shuddering and heaving. Erak's hands twisted in my cloak. I wiped his face.

"Will... Will you sing to me?" he whimpered. I felt like I was going to cry with him. This poor boy was so scared.

"Of course."

> *"Little swallow, so lovely and spry,*
> *Come on and sit on my shoulder.*
> *Whisper your secrets to me as I fly,*
> *Onward and upward to wonder.*

> *Sweet soft sunflower, tall in the wind,*
> *Point out my love in the window.*
> *Show him the way to slip into my arms,*
> *And I may hold him 'fore he goes."*

By this time all of us were fighting tears. Erak had stopped weeping as hard, and now only a few tears were dripping from his eyes. But Reida was crying and I was dabbing at my face.

"Thank you," he whispered. "You're... You're a saint."

"Reida, love?" I said.

"Yes?"

"Would you be all right running to fetch Rosemary? I have some things in my bags he could use."

"I'll be back." She stood and ran into the forest. Her gait was fast, but her legs moved in long, graceful lines typical of an Elf. I turned my attention back to Erak, who was sniffling and shaking from having cried so hard.

"Do you know any more songs?" he asked innocently. I smiled.

"I know lots. I've been everywhere, you know." I thought of songs I'd heard in the giant camp where I was Glukshull, but didn't know the words to. Then one came to mind, one from an Elvish dinner I'd attended years ago.

> *"There was a young maiden*
> *Called Elesa the Fair.*
> *She wore golden dresses*
> *And crowns in her hair.*
> *The men all adored her,*
> *The women ignored her,*
> *The trees all sang with her,*
> *Sweet Elesa the Fair."*

There was another verse that came after that, but it was in Elvish and I didn't know the words. Erak didn't seem to mind, though.

"You're so very kind to me," he said, almost speaking to himself.

"We take care of our own. Reida and I are psychics too. You can't hear us because it sort of... cancels out." He looked relieved.

"I was wondering why I couldn't hear you. I thought they'd... broken me. Are they psychic too?"

"No, dear. I've seen these things before -- magicians and wizards will do some psychic training to try to block off their minds, but there is always a crack. But the Blackhawks, they have something making their walls better, something that links them all together and links them to the beacon strengthening their magic."

"I saw a tattoo that two of the thralls had," Erak offered after some thought.

"That... That could be it. I'll ask Reida when she gets back. She's good with those things."

"Is she with you? Personally, I mean?" he wondered. The question took me by surprise.

"No... I mean, I don't think so." He tried to chuckle but ended up coughing. When he pulled his hand away there were specks of blood on it. He groaned.

"Must be a cut in my mouth." There was a noise from the tree line. I looked up to see Reida guiding Rosemary by the reins. When she got over to us I stood and pulled rags out of my bag and used them to wipe Erak's face. I looked around and saw the sun was going down.

"We should set up camp here tonight, by the cliffside," I said. Reida agreed and together we made a fire. About half an hour later the sky was orange. We found clothes in Erak's knapsack and helped him dress, stripping off the tattered pants he wore. Reida wrapped some cloth from inside her satchel around his torso, protecting the wounds from being irritated by his shirt and cloak. Afterward, Reida went through her own bag. She nearly cried when she pulled out her enchanted necklace from the inside pocket of the bag.

"What does it do, exactly?" I asked her.

"My mother enchanted it so that it would grow hot when danger was nearby. I never thought I would use it, being telepathic and all, but I took it with me when I left for sentimental value. But now I see that it will indeed come in handy. We cannot hear the Blackhawks coming, but this can." She smiled at the necklace and slipped the silver chain on over her head. Reida tucked the blue crystal hanging from it into her bodice.

"Your mother was good with enchanting, then?" Erak asked, leaning against the log wrapped in his cloak. "Tell me, is it possible to enchant a tattoo?"

"Quite possible. Why? Thinking of getting one?" she asked, smiling.

"No," he laughed. "Two of the thralls had their inner left forearms tattooed with the same design."

"That must be their connection to the beacon, then. What was the image?"

"Their seal, the same one they wear above their hearts on the uniforms. A blackhawk with its wings outstretched, a snake in its mouth... Here." He picked up a stick and roughly sketched it into the dirt. Reida nodded thoughtfully.

"It makes sense," she said. "A tattoo connecting all the members together is more convenient than buying each person a ring or necklace, and less expensive too. And the ink used is certainly able to be enchanted."

"And if you burned or cut the tattoo off, the magick would be gone, right?" I asked, a spark of an idea forming inside my head. Reida nodded.

"So, remove the ink, get inside the person's head, and find out where they are and how to get to the beacon!" I exclaimed.

"But we would need someone to do it on," Reida said quietly.

"We have one."

The next morning, I went back into the cave and down into the lower chamber. I looked into the cages. The drene had died sometime during the night, but the man I had kicked across the face was still very much alive.

"You!" he groaned when he saw me. "Have you come to finish me off? Get rid of the evidence?" He spoke through a swollen, bruised jaw. It's a wonder it wasn't broken.

"No," I said lightly, unlocking the cage. "We need your help. You see, we need to find Blackhawk Hall.

But it's, apparently, quite well-hidden. My friends and I happen to know that your little inkwork there connects you to the Hall."

"How could you know?" There was fear in his eyes.

"Deductive reasoning, little one. Drathis, right? Come along now, Drathis. We have ways of getting that tattoo off you."

"What are you going to do to me?"

"Nothing much, if you're a good boy. Come along now." I tied his wrists together with a bit of rope, took him by the bicep, and lead him outside. I tied him to a tree about ten feet from the campfire. Reida flinched when she saw him, and after he was secured I held her close to my heart.

"Drathis, you remember my friends, right?" Shame filled his features.

"They-They kidnapped me, too, you know," he pleaded. Suddenly I was irritated.

"Spare me the sob story, Drathis. They kidnapped you? Well you kidnapped *them*!" I motioned to Erak and Reida. "How *dare* you turn this around on yourself? Reida almost died because of you, you insolent cretin! How *dare* you play the victim? I will rip your goddamn throat out!" Reida put her hand on my arm.

"*Zül, ma lün,*" she murmured. I kissed her forehead.

"*Caiere,*" I replied, using my bit of vocabulary.

"What will you do with me?" Drathis asked in a shaky voice. This time, it was Reida who answered him.

"We shall remove the ink, young Drathis," she said calmly. "But I want you to know that if I were of the *Lan* I should have cut off your arm and painted with your blood by now." The iron in her voice surprised me. Where was the woman who, just yesterday, was petrified to go into the cave? Where was the woman that curled up in my arms like a kitten, crying about the things this very man had done to her? If this was Reida when she wasn't scared, I knew I would like her a lot.

"But," she continued, "I was raised among the *Emï*, and was taught the way of *zül*. I shall put you to sleep and remove the ink by magick. There will only be a scar when you awaken." He gulped.

"And what will happen when I wake up?"

"You will tell us where Blackhawk Hall is, by letting us into your mind."

"And if I don't?" Reida grew a sick smile.

"Then you will discover than my friends were not taught the same as I."

TEN

Reida put Drathis to sleep using the last of her supply of a small, white flower she crushed up and called *nulléan länea*.

"I'll need to stop somewhere and restock," she told me. I promised her we would stop. That contented her, and she prepared Drathis (and herself) for the spell. I sat by Erak and watched as she laid out various crystals and stones on a small piece of leather that was laying before her.

"She's fearsome when she's angry, eh?" Erak said. I nodded, smiling.

"Reida's definitely something. There's mettle in that woman I've been hard pressed to find in some of the men I've fought alongside.

"She's Emïlan, right?" Erak asked quietly.

"Yeah. Mother was an Elf, taught her enchanting and potions and all that."

"What's she doing here in Adaima?"

"She wanted the job as the court alchemist for the Head Counselor for Adaima. But they got her before she reached Silmen..." I paused. Gods, I'd completely forgotten about that. The poor thing just wanted a job, didn't she? She didn't sign up to be a part of my little revenge mission. A deep shame filled my heart. It felt like I was going to pass out. Panicked, I looked over to Erak, but he had been distracted by something and was now interested in what Reida was doing. I looked as well.

She'd started the spell. Her had her hands up above her head and was chanting something quietly in the language of magick -- a form of very ancient Elvish. A bright purple light began to radiate from her palms, and her eyes began to glow the same color. Her aura, the force moving the magick through her and projecting the color, was simply stunning. Each magick user had their own color, but Reida's was by far the most beautiful.

Reida kept whispering the spell as she moved her hands all over Drathis's arm. Slowly it began to fade. The ink rose off of his skin, crumbled into powder and was blow into the wind. There was a speck of blood wherever her hands passed, but it was almost immediately wicked away and layered over with a thick white scar. It took a while to completely remove the tattoo, as Reida went over each spot multiple times, making sure no trace of the ink (or the magick) remained. Her chanting ceased and her aura faded from vision. Deep lines and dark circles took its place. She leaned back onto her heels and sighed.

"It is done," she said softly, picking up her crystals and putting them back into the velvet sack they came out of.

"Are you all right?" I asked warily, starting to stand.

"I'm fine, just... A bit worn out. I haven't done anything like that in months, you see... And I'm still a bit weak," she admitted. I helped her to her feet and she hugged me. Her knees wobbled but I kept her upright.

"Go sit next to Erak and we'll get you something to eat. You'll be right as rain." I assisted her with the movement and then pulled food out of my saddlebag. Culturally, Elves are vegetarians, so I gave her apples and bread to help fill her stomach. She ate them hungrily, even though breakfast had only been about two hours ago.

"You're a witch, then?" Erak asked. Reida shrugged.

"I prefer to think of myself as an enchantress. My specialty is putting charms and hexes on things. But my mother was a healer, so I know lots of different things. What I did was simply a modified healing spell. Instead of closing the wound immediately, it drew foreign substances out of the skin first. My mother showed it to me a long time ago, back from the days of the war when she had to pull shrapnel out of men. Usually I can do it without all the crystals and things, but they were added to the increase power of the spell, since I am not very strong yet."

"Fascinating," he replied. "But, and I am deeply sorry if this comes across as rude, why didn't you use the spell on me? Sorry again." She smiled gently.

"Your question is a valid one. It is because your wounds will heal on their own, without magical intervention. I thought about doing it, believe me. But I decided it would be too hard on me. But the ink would not follow suit, and we couldn't do it easily without hurting him, so I knew I had to." Erak nodded, looking embarrassed that he had asked.

"When is this stuff going to wear off?" I asked, dragging Drathis back to the tree and tying him to it once more.

"Another hour or so," Reida replied, gnawing the rind off a cheese.

"What shall we do to pass the time?" Erak asked. "I have cards."

"I know. Why don't we toss things up in the air and see if Talia can shoot them." She grinned at me. I laughed.

"Well, all right," I said. "Toss your apple core up when I say so." I nocked an arrow in my bow and aimed about six feet above Reida's head. "Ready... Go!" She lobbed it up, and I fired. My arrow soared and struck through the core of the apple, splitting it in half at a diagonal angle. If the core had been just a bit thicker, it would have been skewered onto the tree behind it. But it was just a tiny bit too thin, and so the two halves fell to the ground and my arrow was lodged seven feel up into a white maple. My companions howled with laughter.

"Incredible!" Erak exclaimed. "How did you do that?" I shrugged.

"Practice," I said.

"You should have seen her take out the guards outside yesterday, from the entire way across the field," Reida said.

"Wow..." he looked astonished.

"Oh come now, surely there is something you excel at too, Erak," I said, trying to change the subject.

"I suppose... I can cook. And I sew rather well." Reida gave him a look of surprise.

"Most boys think themselves above the needle and thread," she observed.

"My mother had four boys and no daughters, so we were all taught how to sew. My father thought it was silly, but my mother was the boss."

"You never know, that could come in handy someday," I told him.

"How do your ribs feel, Erak?" Reida asked, getting down off of the log and onto the ground next to him.

"All right, I suppose. I'm sore, and the wounds are tender and bruised to hell, but I'll be okay. Do you want to look at them?" he asked her. She nodded. He unbuttoned his shirt and pulled it back. I sat on the log behind Reida to get a better look at him. She pulled back the bandages. Underneath were thirteen molten whip marks, each about three or four inches long. Each one had a bruise around it, and they overlapped in some spots.

"Does it feel like anything is broken?" Reida asked, pulling off the bandages. "Talia, will you boil some water for me?" I poured my waterskin into the pot I carried with me in my saddlebag and lit the fire underneath it.

"I don't think so," Erak answered her, "but it's hard to tell. Maybe a rib or two, but I can't tell because it hurts so much on the surface."

"Quite... Well, once the bruises fade we can look for ourselves, and by then I should have more herbs and things, so I can treat you further. I'm going to let these breath for a while, and I'll sterilize the bandages." Erak nodded. Reida whispered a blessing in Elvish and gave him a leaf of something to chew on to ease the pain. Soon he was half-asleep and she had relocated to my lap.

"May I ask a question, *lün*?" I asked her, kissing her cheek.

"How were you so firm with him?" I motioned to Drathis. "You were so scared a few days ago." She shrugged.

"I knew I couldn't be scared of him forever."

"It wasn't very long ago, you know. You have every right to be scared of him."

"I know... But I don't *want* to be. Isn't that the trick? You just stop wanting to be. Or, *needing* to be, I guess. Just stand up and say that you're finished being held back by it, and you're free." It made sense to me, in a way. We, as psychics, had more control over our minds than most people did. Wasn't fear just one more thing to control? I pondered for a while, but odd little half-thoughts kept slipping into my head. It confused me, and it took me a while to realize where they were coming from.

"Reida," I said, "do you hear that?" She paused and listened, then jumped up and shrieked.

"It worked!" she screamed. "Oh thank Drünin, Mother of Magick!" She danced around in circles. "Sweet Mother! *Zülle glin!*" I laughed and stood up with her, twirling hand in hand. She nearly leapt into my arms. I caught her and her head found a place on my shoulder. I scooped her up into my arms. Reida looked up and our eyes met. She smiled softly. I returned the smirk.

All of the sudden she pressed her mouth to mine. My eyes opened wide and I began to pull back, but I realized that I really didn't want to do so. My eyes closed and I pressed back. Her mouth was warm and soft, and I felt my face grow warm. It horrified me. I'd seen this woman naked and not been affected, shared her bed and not been flustered in the least. So why did her kiss make my knees weak?

After a moment or two passed, someone cleared their throat. I opened my eyes. It was Erak, sitting in his place near the log with an eyebrow raised and a smug smiled on his face. Reida blushed and pulled back. I laughed at her, kissed her cheek, and then set her down onto her feet. I smiled at Erak, face still warm.

"You're all right, then?" he asked, grinning. I looked at Reida.

"I don't know about her," she said, "but I'm doing just fine." Another thought from Drathis interrupted us, and we all heard it. He was close to awake now.

"It worked. It really worked," Erak marveled.

"Did you doubt me, Erak?" Reida inquired with a smile.

"Would you kill me if I said yes?" he smiled. "Frankly, I'd never even heard of anything like that. But you've made a believer out of me, friend. I commend thee! If I could bow, I would do so a thousand times." He made grandiose hand gestures. Reida laughed. We joined her and moved in closer to Drathis's tree.

Drathis groaned groggily and tried to roll to the side. His bonds kept him from doing so, and he jolted awake with a panicked look. Once he realized where he was and what had happened, his panic was replaced with fear and worry.

"What have you done?" he croaked. Reida gave him a drink from the waterskin.

"Your mind is opened to us now, young one," she said, coolly pointing to her handiwork. He looked and then blanched. Fear spiked even more harshly through him.

"We can hear everything. So either think about it, say it, or I'll dive in and force it out." I was only about a foot from his face. I saw the action coming, ducked to the side, and avoided the spit that came flying from his mouth. I whipped out my dagger and pressed to his neck. "You little whelp!" I yelled. "Look here. I've been quite nice to you, considering all you've done to my friends. My patience with you is slipping, Drathis. Now, try anything else and I'll plunge this dagger into your fucking neck, got it?" He sneered. He knew he was going to die, or at least he was fairly sure.

"Sure," he replied coyly. It took a fair amount of strength not to slit his throat. The only thing stopping me was the fact that he was only way that we would get the location of the Blackhawks. I couldn't kill him because as soon as the heart stops the memories are just about lost. With the demise of the body comes the demise of the mind. I pulled my knife away and slapped him across the face instead, hitting right where the bruise from my kick had already formed. Drathis sputtered and swore. I stood and backed away.

"Now, I'm going to go inside your mind, and you're going to be good and not fight me. All right? All right." I closed my eyes and pushed outward. The prying tendrils sprouted and crawled through the air. When they came into contact with Drathis's consciousness, they began to burrow. I found his mind deliciously open and dived in. He swore out loud and immediately his psychic training kicked in. A wall sprung up between me and his memories and I recoiled. It was only half as strong as before, but it was still formidable. I gritted my teeth and scoured the wall for a hole. I found one, a tiny chink in the armor. I slipped through it and the wall disappeared.

Memories flooded my head. I saw a mother sending a son off to college. I saw a studious pupil of medicine at the Physician's College. I saw a meeting in a pub between Drathis and a man who wore the armor of a Blackhawk drene. I saw the drene slip something into Drathis's drink; one of the things the eyes see but the brain does not process. Then came darkness -- a hood over Drathis's face. Training and breaking of the mind came. They beat him once and he was theirs. His will bent, he was initiated, and I saw the inside of the Grand Hall, all made of wood with furnishings of velvet, and banners of purple and black that bared the Blackhawk crest. The members all dressed in variations of the same attire, getting fancier and of higher quality the higher the rank.

They all faced the back of the Hall, where a man stood on a high platform. He was broad-shouldered, greying, and wore an eye patch over his left eye. Under the patch was a long, white scar going from his hairline to the middle of his cheekbone. He wore a stern look and the grandest uniform of all, complete with a purple cloak and silver buckle bearing the crest.

A name came to me. Commander Worth.

Then Drathis's memory took him out of the Hall and through the wilderness. The route came to me backwards and I saw it in my head. I retreated, wanting to leave before memories of Reida came up. I pulled out and felt my own body once more, then opened my eyes. Drathis was sickly pale, having watched it all with me.

"You... bitch!" he exclaimed weakly. "I ought to... ought to kill you!"

"Reida, what is wrong with him?" Erak asked. Reida looked worried.

"He is weakened. Maybe... maybe the *nulléan länea* was not enough. Here..." she dug around in her satchel and pulled out a small vial of greenish liquid. She went over to him and uncorked it. "Drink this, young one." He opened his mouth and she poured it in.

"It is foul," he coughed, glaring at her. Something seemed to change in her, for Reida's face turned from gentle to furious in a split second. Her aura began to glow from her eyes and fingertips.

"Well," she snapped, "it will help! You should feel grateful I even thought to give it to you, or to put you to sleep while I removed your tattoo! I could have just paralyzed you, and left you to watch as I carved the ink out of your skin! Be thankful you are even alive!" Her aura flared brighter and Drathis was terrified. I wasn't too calm either, though. "You assaulted me, dishonored me, and left me to rot! But you, you tiny speck of filth, will live to tell the story of how you met the three of us." Reida turned and her aura faded, but she left tiny purple flames behind her as she walked.

"Maybe not," Erak said after Reida had stormed away by herself. "I may wipe your memory of the whole ordeal, or build walls around the memories so you can't remember. I'd leave you wondering about that scar for the rest of your life. Maybe you'll wander around the continent, looking for a place you don't *quite* remember how to get to. Maybe you'll even go mad and end up sticking a knife through your eye to carve out the memories." The fear on Drathis's face was obvious.

"Please," he choked, tears falling from his eyes. Now it was my turn to scare him.

"Why?" I retorted. "Why should we show you any mercy at all?" He stuttered, looking for words. "Why!?" I demanded. "You are scum! You don't belong here! A freak! A monster!" He sobbed. I bent down and looked him in the eye.

"Now you know how it feels," I whispered.

ELEVEN

After I found Reida, she pulled the bandages out of the hot water and let them cool slightly before wrapping Erak's torso back up. We sat down and decided to eat something while Drathis recovered. We came to the conclusion that wiping Drathis's memory of the Blackhawks would be the safest route to take. Drathis looked miserable at the news.

"Don't worry, young one," Reida told him, eating a piece of a dried apple. "He'll be gentle." The look Erak gave her told me he had not, in fact, been planning on being gentle. I stifled a laugh.

Erak shuffled closer to Drathis and sucked in a breath, closing his eyes. The world in my head slowed down and I could feel something pervading into the air. I wanted so desperately to touch Erak's mind, but I couldn't reach for it. I longed for it like a child longs to touch its mother, such was the pining I felt in my heart. But even though his consciousness was soft-looking, it was cold and uncomfortable, and the feeling made my skin crawl. I watched in my mind's eye how it passed before me and touched Drathis's forehead. I watched his body shudder in harmony with Erak's. Drathis begged for his memory to be left alone, but Erak was marble as he sat and worked.

A few minutes passed, and suddenly the begging ceased, and a glazed look overtook his face, a single tear leaking out of the corner of his eye. Erak snapped back into his own body and gasped heavily. He quickly tried to stand up.

"Something's wrong!" he shouted, clutching at his torso as he struggled to get off the ground.

"Erak, don't!" Reida cried. He brushed her aside and stumbled over to where Drathis was lying limply. I stood and rushed over to him as well.

"Something's wrong," Erak repeated. He shook Drathis and swore at the lack of response. "I was erasing the thoughts of the Blackhawks, and then, all of the sudden, there was nothing!"

"Nothing!?" I asked, listening to the thrall's chest. His heart was faint and sounded far away.

"I swear it," Erak said. "One second he was struggling and the next... It was like he had died."

"Hold on." I quickly dived into his mind and looked around. It was eerily empty. The familiar buzz of thoughts and emotions was gone, and my presence seemed to echo off the walls like a shout in an empty tomb. I rushed around searching for something, anything. There was only the basest set of memories, almost instructions for life. How to breathe, the inner workings of a heartbeat. He'd been reduced to a child, a newborn. Then something caught my eye. It looked like a trip wire of sorts. I had a horrible realization, retreating quickly before I accidentally killed him.

"Those bastards!" I screamed upon entering my own body. "They've done this."

"Blackhawks?" Reida breathed, too shocked to raise her voice.

"They made it so. They knew eventually someone would try something like this. I saw a trigger, a trip wire of sorts. If you lose the Blackhawk memories, you lose everything." I spat in anger. Erak sat back on his heels and gave the ground a blank look. Reida held him.

"I know what you're going to think, *daén*, and you mustn't think it. You didn't do this, it isn't your fault!" She seemed to be begging with him.

"I didn't see it," he mumbled. "How didn't I see it?"

"Erak," I said. He didn't look at me. "Erak." I cupped his chin in my hand gently and he looked up at me. "Erak. How long have you been away from home?"

"Two months," he muttered.

"Well, see now. You haven't been out for barely any time at all. You aren't experienced, Erak. You need practice..." He was still distant, almost looking through me. I sighed. "Things come with a price, Erak. I know how it goes when someone gets hurt because of what we can do. Trust me, I do. But by the Five, Erak, you're bigger than this incident. You've got to pick up and carry on, okay? Nothing good will come of this until you let it go." He nodded absently and looked away.

Curing this time, Drathis had started to cry. He wailed like a baby, pausing for breaths every few moments. We backed away, repulsed by the man-child before us. He pulled at his bindings furiously. Erak and Reida looked at me.

"Should I... untie him?" I asked hesitantly.

"Surely he cannot do much harm," Reida reasoned.

"Have you ever *seen* a three-year-old throw a fit?" Erak retorted.

"Look at him," I said. "He's helpless."

"Fine," he sighed. I approached Drathis slowly. He whimpered when he saw me.

"Shh," I whispered. "It's okay. I'm going to cut these, all right?" I pointed at his rope. I slowly pulled out my dagger, wondering if he knew enough to be scared of it. Apparently he did not, because he didn't even blink when I pulled it into view. I cut his rope and pulled it off of him. Drathis curled up and whimpered and I hurried back to Reida. I held her to me.

"*Lün*," she whined nervously.

"I know Reida. I know." I kissed her head, comforting her.

"What should we do?" Erak asked after a few minutes of silence between the three of us. We looked at Drathis collectively. Everything was silent except for his sobbing. There was not even a breeze rattling the leaves around us, or a bird singing in the distance. It was as though nature had paused to take in the spectacle.

"In Glïnéa, we have something we call *züllen mori*. It means something like 'mercy death' in your tongue. To take the life of something or someone that is suffering."

"Killing a horse with a broken leg," Erak said grimly.

"Yes. Except we mourn the loss. We treat everything as if it holds the same place in the circle of life as we, the *Emï*, do. And, honestly... I don't know how he will have any life beyond this."

"Is he suffering?" I asked her softly.

"I do not know how he could not be," she replied. Erak let out a vulgar curse.

"This is my fault," he said.

"Now, Erak --" I began.

"No! Don't lie to me and tell me it wasn't. I caused this... And I have to be the one to end it." He staggered closer to what was left of Drathis.

"Don't... Don't hurt him," Reida said quietly. Erak nodded and shut his eyes. He reached into the shuddering thrall's mind. He grimaced. A few seconds later the quivering ceased. Drathis was dead. Erak withdrew and Reida closed her eyes, pressing her face into my shoulder, and I hugged her to me, feeling her tears put hot, wet marks into the cloth.

An hour later, we'd buried Drathis's body and packed everything up. We knew Rosemary would only be able to carry two people at once. Reida was in bad shape, grieving after the *züllen mori* and still less than healthy. Erak's ribs were tender and inflamed, making it hard to walk very far. Therefore it would be those who on horseback while I walked alongside, holding Rosemary's reins. Reida desperately needed supplies for Erak, so I promised her we would stop at a trading post. I knew of one that was east of the clearing, just over the border with Middle Vale.

We travelled for barely eleven miles, hit the border, and then went another mile or so inward. We came to the top of a hill and saw a tall wooden building resting at the bottom of it. A sign hung from the covering on the wide wooden porch. It read "Abrahm's Wares" in big white letters at the top, and at the bottom, under a picture of a sword and a horseshoe, it said "Overnight Rooms and Meals Twice Daily." I tied Rosemary to the trough outside, helped Reida and Erak down. For a guy who didn't look all that heavy, he was muscled and weighed more than I expected him to. Together, Reida and I supporting Erak on our shoulders, we went inside.

The main room was quite spacious, and there were shelves lining every available wall and little knee-to-waist-high tables scattered around the floor. They all held trinkets, furs, books, toys, clothes, jewelry, armor, weapons and jars and vials of mysterious substances. The man standing behind the counter was tall and lean, with coarse black hair he wore in long, thick strand that fell down his back. He was greying near the roots, and his face was beginning to fill with lines of wear, but his eyes were youthful and full of life. His skin was a rich earthy brown, and his eyes a deeper shade of that. A smile spread on his face when he saw me come in.

"Talia!" he exclaimed happily. "I haven't see you in quite some time." I smiled back as we made our way to the counter.

"Good to see you, Abrahm," I replied.

"Who are your friends?" he asked, looking them over.

"I am Reida of the clan Bollaïne," Reida said, smiling.

"Erak Birchdal of the Basin," Erak added, grinning.

"Pleased to meet you both," Abrahm said warmly. "Are you hurt, there, son?" he asked Erak.

"Oh, I'll be fi--"

"Yes," Reida interrupted. "May we have a room with two beds for the night, please?"

"Of course, dear. That's fifteen gold, and here's your key." I paid and Abrahm handed Reida a key on a long leather strip, big enough to be worn around the neck.

"Thank you," we said. Reida and I took Erak upstairs to the third floor and got settled into our room. Erak was placed on the bed nearest the window and stripped of his shirt. Reida pulled back the bandages and grimaced. His wounds had begun to pus and fester. Erak turned pale at the sight of his mangled flesh.

"If I didn't know any better, I'd say you two just like looking at me shirtless," he joked weakly. I hit him on the head with a roll of paper.

"What do you need?" I asked Reida.

"Oh... Uh... Here." She wrote me a list. I went downstairs and showed it to Abrahm. He flitted around the shop, pulling vials and jars and parcels off of the shelves.

"Your friend is an alchemist, then?" he asked as he put them all into her satchel.

"She does a bit of everything, actually. Enchanting, alchemy, healing... She's talented."

107

"You like her," he said. It wasn't a question. I felt my neck get hot. Abrahm laughed. "She likes you too. Tell me, Talia, do you want to be with her?"

"Yeah," I answered quietly. "I do." He smiled and patted me on the shoulder.

"Then it shall be so."

I paid him and went upstairs with the ingredients. I handed Reida the satchel, Abrahm's words still buzzing in my mind. She opened it and looked through it, open mouthed.

"He had everything on the list?" she asked, astonished.

"Abrahm has everything that could be on any list," I replied, smiling.

"I haven't seen some of these things outside Amèni," Reida mumbled. She pulled out her mortar and pestle, a small vial of oil, and a jar of small leaves. She put three or four leaves into her bowl and added a drop of the golden oil.

"What is that stuff?" Erak asked, as if he knew I was wondering, too.

"It's from the bark of the sacred Glïn tree in the capital city of Glïnéa, Rodènsï. The Glïn tree has been there since the beginning of time. The city was built around it," she explained.

"If the tree is sacred, how to people get oil from its bark?" I asked.

"There are two ways, both only done by the Priests and Priestesses of the temple that care for the tree. One a year, in the summer, they take some of from the tree as a blessing from the goddess of nature that they serve, Kynarïn. But even though the Glïn tree is sacred, it's still a tree. The bark falls off sometimes, and they collect it and make the oil to use on the sick and injured people that come to the temple."

The paste was finished. It looked like the green sauce the Valian cooks put on their fish. But when Reida took a bit of the concoction onto her pinkie finger and tasted it, the shudder that made her body quake told me that you certainly would not put it on fish. Reida took a metal spoon and spread the mixture gently over Erak's wounds. He winced, and his flesh seemed to crawl at the touch of it.

"What is it doing to me?" he asked warily.

"By sundown you'll be seeing for yourself," Reida told him. "Now don't touch it, I'm not bandaging over it. It'll be good to get air on the wounds." Erak grumbled and fidgeted, but did as he was told. I pulled out the bag full of papers that I'd taken from the Blackhawks' cave and began to rifle through them.

"What can we hope to learn from those?" Erak inquired.

"I was hoping to find some of the locations of the other dens," I replied. He had a strange look on his face.

A thought struck me. "Can you read?" I asked him. He shook his head.

"My father thought it wouldn't do me much good," he said, a touch of bitterness laced on his tone.

"I can teach you, when we get a moment," I offered. His eyes lit up.

"I'd like that," he answered quietly.

"I can read your tongue," Reida said, taking a few papers off of the stack.

Together we read for a long while. By about seven o' clock I'd found the prisoner and fund reports. I showed them that the Blackhawks had been lying to their headquarters about how much money they'd taken off of Reida and Erak. Reida said she'd been carrying six hundred fifty-seven in coin on her when she was kidnapped -- a number she remembered because she had been saving the sum for over a year -- but the report only counted three hundred seventy. The rest had, undoubtedly been spent on personal things, while the counted sum had been sent back to Blackhawk Hall. The same thing was true for Erak, whose report was missing three hundred of his seven hundred sixty-four gold.

"Rotten little food stains," Erak growled. Reida scowled, an unusual expression on her normally-content face. Luckily for the both of them, there was still one hundred twenty-three pieces in Erak's purse, which he split with Reida (an act that made her tear up a bit and hug him around the neck).

"I'd been saving all that money for a set of proper enchanting robes," Reida said a bit sadly. I reached over and she slipped her hand into mine.

"After this is over, I promise you'll get your robes, *lün*," I said. She gave a small smile and squeezed my hand. I used my other hand to pull another piece of paper in front of me. I looked over and nearly fell out of my seat.

"This is it!" I yelled, letting Reida go to press the paper flat. It was a map. "This is where the dens are. There is one for every province, it seems." Reida looked over.

"There's one in the south of Middle Vale," she said, pointing to an 'X' about ninety miles away, near the border with the Basin.

"When we're ready to go, that's where we should head," Erak said. We all nodded.

"We don't know if they have a prisoner or not," Reida said, "and it would be unwise to let the chance go. Plus, by the time we get there, I should be strong enough to conjure a familiar to go in and scout the place out before we go in."

"And if we do find someone inside?" Erak asked.

"Then we get them into good shape and let them choose if they want to help us or not," I replied. I stopped. "You two have that choice as well, you know." There were a few moments of silence.

"Why would I go home?" Reida asked quietly, wrapping her hand around mine. "There is no one to go home to anymore. And... I like what I've found here."

"Aye," Erak agreed, smiling. "I was a lonely child, left home thinking I'd find something great. Well, I was right. I've got you two now. And, I suppose I have a score to settle."

"We are together, then?" I asked. Reida and Erak smiled.

"Together," they said.

TWELVE

Just as the sun was going down, Reida wet a rag and wiped off the hardened paste from Erak's ribs. He gritted his teeth a little at the sting of water. We all gawked at the results. The wounds had shrunk to half the size, and had closed up. The festering was gone and the welts around the wounds had changed from fiery red to muted pink in color.

"Holy..." Erak breathed. Reida beamed. "Oh Reida, I would kiss you right now if she wouldn't murder me for it." We laughed.

"I'll kiss you," I said, poking Reida's bicep. She blushed. Erak's stomach growled.

"You two can get cozy later. What's for dinner?" he asked, grinning.

"Abrahm has food, if you're insinuating I get some," I laughed.

"I thought you'd never ask. Surprise me!" He pulled five coins from his bag and tossed them at me. I smiled and caught them, then Reida and I went downstairs. Abrahm was haggling with a customer in a grey riding cloak. We decided to browse while we waited. Reida looked out the window.

"Talia, look," she whispered suddenly. I went over and looked with her. Outside was a large carriage painted gold with deep red trim. On the side was an intricate lion, a snarl on its face. The curtains were drawn, but I didn't have to see the occupants' faces to know who they were.

"That's the royal carriage," I breathed.

"What are they doing here?" Reida asked.

"I don't know, there wasn't any word sent out about a royal trip. For all we know, King Altren and Queen Pernelle should still be in Highland. Unless it's something they didn't want the people to know about. But, if that's the case, why travel with the golden carriage?"

"Something isn't right here," Reida said warily. We heard footsteps behind us and turned. It was the stranger from the caravan outside.

"Women," he sneered. "Always gossiping. I suggest you leave now, as you're butting into official business." I glared at him.

"What's the royal envoy doing here?" I asked him.

"What makes you think that's any of your business?" he snapped. I laughed. My mind reached out and dived into his. He shuddered and looked around for a draft. In moments all of his memories of the mission had flooded my head, and I knew all I needed to know. I retracted and he made a face at me.

"Because, sir," I answered, "I am in the business of knowing other people's business." He huffed angrily and stormed out of the shop.

"What did you get?" Reida asked me quietly.

"Decoy," I said. "King Altren isn't in that carriage. But, that pig of a soldier is too low on the food chain to know exactly where he is or what he's doing. He leaves at dawn and he comes back at dusk." We exchanged a look. Reida and I bought dinner and went back to our room. As we ate we relayed the information to Erak. He didn't look worried; he looked almost sorrowful.

"They said something about the king," he said.

"Who?" Reida asked.

"The Blackhawks. They said something about the king while I was there. The king and... And inspections." He looked miserable. My heart nearly stopped.

"No," Reida whispered.

"How could this happen?" I demanded. "And why didn't I know about this?"

"I thought... I thought I was just hearing things. I was delirious, they said a lot of distorted things. I'm so sorry!" he said, almost crying.

"The implications of this are... Astronomical! The ruler of the Empire has the Blackhawks under his thumb. If we try to take them out, we'll have the entire god damned army on our tails!"

"Unless... Unless they don't know," Reida said. We turned to look at her. "Think about it. Most of the people in the army are younger than you, Talia. The Blackhawks were before their time, and Altren would have wanted to keep his dealings secret, right? Chances are nearly no one really knows what he's up to. So, if we were to, say, plant a seed of knowledge into their ranks, we could sway them to our side, and change the course of this campaign in our favor."

"Who is to say they will join us?" Erak protested. "Maybe they'll think us freaks as well."

"Then we simply... Make them forget about us," I said. "Or we kill them. Loose ends." They agreed solemnly. I took Reida's hand.

"I promise it'll be over soon," I told her quietly. She kissed my cheek.

"Are we going to Highland or the Hall first?" she asked.

"Highland first," I said. "We'll spread the truth about Altren's dealings, and see where it leads us, but we'll stop at Blackhawk dens along the way. Alright?" Both of them nodded.

"And if becomes an uprising?" Erak asked, crossing his ankles in front of him. I thought for a second. It was mind-boggling to think that something that started out so simply could turn into a revolt. Yet, it was a possibility I could not ignore.

"Then we play our parts. Whatever they end up being. After all... If they want to fight with us, who are we to stop them?" I smiled a bit.

"Are we starting a rebellion, *lün*?" Reida asked me.

"Not yet," I replied. "But maybe soon."

THIRTEEN

We spent the night at Abrahm's. In the dim morning light I woke to find Reida stripping off the tunic she still slept in. She proudly showed me how much weight she'd gained. Indeed, her skin was drawn less tightly around her ribs and hips than before, and her chest had begun to fill out. I smiled and kissed her bare stomach, then patted her side and recommended she get dressed before Erak woke up. She was just getting her dress on over her head when Erak groaned and stretched.

"Good morning," he said sleepily, propping himself up on his elbow.

"Good morning, Erak," I said, tightening the lacing on the back of Reida's dress.

"Yes, good morning," Reida added. "How did you sleep, *daén*?"

"Pretty well. And you two?" Reida eyed me slyly. I grinned.

"Quite well," I said, laughing. Erak made a childish noise and I laughed. Reida blushed and I kissed her cheek. We packed our things and Reida checked Erak's wounds one last time. They were scarring over already, the healing sped up enormously with the Glïn oil application from yesterday. She was pleased with the results, and Erak was cleared to do nearly anything he felt, as long as it didn't cause his wounds to reopen. Once everyone was ready, we went downstairs and said goodbye to Abrahm.

"Abrahm, my friend, could you tell us which way the caravan went?" I asked him right before stepping out the door.

"East, my old friend," he replied.

"Thank you," I said, and turned to follow the others, who were already out the door.

"And remember, Talia," Abrahm said as I opened the door. "It shall be so." We winked and I smiled back, then left. We headed east until the early afternoon, when we heard carriage wheels in the distance.

"That'll be them," I said, slowing Rosemary down to a walk.

"We should follow them and set up camp when they stop for the night. Then we can spy on them, and maybe see the king returning," Erak proposed. We all agreed. From then on, we followed them about a half-mile back. When they slowed, we fell back to refrain from being spotted. Sometimes we even went off of the dirt and trailed them in the woods, following the road. All in all, it didn't appear that we were seen. Even if we were, no one in their ranks really seemed to care all that much about it. At sundown they stopped, so we did too. We set up camp in a tiny clearing about three quarters of a mile away from their set up.

"No fire tonight," I said. They nodded, and we begrudgingly ate our food cold. I finished first, so I volunteered to go and spy on the caravan. I snuck through the woods and made my way to their camp. I sat in the shadows by the edge and listened.

"Never lending him coin again..."

"How could she bed another man? She said she would wait for me. But they never wait, do they..."

"Lying whore, saying that little whelp is mine. Could've gotten up the spout with anyone in that gods-forsaken brothel."

"The King is back!" someone called aloud. I nearly broke my neck from how fast my head snapped around to look. Everyone was standing and looking the same direction. Two men on horses had appeared. They dismounted and I recognized the taller of the two. King Altren. He was a few inches taller than me, with salt and pepper hair and a thick black mustache. He wore a permanent frown on his weathered face and a black riding cloak was fastened around his throat. A man wearing a pompous red and gold uniform came up to him and saluted. Everyone else did too.

"Easy, gentlemen," said the king in his deep voice.

"Any news, Sire?" asked the man in pompous uniform.

"Not here, Raslin. Come to my tent." The two men began to walk towards a large white tent bearing the royal seal. I snuck closer to the tent, nothing more than a ghost in the darkness of the night, hiding in the shade it threw to listen to them talk.

"Have they made progress, Sire?" the man named Raslin asked.

"Bah, it depends on what you consider 'progress.' They've captured the abominations, yes, but none of them know anything. It appears almost none of them have even *heard* each other. They're like a cat with no teeth; they can catch their prey, but not get what they need from them."

"Why not order them to show some results, Your Highness?" Raslin suggested.

"No, no. They must be made to think they are in control, that we're sharing the power. That Worth fellow isn't intrepid by any stretch, but he is not stupid, either.

He'll turn on me as soon as he sees something that he doesn't like. No, Raslin, we must be gentle in our urging."

"Just say the words, my King, and I shall write them." I heard the rustling of papers and then the scribble of a pen as Altren started to dictate.

"Commander," he began, "You will be happy to know that I have nearly completed my inspection of your... *Stations*. Your men are well trained in the art of torture, but I do not see much in the way of answers. It is of no matter, though, as I am sure they will extract something sooner or later. If I may be so bold, I am asking you how many prisoners you have. I have counted seven alive and two dead, but still have one last station to visit. From what your officers tell me, however, it seems as if none of the vile things knows one another. I wonder, will this be the same for the entire group of them?

"But I digress, Commander. Your men have done extraordinarily well in capturing their nine anomalies. You should be proud, Commander, in having brought up such adequate soldiers. Remember, our meeting in Highland is scheduled for the end of October. I trust that we will speak more about this topic then. In confidence, Altren Domaste."

"I shall make a good copy and send it to the outpost, Sire."

I'd heard enough. I melted back into the shadows and returned to our camp. When I got there, Reida was asleep, wrapped in her cloak. I sat next to Erak, who was whittling something with his dagger.

"What did you hear, Talia?" he asked me.

"The king is definitely involved. He's in control, but doesn't want Worth to think he is. He's been visiting their hideouts, observing their techniques and learning what they know. They haven't gotten to the Adaima den, though. And we need to go before they start on the road. They'll start a search for you and Reida the minute they find the bodies in the first chamber. And Altren has soldiers stationed all over the continent. It won't be a long look if we don't hide."

"Let's go to Glïnéa," Reida said. She'd been awakened by us talking and was now sitting up.

"Why?" Erak asked.

"It's ruled by the Elven Council, not the Empire. They have no power there. And we can stay until we figure out our next move."

"King Altren said he and Commander Worth are going to meet at the end of October. Today is September 26th. We don't have long, and the only way I can see this working is to go to Glïnéa and travel up through the Neck. We'd have to avoid Red Road Pass, though, it'll be swarming with guards."

"So, now we have two things to do in Highland. Spread the word about Altren's dealings, and to see what he and Worth are planning," Erak summarized.

"Yes," I said. They both nodded. There was a lull and Reida snuggled up to me.

"Talia?" she asked me quietly. "When we get to Glïnéa, can we stay in my hometown, Amèni? The harvest festival starts October fifth. That's... ten days." I smiled gently.

"What do you say about it, Erak? Do you think we can drop in on the second-biggest party of the Elven year?" He grinned.

"Hell yes, we can!" he laughed. I kissed Reida hard and felt warmth rise into her cheeks.

"We're going to Amèni, *lün*," I told her. In the dim moonlight I saw a flash of a smile. Her arms wrapped up around my neck and her head found a place resting on my shoulder. I thought back to what Abrahm said.

'It shall be so.'

We left before the sun rose, knowing the caravan would be leaving at the first light of day. We travelled to the southwest, following the road-signs to the Elven-Valian border. We travelled fast, once even riding throughout the night to give us more time. By the end of the third day we'd reached Stillwater Lake.

Stillwater Lake was a huge lake nearly in the dead center of Middle Vale. It was nineteen and a half miles across at the widest point. The center of the lake was curiously still and silent, giving the lake its name. The legend behind the still center went thusly: A young woman had been betrothed to a handsome young man who was caught in bed with another woman the night before their wedding day. She was so heartbroken that she'd drowned herself in the lake, and her body was found floating in the dead center by a fisherman. It was said that her spirit caused the unusual stillness, as a reminder of her sorrow, and on a cold night one can supposedly see the foggy form of the poor woman gliding across the water.

Regardless, we set up camp on the beach and made a fire. I'd shot a rabbit earlier that day, so Erak and I shared it while Reida ate a vegetable soup that Erak had made especially for her.

"Do you think they've found the cave yet?" Reida asked once we'd finished our meals. She was laying with her head on my shoulder.

"I don't know, love. Maybe."

"How long until we get to the border?" Erak inquired.

"At this rate, about three and a half days. Then you have to account for the time to get the passports taken care of. But, all in all, we should get to Amèni before the festival starts." Reida smiled.

"What's the festival like?" Erak wondered. "We had a party in Hell's Creek for the harvest, but I'm sure you Elves throw better bashes." Reida laughed.

"It usually lasts two days and two nights. The morning of the first day is fasting and devotion to Granduil, the god of harvest and agriculture. When the sun goes down, the partying begins. There are dozens of courses with hundreds of dishes, all vegetarian of course. Wine and ales from every region of the province, fireworks... and *magick*. That's where I am. All the summoners and enchanters gather and do a synchronized show. I'll be participating in full since I'm getting stronger. We conjure smoke beings, atronachs, dragons made of blue and green fire, spectral dancers... Everything you could possibly imagine! Each year has a specific theme to the show... Oh, I can't wait to find out what they've picked this year... Miraculous things happen during the festival, especially in the capital, Rodènsï, where the Glïn tree is. Granduil and Kynarïn have been known to make themselves known during the festival; healing people, blessing children, even granting wishes they deem worthy of granting.

"The party lasts until first light. The next day is one of rest and personal offerings to Granduil. Every family selects the best thing they've grown or made that year to give to the burning pile. When the pile is completed, it is doused with oil and incense and lit ablaze. When the fire burns for hours, and when it dies out, the festival ends."

"Fascinating," Erak murmured. I was welling up with excitement. I'd heard of the festival for years, but my travels had never taken me to Glïnéa during the harvest. Now I was getting to see it with two of the most important people in my life. I looked at Reida and kissed her cheek. She smiled, but then her face grew worried.

"Don't move too quickly," she mumbled, "and please do not panic. My necklace is burning hot."

All of the sudden, there was a crash by the tree line. In a second I was on my feet and had pulled out my bow. The vegetation rustled and I nocked an arrow, waiting for someone to come into view. Reida was crouched beside me, hands and eyes glowing purple, and Erak had his sword drawn. The crashing came nearer and we slunk backwards to put the fire between us and the coming person or people. We began to hear voices; at least two distinct male tones, whispering and anxious, but the footsteps suggested many more than two. We looked at each other warily, knowing who they were before they were seen. Finally, with a giant bound out of the trees, they appeared. There were twelve of them; eight men and three women, all wearing the red and gold uniform of the Empire. Their leader, a man with his sword drawn, stood in front of the horde.

"You three are Talia Storm-Cloud, Reida of the clan Bollaïne, and Erak Birchdal of Hell's Creek, yes?" he asked in a gruff voice.

"Indeed," I said, aiming my bow at his head. "And you are?"

"Therm Denne of the Imperial Army. You three are wanted for crimes against the Empire." We looked at each other. Apparently, they had found the cave.

FOURTEEN

We stood there for a minute before I had an idea.

"Do you know who you're working with?" I asked.

"What say you, citizen?" Therm Denne said.

"Do you know who you're working with?"

"We work for King Altren and the king alone," said a woman with a thick Nordic accent. She seemed to be getting a bit irate.

"And who, dear Nordic miss, do you think your king works with?" I asked coolly.

"What are you saying, citizen? I will not tolerate slander of our ruler!" roared the therm.

"Slander, dear Therm, is a spoken falsehood that is harmful to another. What I say may be harmful, but it certainly is not a falsehood. Now, I ask you again; do you know who he is working for?" There was not a sound.

"No," squeaked a man from their side.

"Thank you for answering, Thrall. It seems the king has partnered up with our very own home-grown terrorist organization; the Blackhawks."

"Liar!" screamed the Nordic woman. "Altren Domaste would never do such a thing!" She went to take a step towards me.

"Stop!" I called. "Stop unless you want an arrow buried in your skull. And don't think I am bluffing, any of you. I never bluff."

"We speak the truth," said Erak.

"They vanished," the therm said, seeming to be convincing himself rather than us.

"They came back, Therm," I returned. "And they've started to hunt again."

"Who?" a man asked, his voice melodic and soft.

"Us," Reida said grimly.

"You seem interested in what we have to say. We can all put down our weapons and speak about this like gentlemen and women, yes?" I asked. "Here, I shall be the first." I lowered my bow and put my arrow back into my quiver. I set down my bow onto the ground and slid it away from my feet. Reida's aura faded and she righted herself. Erak sheathed his sword and took off the belt it was attached to, laying it on the sand, and we all looked up at them to see what they would do. The man who has spoken last relinquished his weapon first. One by one, they followed suit. The Nordic woman was the last to put her weapon down.

"Now," I said, "please, come sit around our fire." Hesitantly they made their way over. Reida, Erak, and I sat on one side, and the soldiers crowded on the opposing side, with Therm Denne sitting front and center on a log.

"How do you know that the king and the Blackhawks are working together?" asked a woman from Middle Vale.

"More importantly, how do you know they're even back?" the therm demanded.

"Because they kidnapped me," Reida answered. "And Erak, too." A feeling of fear rushed over the soldiers. All three of us felt it.

"I... I am sorry, miss," Therm Denne said quietly.

"Don't be, Therm. I will tell you everything, if it helps you to understand us." So she did. Reida told them all that had happened up until now. She told them what they did to her, how she was raped and beaten and starved, and the horrible wounds they'd given Erak. He showed them his scars, which were only a day or two healed over. She told them how we'd interrogated Drathis and how they'd set him up to die if we tried to let him go. Reida was strong, only faltering over the parts about her assaults and the bit about Drathis's death. I held her hand, encouraging her to stay solid. A few of the soldiers cried with her, including all three females and a few of the men. Even the therm shed a tear or two.

All was silent when she finished the tale. When someone did speak, it was the Nordic woman.

"How could Altren work with people who do such awful things, even to their own people?" she murmured, genuinely horrified.

"We cannot be part of this," agreed a tanned Nord man.

"I did not leave my home to fight for a man who condones such things," said a Valian man angrily.

"What do you think, Therm?" asked someone else. There was a pause while everyone looked to Therm Denne. His thoughts flashed full of images of his home and his wife, who was with child, and his brother, who had died fighting in a skirmish defending Altren's territory.

"When I was a lad," he said, "my father used to tell me stories about his days in the army, fighting under Altren's father. He used to talk about how glorious and good-willed Emperor Gästil was. He spoke of him like he was a Divine, such was the sum of his adoration for the monarch. It is of no question that Gästil and his wife Malena would be ashamed to see their son now. Hell, Altren took the title 'King' instead of 'Emperor' because he believed the title held less power to corrupt, less of a chance to go to his head... Damn. I will join your crusade, Talia Storm-Cloud. I will fight against this injustice alongside you."

"Aye, and I," said the Nord woman.

"And us," said a Valian man and Valian woman together. One by one they joined our cause, following their leader with pride.

"Thank you," Reida whispered to the Therm, her eyes welling with tears.

"What is the next move?" asked a man with red hair. I realized he was looking at me, and then all of them were looking at me. I was struck by the realization that they considered me the leader now. It flustered me for a second.

"Introductions?" Erak suggested. I nodded, my thoughts collecting now.

"Yes... We can hear all of your thoughts, but it's more polite that you tell us *aloud* who you are and what skills you have," I said. They chuckled. The therm went first.

"Therm Audar Denne, hailing from Farose, Hjellmun. I'm thirty-two, and I've served in this army for eleven years. I've got a wife, Lisbet. She's pregnant, it's our first baby together. She's waiting for me in Highland. I specialize in strategy and swordplay."

"Lismari Guldland, Drene in the Imperial Army," said the Nord woman. "I am from the Basin. I've served for eight years. I'm an expert at stealth and secrecy." The next to introduce themselves were the Valian man and woman who had pledged themselves together.

"I am Chioma Ime," said the man. "This is my twin sister, Akua." The woman smiled demurely. "We come from Masozi, Middle Vale and are experts in archery." Chioma smiled at me and I grew excited for all the talking we would do about my weapon of choice. The tanned Nord was next.

"Thrall Bergliever Rydskov, hailing from Hjellmun as well. I've only been in the army for five months, and so I don't have a specialization yet. I can cook, though," he said, smiling sheepishly. Akua pushed him playfully, laughing.

"I am Eru Søndervik, Emïlan from Adaima. My mother was a Nord and my father an Elf. I do conjuration, and specialize in defensive magick." Reida caught his eye and I knew they would be spending a lot of time together. The third woman cleared her throat.

"Thrall Eliza Heim, from Silmen. I can do a little of everything." She returned to looking at her feet. Shyness radiated off of her like heat from the sun. Another Valian man spoke.

"Thrall Rudo Tumelo, born and raised in Middle Vale. Been in this army for seventeen months. I'm versed in ten languages and I'm good with cultural skills and foreign communications. Pleasure to meet you three." The red haired man went now.

"Henrik Almby. Hjellmun born, Glïnéa raised. My mother moved us there to follow her job with a continental bank. I'm good with the Elvish language, and I can pick a lock in under fifteen seconds." I wondered where he'd learned to do that, but resolved not to pry into their minds.

"Thrall Iwan Eklund," said a brunette man with a facial scar. "I was raised in the army, my father was a hersin under Gästil. I am excellent with military strategy."

"Thrall Vrold Lindberg of Adaima. Combat trained and tested. I've been serving with Therm Denne for three years. You can count on me, lasses and lad." He smiled. The last man to speak was a Valian man with stormy eyes and locs in his hair.

"I am Uduak Tichaona. I am better with a sword than nearly any man alive. I make poisons and I use poisons, and I do both very well. I do not like you, Storm-Cloud, but I dislike the Blackhawks more." There was a short pause.

"Now that we all know each other," Reida began, "we can talk about our plans, yes?"

"We should show them our skills, too, *lün*," I said.

"Yes, enchantress, show us what you can do," said Eru, laughing a little. Reida smiled and stood. Since she'd been gaining weight and eating more, her aura had strengthened and her magick flowed more evenly. Now her eyes glowed and she chanted a few words quietly to herself. Her palms lit up and she circled them around until a ball of light formed between them. It grew from a grain of rice to an orange, and she threw it on the ground. A translucent purple wolf grew out from the ground and howled at the moon. The soldiers were delighted, especially Akua and her brother. They'd never seen such a display, as Eru only focused on defensive shields.

"Most impressive," Eru commented happily. Reida's aura faded and she sat back down, her familiar taking a seat on the sand by her side. She petted it contently.

"Now you, Storm-Cloud," said Iwan. "What skill do you have?"

"I can hit anything with an arrow," I replied. "Deer, rabbit, bird... or person."

"Show us!" said Akua excitedly. She and her twin smiled eagerly. I grinned, retrieving my bow. I pulled out an arrow.

"What shall I shoot?" I asked, looking around. "It's a bit dark tonight." Akua glanced around her. She pointed to a log floating in the water. It was about a hundred feet out, floating slowly on the surface of the lake.

"Shoot that," she said. I smiled and stood, taking my aim in the moonlight. I released my arrow and it flew through the air, hitting the target dead in the center with a *thunk*. It spun in the water, and the Imes beamed.

"And you, Birchdal?" Lismari asked. "What are your strengths?" Erak's neck grew red and a strange emotion filled his eyes.

"I suppose I am in the same boat as Thrall Rydskov," he said shyly. "I can do a lot of different things adequately. But it seems I have yet to find one thing I excel in. However, if any of you decide to teach me anything, I would be happy to learn."

"Ah, a humble lad," Therm Denne said. "And willing to be taught, too. You would have been a fine soldier." Erak smiled a bit.

"So... Where shall we go?" Vrold asked.

"There is a Blackhawk hideout near the Valian-Basin border," Reida said. "If six or seven of you go and clear it out, the rest of us will head into Glïnéa. We can meet in Rodènsï on... October twelfth."

"I can give you the memories of the cave I took Erak from, if you'd like, Therm, to let you know what you're up against," I offered.

"That would be helpful, Talia," he replied.

"You shall receive them in the morning, then, Therm."

"Who wants to go with me?" Denne asked the soldiers.

"I do, Therm," Lismari said. "I'll take any chance I can get to take out those scum."

"And me, Audar," Vrold said. "I go where you go."

"As well as I," Iwan said.

"I will go," Bergliever said.

"Aye, and I," Eliza added.

"I will kill them with you as well, Therm," Uduak said darkly. No one else volunteered.

"The seven of us will meet you in Rodènsï, then, Storm-Cloud," Therm Denne said. "We leave when the sun rises." With that, it was decided that we should go to bed. Reida dispersed her familiar, curled up into my arms, and I was asleep within minutes.

The next morning, I gave Denne the memories and the two groups went their separate ways. Erak, Reida, Chioma, Akua, Eru, Rudo, Henrik, and I all set off to the west. It would take about three days to get to the border, and another length of time to get our passports verified by the guards who watched it.

Glïnéa was the only province that one needed a passport to cross the border to, but that was because it had a different government than the rest. Sometimes it took hours, even a whole day to get your papers "verified." Mostly that just meant that the soldiers took them, looked at them, sat around for a few hours, looked at them again, then gave them back. They were corrupt, most of them, willing to do the job faster for a handful of gold coins. In five days' time it would be October fifth, the day the festival started. We needed to make exceptional time to the border if we were going to make it to Amèni in time.

"Eru," I called behind me. I was leading the group of us, sitting on Rosemary with Reida placed behind me.

"Yes, ma'am?" he called back.

"I know you are half Elf, but have you ever been to Glïnéa?"

"No, unfortunately."

"Then you will be interested to discover that our little excursion has us arriving just in time to partake in the harvest festival." Eru laughed.

"Ah! I'd lost track of time," Henrik said nostalgically, "and nearly forgot about the festival."

"You were raised there, Henrik, tell us about it," Chioma requested. Akua smiled.

"Yes, and you, too, Miss Bollaïne!" she exclaimed. The soldiers had begun to call us by formal titles. I was "ma'am" and Reida was usually "Miss Bollaïne." They called Erak "Birchdal" or just "Sir." We were all fine with it, and Erak sort of smiled whenever they addressed him, since he was younger than all of them. He was twenty-one, older only than Eliza, who was nineteen, but she wasn't here. Either way, Reida and Henrik took turns telling stories of their times at festivals in the past.

"What about you, ma'am?" Rudo asked me. "Do you have any stories?" I laughed to myself.

"Too many," I replied. "What sort of story do you want to hear?"

"Something thrilling," Akua said.

"Something full of danger," Eru added.

"Something fascinating!" Henrik exclaimed.

"Do you want to hear about the time I stumbled into a Dwarven city?" I asked. I felt a bit like a mother talking to her children. They seemed to hang off of my every word.

"*You* walked away from a Dwarven city?" Chioma asked incredulously. He had a right to be skeptical of me. Not many people walked away from an encounter with Dwarves. They were a fearsome people, secretive and ruthless in protecting their hordes of metal, money, and knowledge.

"Yes," I said. "About three years ago. I was travelling through the Neck, in the south part of the range. I stopped in a clearing under some trees for the night. The western side of the clearing was a sheer mountainside, and it was dark, so I didn't see much of any details. The next morning, though, I noticed something odd in the side of the mountain. It was a button of some sort, just flat against the mountain. I ran my hand over it, and it clicked. Sure enough, the damned mountain opened up!

"It was a door, six feet tall and four feet wide. Behind it was a hallway, a long tunnel carved into the stone, dimly lit by glowing fungi on the walls. My curiosity got the better of me, and I went inside. I pulled my bow and I crept further into the mountain. The tunnel sloped downwards slightly, and the air began to get a mustier the further I went. After a long time, I found myself against another door. It was metal, but it had no handle that I could see. My hand brushed against it and it cracked open. It swung slowly, yet silently, despite it looking like it had been there for millennia. I peeked through the slit, and do you know what I saw?

"Dwarves.

"Tall as my waist, long beards to *their* waists. There were four of them, milling about and talking in their thick, guttural language. A rock shifted under my foot and I fell forward, knocking open the door and slamming onto the ground inside the small room beyond the door. They all looked at me, stunned. It seemed to take them a moment to comprehend what they were looking at. Then all hell broke loose.

"They jumped on me, grabbing my arms and my bow. I was dragged to a door on the other side of the chamber. I was telling them over and over that I wasn't going to hurt them and that they could let me go, but none of them spoke our language. They took me through the door and into a room full of steaming water pumps and clanking machinery. I was dragged across the floor, the men gripping me with iron-like strength. They said things to the workers that turned to look, and one of them went over to a lift in the corner and pressed a few buttons. He went up and I was held down. Minutes passed, and I was glared at like I had murdered someone. Finally the lift came back and the male worker had someone else with him, a Dwarven woman. She came over to me and spoke.

"'Who are you? What is your purpose here?' she asked. Her voice was thickly accented and heavy, as if her mouth was unused to forming the words she spoke to me. Not that I could see her mouth. She was wearing the thick veils that all Dwarven women wear.

"'I am Talia Storm-Cloud,' I told her. 'I am here by mistake. I found your secret door and I was curious. I will leave now if you let me go.' I could hear her thoughts, but they were in Dwarvish! It was maddening." Reida giggled. I looked at her over my shoulder and smiled, then continued.

"Eventually, she said something to the men and turned back to me. 'Come,' she said, 'I will take you to the king. He will want to see you.'"

"You saw the king!?" Akua and Rudo exclaimed together.

"Yeah!" I said. "It turns out I was in the city where he lives. A huge city called Urgarum. Anyway, the lady

Dwarf took me to the lift -- on my feet. She was a lot friendlier than the men. She understood that I'd made a mistake, and that I wasn't there to cause trouble, so she was quite nice.

"'My name is Sibra Ironhand,' she told me. 'I am sorry my peers were so rough with you. They are... suspicious of the surface dwellers. But I have studied your kind for fifty-two years! I am fascinated to finally have a live specimen! Tell me, how do you pronounce the word of the animal that humans ride on?' I started laughing, because she meant a horse." Everyone laughed.

"She led me through huge halls with intricate tapestries and paintings, down a huge spiral staircase, to the very lowest part of the entire city. All the while, she was asking me to explain human practices to her. 'Does the male always grow a beard? Why don't the females wear the veils as we do? What is it called when you use your heels to make the horse go faster? And why do you put shoes on your steeds? Is it true that your... your *trees* grow to be tall as the mountains?' It was that all the way to the king's chambers.

"The hallway leading to his throne room was lined with alcoves on both sides. In each was the bust of a former king and how the beginning and end dates of their reigns, reaching back thousands of years. The hall was incredibly long, filled with hundreds of kings. Some of them lasted for a century or more, some for a week. The last stretch of the hall was empty, leaving room for future occupants. The large door at the end of the hallway was guarded by two Dwarves holding six-foot pikes. When they saw me they pointed them at Sibra and I. Sibra explained why she was there and they hesitantly lowered their weapons. They opened the door to a huge room. The floor was covered in silver bars, gold coins, jewels... Riches beyond any I'd seen before or have seen since! And sitting in the middle of it all, atop a throne made of stone, was the king.

"He didn't seem surprised, actually. He looked at Sibra and said something in Dwarvish. She answered him demurely, and he motioned for us to enter. We stepped into the room and the door closed behind us. It made me nervous, but I didn't want him to know that. He looked at me and I looked at him. His hair was graying slightly around the temples, but his beard was still thick and red. He wore it braided, and even then it fell below his waist. His clothes were rich and trimmed with thick furs, and on his belt he wore a sword. He looked a bit taller than the rest of the Dwarves, like he would reach the middle of my chest. He wore a crown on his head that was encrusted with jewels, and above the center of his forehead there was mounted a ruby the size of an egg. He noticed me staring, and spoke to me.

"'You are human,' he said. His accent was thicker than Sibra's. 'Sibra told me why you are here. I am King Valgrim Hammeroath. You seek not to harm us, surface dweller?'

"'No, Your Highness,' I said. 'I mean your people nothing but good will.'

"'Do you wish to learn from us, then?' he asked in his deep, rich voice.

"'It would be an honor,' I replied. So Sibra and I bowed, and she took me to a room a few levels up and asked if I wanted anything. I asked her to see that Rosemary here was well taken care of, and she was quite delighted in seeing a real horse." We all chuckled.

"How long were you there?" Erak asked.

"A week and a half," I said. They marveled at me.

"What did they teach you?" Chioma asked.

"Letters, numbers, some words. I read some books from the library, too. But the really interesting thing is the archery skills they showed me. One of their weapon-masters taught me a more efficient way to hold my bow, and a method of aiming."

"Fascinating!" Henrik exclaimed.

"How brave," Reida said, kissing my neck and laughing. I kissed her on the neck.

"Now I want to hear your adventure stories," I told the group. By nightfall I'd learned that Henrik had met (and courted) a woman who turned out to be a necromancing witch, that Chioma and Akua used to pretend to be one person when they were children, and that Rudo had once almost fallen over a waterfall. We set up camp near some trees on the side of the road and slept soundly until dawn. So went the days. During breaks and at night, Akua was teaching Erak how to read and write. He was intrigued by the way her pen spilled out the letters with such grace and precision, and how she shaped their sounds. It was nice to see him so eager to learn.

On the third night, when we were about ten miles from the Elvish border, he proudly wrote his name for the first time in his twenty-one years of life. I smiled at the happy gleam in his eyes as he did so. He wrote it over and over, correcting the tiny flaws in his sloppy handwriting until he was satisfied with it. Akua watched him jovially. I caught her eye and sent her a thank-you she heard inside of her head. She nodded and smiled at me.

Extremely early the next morning, we rose and ate a huge breakfast, nearly emptying most of our stores of bread, cheese, and dried meats. We finished about an hour after dawn.

"Alright," I began as we were about to pack up, "do you have any civilian clothes in your army packs? It will be easier for us to cross the border if you don't look like servants of the Empire anymore." They did, and so they changed and packed their Imperial colors away. The Elves had a council instead of a monarchy, and they vehemently disagreed with the Empire's way of doing things. They believed in a group of seven whose word is law, instead of each Imperial province having its own small council and the Head Counselors meeting with the king bi-annually.

We crossed the border an hour and a half after we left our campsite. Well, there was more "approaching" than "crossing" in those ninety minutes, really. We were stopped by a group of Elvish soldiers, who had a small station sitting on the border. They searched our packs and took our passports. They eyed the soldiers suspiciously.

"Why are you, who carry the Empire's uniform in your packs, dressed as civilians?" one asked the soldiers.

"We're leaving the army," Akua said.

"Hmph. Good, they could *do* with a few less people. These passports will have to be verified." He took them and sauntered off into the small guard station. Then came the waiting. We spent hours outside the station, watching the men inside do nothing. Rudo, Chioma, and Erak fell asleep, Akua, Eru, and Reida played cards, and Henrik and I got frustrated. Even though the view from our waiting place was lovely -- about three miles from the border was the beginning of the huge forest that housed all of the Elvish cities -- we were quickly less than satisfied with staring at the tree line. After two and a half hours of waiting, Henrik huffed and went to knock on the door. I followed. A bored-looking Elvish man answered.

"We really need to get into Glïnéa," I told him. The man looked at me and I realized he didn't understand me. "Wonderful," I sighed. "A man working the border with the Empire that doesn't speak the Imperial language." Henrik stepped in and began to speak to the man in Elvish, and the Elf spoke back. They returned remarks, the exchange got a bit heated, and the Elf stepped back inside the station with a sniff. Henrik spat a word at the station door, and I didn't need to know the language to understand that it was a curse.

"He said they're 'working on it.' Whatever *that* means." They 'worked on it' for another two hours. It was early afternoon when they finally gave us back our passports and we were able to cross the border. We travelled farther west, heading toward Amèni. Reida's excitement was growing stronger the closer we got to the city. I could tell by the huge smile she wore, and the gleam in her eyes. It was nearly dark when we spotted the gates of the city, after climbing a huge hill that took us over an hour to scale. It was nestled into the trees as if it were part of them, and the city beyond it was illuminated with the orangey sunlight, because it was settled mostly under a group of trees whose growing routes had been changed slightly by magick to angle them back, allowing light to come down onto the city. When we got to the gate the soldiers pressed their faces to it like kids on the window of a sweetshop.

There was a huge marble building in the middle of the city, and I knew it was a huge library and school. Some of the taller buildings were wood or clay, but most of them were made by weaving trees into shapes using magic. It was a beautiful mix-match of styles. I looked at my companions. Reida was beaming, Eru was wide-eyed, Henrik looked nostalgic, and the Valians were astounded. I held Reida's hand as the gate opened. It was the night of October 4th.

FIFTEEN

The next morning, Reida rose early, waking me up by slipping out of bed. She whispered to me that she was going to a shrine to devote herself, and that I should go back to sleep. But as she left, I was already awake. I looked around. It took me a moment to remember what was going on. We were staying in the Lotus, a huge inn with a hundred rooms and a bath house connected. Reida and I had bought a room just for ourselves. Erak and the soldiers had split into groups and gotten rooms on the same floor.

I sat up and decided that I was going to take a bath. I went through my bags and pulled out my soap, scented oils, comb, and the best dress I had. Taking a room key with me, I walked out into the hallway and made my way to the bath house. When I got there it was all but deserted. I then, of course, took the largest room for myself and opened its door.

The inside was lit by a large orb in the middle of the room, which floated about and cast white light onto the ground, which was made of stone and cool to the touch of my sleep-warmed skin. The tub was set into the floor, and was about four feet deep. There were little benches set into the sides and stairs that led into it, and a faucet and knobs on the side with different labels on them. There was a paper posted on the wall near the door explaining how to use the bath, written in my language and in Elvish. The knobs controlled the hot and cold water that came out of the faucet, using a pump somewhere else. I tried it out. The water flowed seamlessly. I resolved that the Elven engineers were a clever bunch and stepped down into the water.

I soaked myself for a while, just enjoying the warmth and the tranquility around me. Then I sat on a bench and washed my hair, and scrubbed myself with soap. The orb floated around peacefully and I sat in the bath and enjoyed myself. An hour after I got in, I got up and walked up the stone steps onto the floor of the bath house. I wrapped myself in a towel that was sitting on a shelf nearby. I dried my hair with another, smaller one, then combed it out and left it hang naturally instead of braiding it. I looked myself over in the mirror that hung on one of the walls and then exited the room.

I went back to the room Reida and I had rented and found my partner meditating in the middle of the floor with folded legs, a few crystals and stones laid out in a circle around her. Her eyes were shut and her aura was gleaming brightly.

"Hello, my love," she said quietly when I walked into the room. Her eyes were still closed.

"What are you doing, dear?" I asked her, setting my old clothes down onto the mattress.

"Meditating on the Stones of Granduil," Reida replied. "Pray tell, what is the time?"

"About eleven in the morning."

"Mm... Then I will be here for quite some time. Why don't you go find something to do to pass the time, *lün*?"

"Alright," I acceded, strapping on my dagger-belt (not that I thought I would need it, but one can never be too prepared).

"Have a nice day, Talia," Reida said serenely. I smiled at her and then left the room once more. Once I got out onto the street, which was made of earth and plant matter, I looked around and found that there was nearly no one outside. Those who were seemed to be working slower than normal, walking at peaceful, stately gaits and observing the city as they passed, like it held a sense of nostalgia for them. I joined in the sightseeing. Everything here seemed to be connected with the earth, even the modern marble buildings. They had ivy hanging off of them, and around the school there was a little brook babbling by.

I decided to go into the school and do some reading. This library was different than the one in Silmen -- it didn't have guards or heavy metal doors, and you were never routinely searched. It was based off of a more trusting system, where the librarian on each floor simply gave you the book and you were expected to put it back. They didn't hound you, or scold you, simply handed it over and told you where it belonged. This was due to Elven society putting a higher value to education. In Nord and Valian societies, education was a luxury -- nice to have, but not essential to the lives of the majority of people (farmers, laborers, and so forth). In Elvish culture, though, it was seen as unacceptable to be uneducated about things like language, rhetoric, history, grammar, and mathematics.

Either way, I entered the school through the front entrance, where the doors were wide open. Inside was a huge room with bookshelves forming rows. There were wide aisles, with open areas where tables and sitting pads were laid out so people could read. In the corner was a hole in the ceiling with a sort of tunnel of light passing through it. I'd seen them before -- it was a telepathy-based levitation system. The art had been perfected many generations ago, as the Elves were very aware of telepathy, and those who had the gift were revered instead of isolated. For this system, one simply stepped into the light, thought of the floor or genre they wanted, and were raised to that section. Only one person could use the magick at any given time, which lead to occasional lines. But other than that minor inconvenience, it was a rather efficient and fast way of getting to the proper floor.

I stepped into the light and thought of the section on religion. There was a short pause and then I was lifted up off the ground. I floated up and stepped off when the tunnel stopped my movement. I looked around. The floor was filled with priests and priestesses and monks dressed in robes bearing the colors and symbols of the deities they served, along with quiet devotees. This was the Religious Studies floor. I'd decided to learn more about the beliefs of the Elves to better understand what or who Reida and so many others were devoting themselves to. I approached the front desk. The librarian of this floor was an older, gentle-looking Elven matron. Her yellow robes signified that she served the goddess Kynarïn.

"*Mélla, daén*," she said cheerily.

"*Mélla*," I replied. "I need a book on Elvish mythology."

"Just in time for the festival, no?" she asked in a voice that sounded like the twinkle of tiny bells.

"Yes. My *lün* is devoting herself to Granduil today and I wish to know more about him, and the rest of the gods and goddesses." The matron smiled.

"She is lucky to have a partner who is so interested in, and eager to learn about the culture of her lover," she said. The matron led me to a huge bookshelf and pulled out a huge, leather-bound volume. She handed it to me and smiled. "This is the only non-Elvish copy. You're in luck; usually it's out for use translating or teaching students. But here, it has the creation story, information about all the divinities, and then many parables about them."

"*Állé me,*" I said. We smiled politely at each other and then I sat down at a desk in the corner and began to read.

The beginning of time saw only one thing, said Elvish mythology. Méllék, Creator of Elves, stalking through time and space, feeling it was missing something. Méllék created the world, the stars, and the ten other gods came into being as they were needed, simply willed into being by Méllék. Nature was the first thing to be created, and so the goddess Kynarïn was brought into existence too. She ruled over the water, the sky, the animal, and the plants. Then, thing began to die, as everything does, and so a god of death was needed. Baerü was the one who took rule over the Afterlife, and controlled the life-strings of every living being.

Méllék thought his creation incomplete, and so he created Elvenkind. With these new beings came new needs, and so, new gods. They needed to grow food to sustain themselves, so Granduil became the god of agriculture. They needed to reproduce and connect with one another, and fall in love, so Taranma took the place of goddess of love, marriage, and fertility. The mortals began to grow in numbers, and they found that they needed guidance, so Gaené became the goddess of wisdom and truth.

The Elves wanted to sell, buy, and trade their goods, so Vülléna became the goddess of commerce and business, and also of wealth and financial prosperity. With riches come alliances, and with alliances come feuds, and with feuds come wars. Adröne was put into the place of god of war and power, to guide those in the waring path on their way. Then came Ceisaré, goddess of misfortune and tragedy, and Ollünen, god of mischief and deceit. And last of all the divinities was Drünin, goddess of magick. The mortal Elves worshipped, and still worship, all of the gods and goddesses; some were favored by certain sects, and each had their own temples and priests, but all were respected and feared. They cast their power onto those who believe in them, sometimes granting wishes and favors onto the devout, as a sign of their lingering power.

I looked up from my book and out the window. It looked to be about three in the afternoon. I closed the book and returned it to the matron. She smiled jovially and bid me a sincere goodbye, saying she would look for me and my lover at the festival. I floated down to the main floor and left the library. The sun still had a while to go before it set, so I walked slowly back to the Lotus, admiring the scenery instead of rushing. It must have been nearly four in the afternoon when I got back to our room. Reida was still meditating.

I gawked at how bright her aura had gotten. It was if a star had fallen from the sky and was now glowing instead in our room, shining with incredible force. Reida did not seem to notice that I had come in. Her power had increased to the point that she was now raised a few inches off the ground, even though she was in the same position she had been in when I left, legs folded and arms slightly outstretched, palms to the sky. Her eyes and hands, and now the center of her chest as well, were still leaking purple light, and the room seemed to hum with energy.

A few minutes passed and her lips parted, more light beginning to pour out from between them too. I felt my eyes widen. I had heard some Elves and magick-users speak of this state before; the "ultimate" place of calm and connection to one's inner aura. Reida began to whisper something in Ancient Elvish to herself, repeating it over and over so quietly I couldn't make out the words. Every few seconds she would say it again, a bit louder. Her aura shuddered and pulsed, and I was finally able to hear her words.

"Ai süllèrna mamül en raccü." Reida repeated it three more times, her aura pushing ever outward, eventually encompassing me. All the skin on my body tingled and I got bumps on my arms and legs; it felt like raw, untamed power. The final time the phrase was said, Reida's aura changed. It turned pure white, brighter and clearer than any white I had ever seen. She held the light for a half a minute, then it slowly faded back to purple, and got smaller, until only her eyes and palms were lit. Then she floated back down onto the ground, and even that light was gone. It took a moment for her eyes to readjust, and she smiled when she saw me standing there.

"How long have you been here?" she asked, resting her elbow on her knee and her cheek in her hand.

"A bit before you started to talk," I replied, setting down the clothes and containers.

"What did it look like?" Reida inquired. She looked content and relaxed.

"Your aura got bigger, and brighter, and your mouth started to leak the light as well... and then it all went white." She smiled.

"How white?"

"Pretty white."

"Blinding?"

"I'd say more 'dazzling,'" Reida laughed and got onto her feet. I held her to me and kissed her gently on the mouth.

"Where did you spend your day?" she asked me.

"To the library. I read about your deities," I told her. She smiled to herself, then looked out the window.

"There is still time to be spent before the sun goes down. What do you want to do?" I smiled slyly.

"There's enough in this room to keep me occupied for any length of time." I kissed her neck. Reida shivered and pressed her mouth against the skin of my collarbone, then my lips. I picked her up and set her down on the mattress, still kissing her. She trailed the tips of her slim fingers over my sides.

"You look beautiful in that dress," she told me. I smiled a bit and flipped her over gently so I could unlace her clothes.

"And you look beautiful out of yours," I said. Just as I was pulling out the last lace, there was a knock at the door.

"Come on, ladies!" yelled Erak from the other side.

"We're busy," I called back, kissing the back of Reida's neck. She giggled.

"Oh come on," he said. "I don't believe you."

"You can come in and check if you don't believe us," I retorted. Reida was still laughing as the knob turned. Erak's startled face appeared in the doorway.

"Oh," he said quietly. We laughed at the way his ears and cheeks reddened. "The, uh, soldiers want to get to the square early."

"Tell them we will be down in a few minutes," Reida said. Erak left quickly and Reida rolled over to face me. She kissed me.

"So... Anything I should know before we start to party?" I asked, grinning. She chuckled.

"Make sure you listen to anyone who sounds suspicious. It's even worse of a crime to harm anyone during a religious festival, but it still happens. Oh, and I have something for you." She sat up and pulled a small wrapped parcel out from her satchel. She unwrapped it to reveal a silver circlet with a single, tiny green stone in the center. I unconsciously put my hand over my mouth.

"Reida..." I mumbled. She grinned.

"I got it while I was out earlier," she said, "when I told you to leave." She put it on my head. It fit like it was made for me.

"Thank you, *lün*," I said, taking her face in my hands and kissing her. She smiled against my lips and kissed back.

"Now," I said once I'd pulled away, "let's go have some fun, shall we?" We laughed and left the room hand in hand.

SIXTEEN

The sky was pinkish-orange when the eight of us reached the square. Chioma and Akua beamed the whole way there. Henrik looked excited, too, and Rudo was speaking to him quickly. Eru seemed to be nearly trembling with excitement and Erak was laughing at something he'd said. The square, a large, open plot of space in the center of the city, was lined with dozens of tables laid with grass-green tablecloths, the color of Granduil. There was a platform on the eastern side of the square. A noble-looking Elvish woman was standing atop it.

"*Daéns!*" she called to the crowd. Everyone looked up at her. She continued in Elvish.

"That's the matron of the school," Reida explained. "She leads the meal part of the festival, since she's the highest authority we have in Amèni. In Rodènsï, the Head Counselor would speak now. Tomorrow it will be an actual priest of Granduil. Anyway, listen, she's saying a blessing."

"... *Ai süllèrna mamül en raccü*," proclaimed the matron. As everyone repeated the phrase, I recognized it as the same string of words that Reida had said to herself earlier.

"Reida, what does that mean?" I whispered to her.

"Something like, 'I devote myself to you,'" she replied. I nodded. The matron spoke once more.

"*Accï dé hülian Granduil comcé*!" There was a boom and a streak of light. It raced into the darkened sky and bloomed into a huge sphere of sparks. Fireworks. The crowd roared and more fireworks soared into the air and exploded, creating a sea of color above us. Reida flashed me a smile and all eight of us went to find seats. Once everyone had found a chair together, a bell was sounded and we all looked up. A building on the side of the square had been turned into a huge kitchen, and now dozens of Elvish women streamed out carrying covered dishes. They set them down along the tables, one for every four people or so. They uncovered them to reveal the first course.

The opening of our very traditional, very vegetarian, very Elvish meal consisted of fruit. Apples, pears, peaches, melons, and oranges; raw, stewed in sweet sauces, and made into tiny salads. There were bowls of various nuts too, both roasted and not. Pitchers of wine, ale, and water were also handed out. Every half hour the bell would sound again, meaning that the next course was coming. The second round of food was comprised of potages -- thick soups made from mashed vegetables and gourds, with crusty Elvish bread to wipe the bowls with. I found myself particularly fond of a carrot-and-parsnip variety, and ended up eating two bowls of the stuff before the half hour was up.

The third course was the main one. There were mountains of roasted vegetables, more soups, ten types of bread -- both unleavened and risen -- and more red wine than I'd seen in years. This course was left out for an entire hour. Reida and Chioma found the pumpkin stew to be rather to their liking. Akua ate more bread than I'd ever seen a human being eat. Henrik and I stuffed ourselves with a vegetable that Reida called *outérne*, Erak inhaled three helpings of sprouts roasted with garlic and oil, and Rudo and Eru ate a blend of peas and another, alien vegetable none of us really knew the name of in our semi-drunken state.

When the fourth and final course came out, we were sure we couldn't eat anything else. It was made up of cheeses, wafers, heavy almond and cinnamon pastries, and tarts filled with fruits. A cloyingly sweet wine was also poured with the course. All of us, with the exception of Eru and Reida, who were Emïlan and therefore handled alcohol like Elves did, and I, who had more experience drinking than most of the soldiers, were stone-drunk. We giggled and slurred and drank the berry-flavored wine while choking on how sweet it was. Before long, an Elf came up to our table and told Reida that she had been summoned up to the stage. Everyone turned to look.

Five summoners, including Reida, were standing up on the platform in an inward-facing circle. A hush fell over the crowd. The enchanters raised their hands above their heads, palms to the sky, and began to whisper an incantation. Their palms began to glow, each one having their own hue; red, green, blue, white, and my Reida's purple. Their mouths moved in tandem, feverously chanting something, but their words were too quiet for the crowd to hear. Tendrils of their auras sprouted from their fingertips and twisted together in the air. Above their heads, a human-like form began to take shape. It was feminine, with bare breasts and wide hips, and made of greyish-white smoke. When it was fully formed it stepped down onto the stage like it was descending an invisible staircase. The crowd gasped. A group of minstrels began to play a haunting tune.

The crowd oohed and ahhed as the smoke-being began to dance and leap along, waving its arms dramatically.

The music, a heavy drumbeat with a single flute trilling a frantic melody, made the being twirl and flit until, suddenly, both the song and the figure stopped. A softer melody began to play, sending the figure to swaying its hips and floating out into the audience. It went around to various people sitting at the tables, dancing seductively and touching their arms and faces. It stopped to seduce an Elven man nearby, and I was admiring its curves, when suddenly the figure turned its head and looked at me. I felt my stomach tense up as we locked eyes.

The smoke-being glided over to me, its toes barely grazing the ground. It knelt, still hovering a few inches off the ground, and put itself at eye level with me. Cautiously, like it was testing to see if I would burn its faux-flesh, it laid a hand on my cheek. I shuddered; the figure's hand was cool to the touch. It looked deep into my eyes, the icy-grey of its gaze chilling me to the bone. In the moments that we shared, the figure seemed to change. It became less of a conjured pillar of smoke, and more of a real, living being. As it peered into my eyes, I could see emotion in the cloudiness that seemed to stare straight into my mind. There was sorrow, there was wonder... There was life. The smoke-being parted its lips and hissed, like the sound of water hitting a hot pan. Then it spoke.

"You will... reign." The voice was hoarse and hushed, like someone with a sore throat trying to whisper. The being shuddered and then righted itself. It floated upwards, twirling in slow circles. It stopped when it had risen about ten feet above the ground. Then it began to break apart, being unhurriedly swept away by an unfelt wind. It began at the smoke-being's feet, and rose up its body like a growing gale. The figure was surprisingly calm at seeing its body ripped apart, simply watching it happen. When all of the being's legs had vanished, it began to sing. This time, its voice was cold and clear.

> *"Ai marèllü cé d'anaata éa,*
> *Doh nulléan, nulléan, nulléan,*
> *Sü méll me cé masüléa."*

As the final note rang out, the magick gale swept away the being's mouth, leaving nothing left. There was a moment of silence, and then the crowd erupted into a bundle of emotion. Some cried, some cheered, and everyone shouted praise at the summoners who were standing triumphantly on the platform. The minstrels began to play a lively song and everyone got up to move the tables to the edges. I stood to allow my seat to be removed, but I was momentarily numb to the surroundings. I watched as Erak took Akua's hand and the others found partners to dance with. I looked around and pondered the message the figure had given me. It worried me, but my mind was far too blurred with alcohol to speculate, and I'd caught sight of Reida, so I made the decision to leave such thoughts for the morning.

Hours passed, and we danced and got drunk together. One by one, soldiers began to sneak off with their partners. Eru was the first to go as he tiptoed off with a tall, blonde Elvish man. Then Chioma went off with a brunette Elven woman, Henrik snuck away with Rudo, and Erak swept Akua off her feet and carried her towards the Lotus. Finally, Reida and I stumbled back to the inn. We found our room (barely) and tumbled inside, giggling and kissing each other. Reida pulled off my circlet and set it down on the chest at the end of the bed. We stripped each other and I kissed her so hard that she lost her balance and flopped onto the mattress. I fell on top of her and laughed. She just kissed me harder.

Together we spent the night wrapped up in each other's limbs, writhing blissfully in perfect sync.

The next morning, Reida and I woke to the smell of coffee from another room. It wafted through the hallway and under the door, making me crack open my unwilling eyes. The midday sun didn't burn, but there was a soft ache present in my skull. Thoughts drifted into my head, but I ignored them, like I did most of the time. Reida was still asleep, her back pressed into my chest. I smiled to myself and kissed her on the back of the neck, running my fingertips over the soft skin of her hip.

Reida groaned softly, stretching and rolling onto her stomach. I looked over her body, observing how it had changed. She'd filled out a bit during the last few weeks. Wait, weeks? It astounded me suddenly how little time we had really spent together. She'd run into my camp on the night of September nineteenth, and it was the morning of October sixth. If this day was not to be counted yet, it was only twenty-four days. Just over three weeks, and yet I'd already shared more with her than any other lover.

Yet, taking all this into account, I had no doubts of myself or my actions. Reida smiled in her half-asleep state, and I couldn't help but smile back. I was sure; this was the woman I wanted to -- *needed* to spend my life with. She opened her hazel eyes a bit, which looked nearly green in the sunlight, and deep inside me something swelled with happiness. Yes, Reida was my soul mate. I wrapped her in my arms and kissed her softly. She kissed back sleepily, wrapping her arms loosely around me.

"Good morning," she cooed.

"Good morning, *lün*," I murmured back. She curled up next to me and played with my hair. That was how we spent most of the day -- wrapped in each other, whispering lovely little secrets and laughing about silly things and sometimes getting a bit closer than that, too. Eventually, though, the sun dipped a bit low and the shadows began to get longer. Reida warned me that the burning of the offerings to Granduil would be beginning soon, and that she rather wanted to see it. Reluctantly, and with much encouragement, Reida got me out of bed and dressed. We packed our things, so that we would be ready to leave early the next morning, and then went next door to the room that some of the soldiers had rented. I knocked on the door, my other hand holding Reida's, and waited for an answer. Erak answered the door.

"Hello, ladies," he said, smiling. Akua was lounging on one of the two beds in the room, her torso sparingly covered by a sheet. In the other bed were Rudo and Henrik, both shirtless. Henrik had his head across Rudo's thighs. His face turned red when he saw me, and he turned into Rudo's torso. On the floor laid Eru, who had found his way back to the Lotus during the night, and was nursing a seemingly-horrendous hangover.

"Good morning... err, *afternoon*, everyone," I said. "The sun will be setting sooner than not, so it would be prudent of us all to get dressed and ready to see the fire of offerings being lit."

"Yes ma'am," came Eru's muffled reply from the ground. I chuckled and closed the door to let them get ready. Reida and I had just turned to go towards the room that had originally been Akua and Chioma's when the

169

door to said room swung open. A disgruntled-looking Elvish woman stormed out. I recognized her as the same person that Chioma had left with the night before.

"Wait, sweetheart! Hold on," Chioma said, coming out from the room as well, wearing only his breeches from last night.

"*Slün!*" she screamed over her shoulder at him. I bit my lip, trying hard not to laugh. Chioma sighed.

"What did I say?" he asked, defeated.

"Based on that, probably something you shouldn't have said," Reida said, fighting laughter as well. "Come on, get dressed, the final part of the festival should be starting soon."

"Meet us by the front desk," I told him. Ten minutes later, all eight of us had gotten ready and were walking down the street towards the square. When we rounded the corner into the open area, we saw in the center a huge pile of crops and plants. It must have been a whole five feet higher than the head of the tallest man in the crowd, which had gathered again. The pile was made up of all sorts of things; corn, greens, wheat, flowers, herbs, apples, oranges, pears, and berries. A portion of the entire town's harvest had been deposited here, simply waiting to be set fire to. Nords might think this tradition to be impractical, but their gods didn't require such amounts of sacrifice (typically just a cow or goat annually, and one more on special occasions like a wedding or birth), and so they simply didn't understand.

As we watched, two Elvish enchantresses levitated themselves up to the top of the pile with jugs of oil in their hands. They poured the entire volume of their pitchers over the pile, making sure to get every angle, then gently put themselves back onto the ground. A man wearing the green robes of Granduil approached the pile with a lit torch in his hand. He was tired-looking, as if he'd ridden into town that day. He stopped at the base of the mountain of crops and began to speak. Reida interpreted.

"He's talking about how blessed we are to have received such wonderful gifts from Granduil this year, and how we as mortals under his whim should return some of the bounty. Hence the burning of the crops." We watched as he dramatically turned and lowered the torch to the pile. The oils caught fire, and then the entire structure erupted into flames. The priest and the women with the jugs stepped back from the pyre and retreated into the crowd so that they would not be showered with sparks.

The priest began to sing, his voice rich and melodious. The crowd began to sing along, a chorus of Elven voices singing harmonies with him. I'd heard the song before, but I didn't know the words, and so I simply hummed the melody. The song was slow but happy, a sort of joyous contradiction. I felt Reida's hand slip into mine. I turned my head and smiled at her. Henrik and Rudo were humming along and holding hands, too, and I could see that Henrik had his head on Rudo's shoulder, which was just the right height for him. I smiled at them but they did not see me, as they only had eyes for each other. We stood for a while, just watching the fire roar, and it grew dark around us.

SEVENTEEN

The next morning we left Amèni, heading northeast toward Rodènsï. We didn't have to be there for five days, and at a medium pace it would only take three and a half. It was the seventh of October. I kept us going at an easy pace, keeping a loose grip on the soldiers and letting them goof off a bit. The road to Rodènsï was quiet and smooth, winding through ancient forests and crossing peaceful streams and meadows. We talked about silly things, told stories, drank and sang. Erak spent most of the trip with Akua. I overheard some of their conversations, even the ones that were half-mental, and I knew that Erak was fancying her to be more than a tutor. He knew she felt the same.

For a bit I was worried about how Chioma was handling it. He was, after all, her twin brother, older by nine minutes as he always said. Akua was worried about it too, and for the first day we travelled she looked nervous whenever he was near them. But Chioma didn't care much. He pulled Erak away from the fire the second night and talked to him.

"I don't need to tell you that she can take care of herself, I think," he said. "I am her brother, but she is better a warrior than I even so. If you hurt her, I won't need to come after you. Akua will do it herself. So... I guess I should tell you to watch out for her left hook. It's caught me off guard more than once."

I was sitting on the other side of the fire, but I heard everything he said. I smiled to myself -- he gained quite of bit of respect from me for that. He didn't treat Akua like some porcelain doll that needed coddling, even though she was his "baby" sister. Chioma knew full well what Akua was, and it was anything but fragile. Akua was a soldier, as good as or better than any man in the group. If anything else rose in me that night, it was the urge to see her fight.

Later on that night, while Reida slept with her head on my shoulder, and the rest were playing cards a way off, Henrik approached me cautiously. His mind flashed with images of Rudo and their night together. There was hesitation in the way he sat down next to me.

"May... May we speak, ma'am?" he asked quietly.

"Of course, Henrik. Would it be too predictable for me to ask what is on your mind?" I chuckled. He smiled nervously.

"Uhm, I just wanted to ask... Are you all right with... you know..." his voice trailed off. I knew what he was asking. I also knew from peeking into his mind that he daydreamed quite a bit, and was forgetful, didn't know that Reida and I were lovers. I bit back a smile.

"Thrall," I said sternly, "I am very disappointed in you. You know the rules. Actions have consequences." Henrik's eyes filled up with tears.

"I don't know why I'm like this, ma'am --"

"Surely," I interrupted, "you know that relations between two soldiers in the same regiment are forbidden." He stopped.

"But... You don't care about us being together?"

"Henrik, I'm with Reida. She's my *lün*." A sudden feeling of stupidity and shame washed over him.

"Oh," he said, blushing. He burned with inadequacy.

"Oh come now, Henrik. Don't feel that way. You just were a bit inattentive, is all."

"Yes ma'am," he said, lightening a bit.

"Do you love him?" I asked.

"Yes, ma'am, I do. Very much." I smiled.

"He loves you too, Thrall." Henrik's ears grew red as well as his face.

"He does?" I nodded and tapped my temple with one finger. He smiled widely.

"Thank you, ma'am," he said, hugging me tightly. He got up excitedly and went over to the place where Rudo was sitting. Without warning Henrik bent down and directed Rudo's chin upward and kissed him hard on the mouth. I smiled to myself. Reida groaned softly in her sleep and rolled the other way, off of my shoulder. I looked around at my companions. Everyone had someone. Except for Eru and Chioma. Chioma didn't look outwardly envious, but there was a little pain nipping at his heart. Eru, on the other hand, looked quite sad sitting on his log all alone. I frowned and went over to him.

"Good evening, Eru. May I sit with you?" I asked. He nodded. I sat on the log next to him. He was thinking about his one night stand at the festival. I smiled a bit.

"What was his name?" I asked. Eru gave a sly smile.

"I never got it," he replied. "We saw each other, I brought him a drink, and then he bedded me." I chuckled.

"I've had a few nights like that myself," I told him.

"With women only?" Eru inquired. "If you don't mind me asking, that is, ma'am," he added quickly.

"I've never bedded a man, Thrall Søndervik. And I don't care to ever do so." He shrugged a bit.

"Hey, that's your preference. I've been with everyone," he laughed. "Men, women, even a few people who were neither. It's all good to me."

"That last bit is something I've never done," I replied.

"It's not astonishingly different, really. They were very beautiful though... But anyway, how have you and Miss Bollaïne been? She's been quite happy since the festival." I smiled.

"We have been well, Eru. Has she told you anything, said anything about me?" I felt like a little girl asking, but I didn't mind very much.

"She says sometimes, when we are conjuring things, how lucky she is to have found you in that clearing, instead of someone who would have taken advantage of her. She talks about how gentle you are with her, how ferocious you are with other people..."

"I am lucky to have her as well," I said quietly.

"You should tell her that."

"I will."

The night passed with Reida in my arms, Henrik in Rudo's, Akua in Erak's, and Chioma and Eru wondering what it was like to be in love.

We arrived in Rodènsï on the night of October eleventh. I could tell, even in the pitch blackness of the night, Rodènsï was much, much older than Amèni. The buildings we passed were hardly buildings at all -- they were trees grown into living spaces and shops. Some were squat and low to the ground, and others were tall with parts of the trunks turned into ramps leading to the door. The only proper structure was the palace of the Elven Council, called the *Maïleniau*. It was a huge stone building on the Northern edge of the city. We rode through the gates near the palace and were directed to a strange building, the only thing resembling an "inn" in the whole city. We exhaustedly rented our two rooms and settled down for the night. With Eru, Chioma, Rudo, and Henrik in one, and Reida, Erak, Akua, and I in the other, we fell asleep quickly.

The next morning things went slower. I woke up to the sight of Erak and Akua wrapped up in each other and the warm feeling of Reida's long limbs tangled in mine. I kissed Reid awake, planting little seeds of my love on her head and neck. She opened her gorgeous green-brown eyes and smiled at me.

"*Mél*," she murmured.

"*Mél, lün*," I replied, kissing her on the forehead. On the other bed, Erak groaned and rolled over. We looked up at the other couple, who were both being dragged from sleep. Akua stretched and yawned.

"Good morning," she said groggily. We smiled at her.

"When's the other group going to get here?" Erak mumbled.

"Whenever they arrive," I said. "I left instructions with the gate guards to send us a note when they arrive." He nodded and kissed Akua's shoulder. She used her arm to hide her smile.

"Do you two have plans with each other?" Reida asked. Erak and Akua looked at each other.

"Not particularly," Akua said. Her thoughts wandered and Erak's face reddened. Reida and I laughed, since we heard them too.

"Talia, dear," Reida said, "my stomach hurts. Do you think you could go get some breakfast? A pastry, maybe?" She stuck out her bottom lip. I laughed and kissed her on the forehead, and then on the tummy.

"All right, love. Akua, Erak? Do you two want any?"

"Yes please," Akua said. Erak nodded with his head in the pillow. I pulled on my socks and boots and then went downstairs. I bought four apple-stuffed tarts and brought them back upstairs. I'd only been gone for about five minutes, but when I got back to our room, the whole scene had changed. Reida was sitting up with a strange look on her face, Akua was searching through her bags, and Erak had buried himself in blankets, clearly uncomfortable.

"What's going on?" I asked, setting down the wrapped pastries.

"I'm bleeding," Reida said absentmindedly.

"What? From where? Let me see!" I took a step towards her, searching her exterior for a wound.

"No, Talia," she said. "I'm *bleeding*." She motioned to her pelvis. It took me a moment to comprehend.

"Oh. Oh! *Oh*! Do you need anything?"

"I've got it," Akua said, pulling a cloth pad from her knapsack. She handed it to Reida. She made sure Erak wasn't looking and then slipped it into her underwear.

"Can I have my pastry?" she asked, looking tired and pale. Akua and I smiled at her.

"Here," I said, pulling one out from the wax paper and giving it to her. She bit into it hungrily, moaning and leaning back as it hit her tongue. I chuckled.

"You're all so... calm," Erak noted, popping his head out from the blanket fortress he had built to protect his ears. "I would have thought that one of you starting to bleed profusely would have had a greater impact."

"Oh come on, it's not like she's our firstborn girl and it's her first cycle," Akua snapped. "She stopped cycling because they starved her and now she's gaining her weight back, so it's returned."

"Ah," he said. Erak stewed over that bit of information for a while.

"It won't be a heavy or long one," I predicted. "But..." I kissed the top of her head, "it's most definitely a good sign." We all settled down to eat our breakfast. As I finished my tart, there was a knock at the door. The owner of the inn called something in Elvish through the door.

"A messenger is here," Reida interpreted.

"*Allé!*" I called back. "Well, my friends, it appears that the therm has arrived."

EIGHTEEN

We got dressed and roused Chioma and Eru, who'd slept in the next room to the right. They were playing cards and using some candies as chips to bet with. Their eyes brightened up when I told them that Therm Denne and the others were coming. They said they would help me go get them, and so Erak, Chioma, Eru, and I all made our way out to the gate to receive the rest of the company. They were waiting for us just inside the city walls.

"Therm," I greeted Denne. He smiled kindly.

"Good to see you again, lass," he replied.

"How did it go?" I asked, motioning for the tired-looking group to follow us.

"There were twelve of them" Lismari said.

"Mean bastards," Vrold added.

"They're absolute monsters," whispered Eliza.

"They had a prisoner," Iwan said.

"She died before I could give her anything for the pain," Uduak muttered.

"Died right in my arms, the poor lass," Lismari sighed.

"Did you find any information?" I asked.

"No," Denne answered, "just more maps and lists. But we did find a sizeable amount of gold and loads of supplies. We figured that you guys would want some of the materials as well, so we haven't divided it up yet."

"Good. We'll retire to my room and split it all up there." I led them to the inn and they piled into the room that Erak, Akua, Reida, and I had been sharing. Everything that they'd recovered was dumped onto the floor. I looked at the array. There were ropes, knives, a satchel, a cooking pot, a pack of new fire starters (ones that had recently been developed by a Valian inventor), a few bandages, a bundle of dried herbs, a slab of cured bacon, some salt, a hammer, and, finally, the large bag of coins.

"All right," I began, "I'll pick something out of the pile, hold it, and anyone who wants or needs it can make a case for themselves. Whoever makes the better argument wins it. Does that sound fair?" They all nodded their heads and sat down in their chosen places.

"Let's start with the ropes, hmm?" I picked up the coiled piles. "Who needs some rope?"

"I do," Lismari said. "My rope snapped two months ago, and we haven't been able to find another for me."

"Aye, it did snap," confirmed Iwan.

"No one else needs any rope?" Silence. "Then congratulations, Drene Guldlund, you are now the proud owner of two coiled ropes. Now the first knife. Looks like it would be good for whittling or something of the like."

"I'd like to have it," Henrik said. "I lost my backup knife some time ago... Forgot it somewhere... And that would do nicely." I chuckled. Poor Henrik. He gave off the impression that he would lose his own pants if it weren't for Rudo. No one contested, so it became his.

"And now a carving knife," I advertised.

"I'd like it, ma'am," said Bergliever shyly. "I'm the cook of the group, I'd likely get the most use out of it."

"You would indeed," Denne said. "Let the boy have it."

"Now this last knife. It's used for quick, silent, stealthy attacks. It's small enough to fit in a boot or a corset, but sharp as all hell. It has a ring on the handle for your thumb, see, to give more control."

"Can I have it?" Akua asked. "It would fit in my skirt, so I don't need to carry my dagger belt with me everywhere I go."

"You don't sneak around much," Lismari said. "I do."

"You already have several small knives, though, Lismari," Akua replied.

"True enough." She smiled lightly. "Though, a woman can never have too many weapons. You may have it, Akua. I'm sure I'll expand my collection soon enough."

"Very good," I said happily. This was running considerably smoother than I'd thought. "Now the cooking pot."

"I'd like to have it, *lün*," Reida said. "Eru, Henrik, and I are all vegetarians. It would be helpful for us to have our own pot."

"Yes," agreed Bergliever, "so then I wouldn't have to cook two different meals."

"Quite efficient," Denne commented.

"You may have it then, *lün*," I said, handing it to her. Reida took it and kissed me on the cheek.

"The satchel, now?" asked Rudo.

"Of course," I said, picking it up. "Do you, perchance, want this, Rudo?" He smiled.

"Why yes," he laughed. "I've been in need of a bag to hold my armor in now that we're going as civilians. There's simply no room in my knapsack."

"Seems reasonable to me," I said. "Congratulations, you're the new holder of this marvelous bag." We chuckled. "Now, the fire starters. There are only a dozen, and fifteen of us. So three will need to waive this."

"I don't need one," Eru said. "I can start a fire using magick."

"As can I," Reida said. There was a moment of verbal silence, everyone contemplating their need for one. They all agreed in their own heads that they couldn't start a fire in an emergency like Eru or Reida. Denne was the last to come to that conclusion, but, ever the altruist, he decided to relinquish his claim. He let out a short sigh.

"I'm sure that if push comes to shove, I'll be able to start my own fire," he said. "Plus, I'll probably be with one of you knuckleheads anyway." So the little wax-wrapped tubes were given out to the rest of the group.

"Who wants these bandages?" I asked.

"I do, ma'am," Chioma said. "I used mine a bit too harshly -- got shot in the thigh by a bandit's arrow a few months back -- and they're ruined."

"I can testify on that, ma'am," Akua said. "It was quite a nasty wound, and took a lot of work to heal."

"Then you may have them. Now the herbs."

"I can use them," said Uduak, speaking for the first time since we got back from the gate.

"What is in the bundle?" Reida asked.

"Barberry bark, ginger root, hawthorn berries, mint leaves, pine bark, and some dried *nulléan länea*," I said, looking through the twine-tied packet.

"Shall we share, enchantress?" Uduak asked, his deep voice rising into waves of respect. "I am in need of hawthorn berries."

"Shall I take the ginger root and pine bark, and you take the rest, sharing the *nulléan länea*?" Reida asked.

"It is a deal." So Reida took hers and Uduak took his.

"I suppose our own Thrall Bergliever would like the bacon," I said with a smile at him. He grinned bashfully. Eliza flashed a tiny smile at him. He took it and wrapped it in a cloth. "The salt?" I asked.

"I'll take it ma'am," Eliza said.

"I'd like some, too," Vrold said. "I used all of mine up curing our meat rations last month."

"My salt went into curing all that meat too," Eliza replied hotly.

"Split it then," I said easily. I broke the block in half and handed them each a piece. "Now, who would like this luxurious hammer?"

"I'll take it, lass," Denne said. "Since I've passed on everything else." He chuckled to himself and I handed it to him. Now all that was left was the bag of coins. I set it on an end table and put it in the middle of the room.

"Now, has anyone counted the coins out yet?" I asked the group around me.

"We figured you would like to do it," Iwan said.

"Thank you, Iwan." I dumped the coins onto the table and began to count. I sorted them into fifteen piles, adding one to each pile as I went around. There ended up being 376 coins -- 27 for each person, with one left over. Everyone took a pile and slid its contents into their purses, until just one coin was left. We looked at it as it glinted in the afternoon sun that was filtering through the window.

"So," Henrik said.

"So," I agreed.

"Therm Denne should get it," Chioma said.

"Now Thrall -" Denne began.

"No, he's right, sir," Lismari interrupted. "You should take it. Give it to your baby." She smiled and Denne gave a crooked grin to himself.

"All right, Drene," he said, slipping the coin into the inside breast pocket of his vest. I smiled at him.

"We shall leave here in the morning, everyone," I said. "Get a long rest and eat as much as you can. Don't spend your share all in one place, remember," I chided jokingly. The room cleared out and everyone who chose to remain (just the three who were sharing the room with me) busied themselves. Reida whispered an incantation which produced a tiny orb of light above her head, then busied herself in an Elvish fiction novel. Erak and Akua had a quiet conversation in their bed, holding hands and looking at each other like they were quite in love. I smiled and looked at my own partner. She sensed the gaze and glanced up to return it. I laid my head on her hip and that was how the day passed.

NINETEEN

We left the next morning at dawn. Or rather, we attempted to. The gatemen gave us a hard time because we arrived fifteen minutes before the gate was supposed to open. We ended up having to wait another ten minutes after it opened because a huge trading caravan came up to the gate and, apparently, had priority over us. Probably because they were full-blooded Elvish and we were a rag-tag bunch of humans and Emïlan (it was no secret that the majority of the Elven Council was largely xenophobic and racist against the Emïlan, though the Elvish populace, as a whole, was not). Nevertheless, we got through and began our journey north.

The gods seemed to be against our traveling that day, because when we finally got on the road, we made incredibly slow time. The roads were muddy because it had rained overnight, and Rosemary, being a snobbish little princess, refused to walk through the puddles. We had to physically push her through one particularly-muddy spot. She huffed and snorted indignantly at me for a while, swishing her tail. That ended abruptly, however, when she remembered that I am the one who feeds her.

And besides Rosemary's opulent expectations of our journey, there were several attempts by wolves and wild cats to attack the group. A broken wagon blocked our path for half an hour while its owners fixed the wheel. A fallen tree cut us off of the main road, and so we had to take a longer side path to get around the area, which cost us an hour by itself. We'd only made it about nine miles when the sky began to darken. I swore quietly and told everyone that we had to stop.

The next two days were more productive, but there was still a long way to go. The trip took most travelers two weeks on horseback. We'd lost a day, but at the pace we'd been going I calculated that it would take thirteen more days. Sixteen days wasn't terrible, considering we were a large group with one horse between all fifteen of us. By day eleven we'd reached the halfway point. But, such was our luck, things got exponentially more difficult then.

On a rough patch of road, one made of cobblestones and rocks that had been turned up over time, Rosemary let out a whiny. I turned around quickly, as I was leading her by the reigns, panicked that she was hurt. There was a *clang* against stone and she shuffled her feet quickly. I looked down at her hooves. There, on the ground, was her horseshoe.

"Therm!" I called. "Tell me the nearest town where we can get a horse shoe."

"Kimball's Landing, about three miles to the west."

"Lead us there, please. Rosemary's shoe just came off." I pulled out a large rag and wrapped up her hoof as best I could. I picked up the shoe and we hurried to Kimball's Landing, carefully leading my horse around the worst spots of upturned road. We arrived in town twenty minutes later and made our way to the stable on the edge of the little settlement. We split off into three little groups to look for supplies. I explained what happened to the owner of the stable, a burly Nord man with greying hair.

"You've come just in time, lass," he said. "Another two of her shoes are falling apart, and the other isn't exactly in mint condition. I can replace all four for you, if you'd like."

"That would be wonderful, sir," I replied. "Please use the highest quality shoes you have for her. I'll gladly pay the extra they cost." He laughed to himself gruffly.

"You must really love your mare, there, lass," he observed. I shrugged.

"She's special."

"Right. Well, it should take a few hours. See you then, lass." I rejoined my group (Denne, Chioma, and Erak) to go and look around for the time it would take the stable owner to fix Rosemary's shoes. We found a tavern and went inside, sitting at the table in the corner and ordering a few mugs of ale. We drank and chatted.

"When do you think we will arrive?" Chioma asked me.

"This little sojourn only costs us about half a day, and we can easily make that up if we hurry the rest of the way. We should arrive the morning of the twenty-eighth if we pick up the pace a little," I replied, taking a sip.

"That only gives us two days to spread the word," Erak said, a touch of concern in his voice.

"Ahh, don't worry, son," Denne told him happily. "Highland is crawling with us, and soldiers spread rumors faster than housewives at a knitting circle!" I chuckled.

"We'll make it," I promised Erak. He nodded and took a drink. His eyes wandered around the room for a minute, then locked on something, and he nearly spat his ale onto the table. He sputtered and choked, leaning close to the table. Alarmed, I smacked his back and looked back at the barmaid, who was giving us a suspicious look. Erak gasped for air.

"What's the matter?" Denne asked.

"Talia, turn around slowly, and look at the poster behind the bar," Erak instructed me quietly. I turned my head and the blood all fell from my face. It was a bounty poster. And the faces staring back at me from the parchment were mine, Erak's and Reida's.

I turned back around and shot Denne a worried look.

"We need to go," he muttered.

"It will be hours before we can leave," I whispered.

"My face is on there," Erak muttered in disbelief. "And Reida's!" Anger and fear tied a knot in my stomach.

"We need to get to Reida and the others. Chioma, Denne, you two can move without fear. Go to the other groups and tell them to meet us by the stables in one hour. It's far enough away from the center of town that we should be able to go without attracting too much attention. We are just a group of travelers, okay?" I reminded them. They nodded and we started to move.

"Hold on just a pip!" called the barmaid, her voice shrill and piercing. My gut clenched and I lowered my head. Erak looked into his mug like he was studying it, or maybe drunk.

"Is something the matter, ma'am?" Denne asked calmly as she stood beside our table.

"Haven't you forgotten something?" she demanded, thrusting out her open palm. Denne went into his coin purse, pulled out a few coins, dropped them into her hand, and then smiled politely. She sauntered over to the bar, counting them aloud. We left while her back was turned.

Chioma and Denne went their ways and Erak and I went ours. We traveled between houses and through the yards of villagers, keeping out of sight. We arrived at the stables to see Chioma, Iwan, Akua, and Reida already there. Reida nearly dived into my arms when she saw me.

"Oh, *lün*," she cried. "What will we do?"

"You all know about the poster, yes? We need to rush. We're not stopping between here and Highland," I told everyone. Erak held Akua to his chest and told her quietly that it would be okay. The others rounded the corner, then, and joined us. They all looked worried and discontented.

"I'm going to check on the farrier," I told everyone, ducking into the stables. The owner was sitting on a stool with Rosemary's left hind leg on his lap, hammering away.

"Ah, you're here!" he exclaimed when he saw me. "Impeccable timing; this is the last shoe. You've got a patient, well-mannered, horse here, lass."

"Thank you sir. I hate to ask, but I am in a sort of a hurry, so will you please tell me the cost?"

"Hmm... Sixty gold per horseshoe -- since you asked for the best I had -- and my time and skill included... Tell you what, if you promise to come back soon, I'll call it 300 even." He smiled. I returned the smile. "Oh, I just realized you can't very well come back if you don't know my name. I am Hallur Steel-Arm."

"Nice to make your acquaintance," I said. I walked over to his coat, which was hanging on the side of the stable. I counted out the gold -- six fifty-weight pieces -- and slipped them into the inside pocket of his jacket.

"And... Done!" Hallur said with a final swing of his hammer. He set Rosemary's hoof down on the ground and stood, stretching out his back, then handed me her reigns.

"Thank you kindly, sir Hallur. I promise I shall be back before too much time passes." I led my horse out into the open road and rejoined the group. Reida embraced Rosemary around the neck and whispered things in Elvish to her. Rosemary arched her neck to wrap around Reida slightly, seemingly hugging her back.

"All right, everyone," I called to the others. "No stops unless someone's dying, so watch your step and keep your weapon where you can get to it, yeah?" They all nodded. Just as Denne was going to add something, there was a shout from a few dozen yards down the road, near the edge of the last house. I looked up and swore loudly. Two soldiers were standing there in the intersection of roads, pointing and shouting.

"There they are!" called one to someone else around the corner. Six more soldiers came running from the town, drawing weapons.

"Aim to disarm, not to kill! They're outnumbered!" I yelled to everyone, drawing my dagger. Reida's hands lit purple and Eru's glowed green. One soldier, heading the advancing group, swung his mace at Denne, but he dodged it deftly and elbowed the man in the back. Lismari dropped onto her left shin and used her right leg to kick out a woman's knees, then knocked her out using a pressure point on her neck. Akua and Erak took down two soldiers together, Akua using her new knife to cut a neat, shallow line across a man's forearm, causing him to drop his sword and clutch the wound. She then used Erak as a launching point to tackle another and pin them to the ground with her foot. Erak went off to help someone else, and I smiled a bit. I was right to think she was a force to be reckoned with.

Four were down, and then one came for me. A Valian woman ran at me brandishing her sword. She swung at my neck, but I ducked out of the way and ended up behind her as the momentum she put into the move caused her to stumble forward. I kicked her to the ground, knocking the weapon from her hands, and held my boot on her neck.

"Move and I will have no problem stomping," I warned her. She was still, her ribcage moving like she was panicked. I pulled my bow and looked around, then shot an arrow into the calf of a man who was about to deliver a death blow to Reida. Stunned, he stopped in mid swing, and Reida saw the opportunity to move. She sent him tumbling backwards with a gust of magick wind and looked at me thankfully. A few minutes later, every soldier was down for the count. They were battered, cut, and bruised, but no one had been killed.

"We've spared your lives for now," I called to the people on the ground. "But if any of you so much as lift a finger off of the ground I *will* kill you!" I mounted Rosemary and we all sprinted north.

We didn't stop. We slept in small intervals, sometimes during the day and sometimes at night. We made up the lost time and then some, traveling ever faster as more and more posters of us appeared on the sides of roads. We made the rest of the journey in four more days, covering another 150 miles, traversing a mountain and crossing the plains that surrounded Highland. On the morning of October 27th, we stood about a half mile outside the gates of Highland debating how to enter.

"They'll know our faces, no doubt," I told Reida and Erak.

"They might even know yours from what happened in Kimball's Landing," Reida lamented to the rest. "Oh, my necklace has been burning for days..."

"We should enter in small groups," Akua suggested. "You know, stagger ourselves over an hour or so." Others nodded and chatted amongst themselves.

"Hold," Reida said. "I know what to do." She pulled out her satchel of ingredients and the pot she'd won in the separation of supplies back in Rodènsï. "I'll make a potion. One that will distort our faces." The soldiers looked at her like she was mad.

"As in, make us look like someone else?" Iwan asked.

"No, more like a blurry screen over our own faces. Like when you're crying, or you've got dust in your eyes, and you can tell what you're looking at, but the image is slightly unclear. Let's see... I need oak bark, newt livers, and... Ahh yes! Here we are. Talia, dear, build me a fire please. And fill up this pot for me, yes?" We got to work. I built the small fire and Eru lit it with magick. The others poured their waterskins into the pot until it was about three-quarters of the way full. Reida worked on the ingredients.

"I've chopped the livers, peeled the bark," she mumbled to herself. "Yes, it's all here." Reida picked up a vial of a syrupy blue liquid and poured a bit into the water as it boiled and rippled. The water shimmered as it mixed and turned the same hue as the mystery syrup had been. Reida produced a large gold stirring spoon and swirled it around in the liquid. Then she dumped in some yellow powder, the chopped newt livers, and a pinch of salt. The watery goo kept bubbling and shimmering. The smoke from the fire underneath the pot suddenly turned green; a piece of newt liver had accidentally fallen from Reida's hands and landed in the pyre.

We waved the rancid smoke away, coughing and gagging, then watched as Reida dropped the peeled strips of bark into the concoction. It turned a sickly, pale yellow, like the face of a fever victim. Henrik and Eliza both physically recoiled at the sight of it, and others made faces into the brew.

"Now," instructed Reida, "we wait and let it simmer for a bit before we can drink it. In the meantime, why don't you soldiers get back into your uniforms? They'll be more likely to let a bunch of soldiers into the city without question, even if they think they might know you."

"That means that you three civilians will need to go in on your own, seeing as the only reason to have any of you in regular clothes with us would be if you were prisoners," Rudo told us.

"So, half the soldiers, then us, and then the other half?" Erak reasoned.

"Spaced out over an hour or so," added Bergliever.

"Yes," said Denne, "that should work."

"Quite," I agreed. "Now, let's pray it works." The potion stewed and the soldiers changed, and then fifteen minutes later we assembled the first group of soldiers to enter the city. Denne, Chioma, Eliza, Bergliever, Iwan, and Vrold all took sips of the potion and shuddered like they'd been touched by an icicle.

"Gods, it's awful!" Vrold coughed.

"It's a cloaking potion, not goat's milk," Reida huffed defensively. I chuckled and kissed her hand. We waited about a minute or two, and then their faces began to change. It was slow but prominent. At the end of the brief metamorphosis, they'd become unfocused, and you could only make out the vaguest details if you squinted very hard. It looked as though I was seeing them through a heavy mourning veil.

"How do we look?" Denne asked. Reida smiled.

"Positively out of focus. Now hurry, it's powerful but it won't last more than twenty minutes, at most." They packed their things up, checked them twice, and then set out hurriedly toward the city gate. We waited about forty minutes, sitting quietly while we waited for them to have a chance to get to the inn. When we decided that enough time had passed, Reida, Erak and I packed up our things and choked down our portion of the concoction Reida had made.

I decided, as I was gagging on the foul liquid, that it tasted like moldy bread and dirt. I nearly vomited at the aftertaste, as I found it to be even worse than the potion itself. I coughed a bit and then my face grew warm.

"Is it working, dear?" Erak asked Akua. She nodded. Our faces were humming and buzzing, almost shimmering. If I didn't know what was happening, I might have thought I was going mad.

"All right, off we go!" Reida proclaimed. "Lismari?"

"Yes, Miss?"

"Will you please pack up my pot in your bags after you've drank your share?"

"Of course. I'll return it when we've all reached the inn."

"Thank you, Drene." We packed all our things and set out. I led Rosemary by the reigns as we approached the gate. We were stopped by two soldiers, who were positioned on either side of the main gate. They each had swords strapped to their sides.

"What is your business here?" asked one of them.

"We're here to visit family," I said. Their eyes were wide and transfixed onto our faces, and they occasionally rubbed their eyes in disbelief and confusion.

"You don't look like you're all related," commented the other guard, eyes on Reida and her skin color, which was obviously darker than ours. She seemed embarrassed.

"She's me wife," Erak said, wrapping an arm around Reida's waist. "And the other lass is me *dear* cousin."

"I see. Well, err... Go on in, then. Enjoy your stay in Highland." They both rubbed their eyes again, then one called up for the gate to be raised.

"Must be all the dust from the road in our eyes," one said to the other as we walked past them and into the city. Once we made it through, we all let out a collective sigh of relief and hurried to the inn.

"That was quick thinking," I told Erak on the way.

"Thanks," he said. "I was part of an acting troupe for a couple years back home."

"An acting troupe?" Reida said, baffled.

"Yup. I was the leader," he grinned. We giggled and kept moving through the city. The marketplace was busy, and we barely made it to our destination before our time was up. It was a sleazy little place called the Raven's Beak, where the innkeeper was easily bought and sold to protect identities from the guards and others who might inquire.

By eleven in the morning all fifteen of us had made it into the city. By eleven-ten, we were all in a room in the inn, unpacking and making a plan for spreading the news through the streets.

"The innkeeper told me that the reason the posters were put up was because the king decided that my group and I must have been killed in attempts to apprehend you," Denne said. "They think you three are murderers, and that's the only reason the matter went public. Killing a soldier can land you in the Imperial prison, not just some jail on the outskirts of a trading post."

"Now it makes sense," Erak said, rubbing his temples.

"I say we go see some of our friends in the city and surprise them with our liveliness," Lismari suggested.

"Yes, and then we may relay to them what you have told us and what we have seen of the Blackhawks," Akua added.

"That's the best idea we've got," I said. "And tell them that they must spread the word as well. We need to be ready when Worth comes to the city. I'm planning for the worse here -- planning on a rebellion. Having the capital at our backs will make things tremendously easier in that case."

"Then we will go," Vrold said. The soldiers stood and, one by one, told me the approximate place they were going and the name of the person they would speak to. Denne was the last to speak.

"Talia, may I ask something of you?" he asked when everyone else had gone. He was full of nostalgia and eagerness, and his thoughts flashed of his wife and how she'd cried when he was sent out four months ago.

"Of course, Therm, you may go to her."

"She's due so soon," he explained, seemingly apologetic. I smiled kindly.

"Audar, you never need permission to see your wife. I know how much you love her." He nodded and then squared his shoulders a little.

"Thank you, lass!" he said, then hurried from the room.

"So," Erak began after a moment of the three of us sitting in silence, "what are we going to do? We can't leave the room. Our faces are plastered on every street corner from here to Hjellmun."

"I know what I'll be doing," Reida said. "I'll be meditating on the stones of Drünin, to prepare to conjure the familiar I'll be sending into the meeting."

"Do you need anything special?" I asked her.

"No, thank you. I just really need to get in touch with my aura. Who knows? It might be like the festival, and I can hear Her speaking to me."

"Why do you have to prepare to conjure a familiar? You've been conjuring them constantly since you got your strength back," Erak observed.

"To conjure a familiar is nothing. It's something they teach children of Drünin from the age of 13. But to sustain one, to see through its eyes and hear through its ears? That is an art, and requires a constant and steady flow of the summoner's aura. You have to learn how to portion and maintain your flow, so to get clear images and sounds. I learned how to do it forty years ago, but I still must prepare myself for the exertion." Erak nodded and sucked the corner of his mouth in, making the face he made when he was thinking about something.

"And may I also ask something, dear?" I inquired.

"Of course, *lün*," she replied.

"How do the stones work? I mean, how do you meditate on them?"

"Well, first you have to know about how Elvish children choose a patron or matron to devote themselves to at the age of thirteen. I, obviously, chose Drünin, goddess of magick, to be my matron. One of the duties of the devoted is to try to become as close to their chosen god or goddess as they can be. Part of that is following the example of their patron, but another is meditation. There are eleven gods, of course, and each have a certain set of stones and gems that one uses to meditate upon. Two of them are the *Dïvae Pania*, engraved with the name and image of the divine in the color that symbolizes them. They hold pieces of the divine's influence in them, and so they allow you to get closer to the god or goddess you are trying to ultimately connect with. The divine has other stones that they like as well.

"Drünin, for example, uses amber to enhance magical abilities, amethyst to make your senses sharper (which is essential to a good magician), and rutilated quartz to boost your aura and make it easier to connect to Drünin's higher power, as well as stones that all divines use in their devotion, such as azurite to ease progress into meditation and jade to keep the devotee in a serene state of being and mind. I keep these stones in a pouch in my bag, hidden in one of the inner pockets. When I meditate, I place these all in a circle around me as I sit. The *Divae Pania* are always placed in front and behind of the devotee, like a straight line through their middle. Then I call out to the goddess and push my aura outward to try and feel her."

"Do only the devotees of Drünin use their auras in this way?" Erak wondered aloud.

"In a way of connecting to their divine?" Reida replied. "Yes. The aura is itself a thing used to channel magick energies. It is carefully controlled by the magick user's emotions. It takes years of practice and guidance by Drünin to gain complete control your aura."

"Can't some devotees of Kynarïn use magick to heal the sick?" I asked.

"Yes," she responded. "But only limitedly. Their magick comes in the form of a gift from Kynarïn, gotten only through constant prayer in a time of need. Most of their knowledge of healing comes from Kynarïn's dominion over nature and her gift of knowledge about natural cures. They are still the premier healers, but those with more severe injuries and magical wounds always come to the followers of Drünin for help."

"Magick can heal everything, though. Why would people prefer the longer way of healing, one without Drünin's influence?" Erak asked. Reida shrugged and began to dig in her bag for her stones.

"It is part of our culture. We are taught to honor the earth, and we prefer doing things the way they are most in tune with the world around us. Magick is for tricks and protection and warfare, and only sometimes for healing. My mother and I owned a shop where we sold remedies for ailments not serious enough to turn to Kynarïn for help with. Our specialty, though, was not healing, but enchanting items with charms and hexes for a price."

"I see," he replied. He made his thoughtful face and leaned back against the wall. Reida smiled and began to place the stones in a three-feet-across circle, placing the *Dïvae Pania* in their aforementioned places.

"I, of course, carry more than one divine's stones with me, because I serve a lesser patron than some of the more powerful ones. I carry the stones of Adröne for power, Gaené for wisdom, and Baerü, in case someone is wounded or hurt beyond what I can fix. He will take their souls to the afterlife and let them rest in peace. Of course, every god can be contacted without meditating, if one only prays to them. Meditation is a much more efficient way of doing the same thing, though."

When she was done, she sat with her legs folded in the center of the circle, closed her eyes, and laid the backs of her hands on her knees, palms up. She took a deep breath, blew it out between her teeth, and began to meditate. Her aura glowed from her hands and her face became one of tranquility and peace.

I smiled and settled down onto the mattress of the bed that Reida and I had claimed, and rolled onto my side facing away from her. I closed my eyes and dropped off into a dreamless, heavy sleep.

By dusk, everyone was back in the inn. Denne was the last to return, just before nightfall, and he was brimming with smiles and news about his wife and their unborn child.

"She's due on the thirteenth of November," he announced proudly. "The doctor and the midwife are both certain it is a girl. My Lisbet is so big, though, I have a hard time believing there is just one baby in there!" We all laughed.

"When my wife was with child," Vrold chuckled, "I thought the same thing. Course, I was right. Ended up having twin boys. Come to think of it, they should be having a birthday soon. Six, I think."

"Our mother used to say that it looked as though she'd swallowed a winter melon," Chioma said. Akua laughed.

"It was all the space your big head took up," she teased him.

"I can't wait to meet our little girl," Denne said thoughtfully.

"What will you name her?" Reida asked. "Names are very important."

"Lisbet wants to name her Cora, but I think the name Eldri is nice as well. That was my grandmother's name after all."

"Could always name her after me," Lismari joked. We laughed. "Just a jest, of course. What a horrid name I have! My brothers always used to tease me about it, called me 'Lizard.' Of course, I was always able to beat them up until they took it back."

"I'm happy for you, Therm," I said. "How was everyone else's day?"

"Very good," replied Chioma.

"Everyone was shocked," Eliza said.

"My contacts are eager to fight with us," Uduak added.

"Good," I said. "We need all the help we can get."

"Mine said they would surely pass it on," Bergliever told us.

"As did mine," Eru chimed in.

"Good, good. By the thirtieth, we need as much of this city knowing about the atrocities hidden from them as we can get. So, get a good night's sleep and find more people to relay the information to. Make new friends, get them interested in joining us. Oh, and try if you can to get as many gate guards knowing as you can. They'll be essential if something were to go wrong and we needed to make a quick escape."

"My cousin works the gate," Eliza said. "It will be good to see her, even if it is with such bad news." I nodded.

"Sounds like a very good plan. Tell her I said hello." She twitched out a smile and we all retired to our respective rooms. That night, I held Reida in my arms and slept on a nervous head, my dagger kept under my pillow.

The next day was more of the same. Reida meditated on the stones of Adröne and Drünin, taking a small break between the two, Erak practiced writing and looked at the maps, and I read and observed my lover at work. Her aura waxed and waned, glowing purple and sometimes even growing and turning white on a few separate occasions. The hours passed slowly, and soon all of us began to itch and pace from the boredom and stress of being pent up in the room. The people staying in the rooms around us were horrible, and their days were full of disgusting thoughts and deeds. I was positive at least one of them was the workplace of a prostitute, and her clients wanted the most horrid things from her. I made sure to send good thoughts to her through the wall.

It was after dusk when Reida was about to transcend her aura into whiteness once more. She was peaceful, her lips parted and leaking light, her aura big and powerful, when suddenly there was a loud bang on the wall and an obnoxious laugh. We all jumped, but Reida's eyes shot open and she was on her feet in the blink of an eye, looking around expectantly. Her hands were flexed like talons with defensive fire burning in them.

"Reida," I said, sliding off the mattress. I reached out and took hold of her arm, careful not to touch any of her stones. "It's all right, nothing's wrong." She relaxed, standing up straight. Her aura faded a bit.

"But that means... *Pinüt*! *Slün*!" she swore angrily, her power flaming up again. "Damn it! I was so close, I could *hear* My Lady's voice! Bah!" She sent an angry bit of energy at the wall, screeching through her teeth. A small burn mark appeared where her magick had struck. Reida plopped onto our mattress mournfully. There was a knock at the door.

"It's me," Denne called in from the hallway. I got up and answered the door. The therm looked over his shoulder and then entered, shutting the door quickly behind him.

"What's going on?" Erak asked.

"Eliza's cousin and several of the squad leaders want to speak with you. Tonight."

"Me?" I stammered.

"Yes. They want to hear the story directly from you. There is a theater about eleven blocks from here. They want to meet there at midnight. That's two and a half hours from now."

"By the Five," I muttered, putting a hand behind my head. For some reason, fear welled up inside me now. I wasn't normally this nervous about... Well, about anything, really. Why was this so terrifying? "This is a huge risk. If they decide to ignore us and remain loyal to the king, we're all doomed."

"It was a huge risk coming here in the first place, and we'd have been doomed ten times by now if there was an inkling of loyalty in the soldiers here," Denne said. "They are unsure exactly what to believe. Coming from you, they will surely be completely swayed."

"Why must it be me? I know I have played leader for all this time, but do you truly think I can convince an entire crowd of armed soldiers that the person they've served for ten years is corrupt?"

"Yes," he said. I was caught off guard. He came over and put a hand on my shoulder. "The reason we listened to you that night in Middle Vale, the reason we defied the king and followed you here is because we trust you, Talia.

We're your friends. We're here for you, we believe in you... Those people, they're confused. They don't even know if there are such people as psychics. They need someone to show them the truth, and they're asking for you." I nodded. As reluctant as I was, Denne was right. I took a few breaths and felt my confidence returning.

"How many will be there?" I asked finally.

"Nearly everyone we've told."

"No, no, that won't do. Tell them to send only two or three from their squads. If every soldier in the city comes, the nobles will notice and word will spread to the king."

"I will tell the others to spread the word." He turned and walked toward the door.

"Oh, and Therm?" I asked. He looked back over his shoulder.

"Yes?"

"Please also tell the soldiers to be sneaky about it. No yelling, no lanterns in the dark, and draw the curtains in the theater before lighting the lamps. I want no clues to anyone as to our movements." Denne smiled.

"Of course." He left the room and we heard his footsteps creaking down the hallway. I sat down for a second, Reida's arms curling around my shoulders and hugging me from behind. I leaned back into her.

"Should we come to?" she asked, pressing her lips to my cheek.

"No," I said, kissing her in return. I stood and began to pack one of my bags with essentials. "If it ends up going south, I can probably cut my way out. I don't want either of you to get caught up in that. I know you can both hold your own in a fight, but I am not taking chances tonight. And if something happens, I'm not leading them here. I'll take Rosemary and ride back to Glïnéa. In that case, and I mean that as a worst-case scenario, meet me in Rodènsï in a month's time."

"Be careful, my love," Reida said pleadingly. I smiled gently and kissed her on the forehead. I then turned to Erak.

"I know you can handle yourself very well, Erak. You're smart, whether you know it or not, and you're not terrible with a sword either." He grinned.

"Just don't let the next time I see you be in a lame ward, all right?" he joked. There was worry in his eyes, but he didn't let it into his voice.

"I'll be fine," I assured them, clipping my cloak on. I strapped on my weapons, swung my bag over my back, and left the room.

TWENTY

The streets were empty that night, and there were puddles on the ground from the rain that had fallen in the afternoon. In those puddles the streaks of green and yellow that glowed in the sky were reflected. I slunk along in the shadows, cowl up, turning my face from the oil streetlamps and light from windows. I walked slowly and methodically, thinking. The giant clock tower in the center of town began to ring its bells, counting out eleven strokes. I arrived at the theater on the last *bong* of the bell.

It was a large building made of brick, plaster, and wood, with small slots of cloudy glass serving as windows and a high ceiling. I slipped in the stage door and ended up behind a curtain. I put down my things and sat down on a stool to wait and listen to the crowd. I opened my mind. There was excitement and fear and anxiety in their thoughts.

"I hope she can't read my mind..."

"What if the king really is deceiving us? The shame..."

"If she slaughtered those Blackhawks by herself, she could make short work of us..."

I'd heard enough, and I tuned them out. I didn't want to make myself any more nervous than I already was. The time passed slowly, marked by my breathing and the beads of sweat that began to drip down my forehead on the dusty, hot stage. Five minutes before midnight, Denne came back onto the stage to find me.

"Everyone who was sent has arrived," he reported.

"Thank you, Therm," I said. I stood and peeked one eye out from behind the curtain. There must have been a hundred soldiers out there, sitting in the seats chattering nervously. I took a shaky breath and steeled myself on the exhale, then swept back the curtain and stepped through it. Denne walked to the right, over to the edge of the proscenium. All talking and whispering in the theater ceased. There was a cool silence.

"I assume introductions are unnecessary," I said after a moment. There were two or three chuckles. I began to relax. "I'd like to know what you've all heard about me before I tell you the truth. So... if someone would please give a summary...?" Silence. "Come now, I am not asking for your blood oaths to me." It was another moment before someone stood, a short Valian man near the middle of the crowd, looking scared.

"Your companions told us about the other two telepaths, the enchantress and the Nord man. We were told that the Blackhawks have returned to our land, and that they have begun to hunt once more. They're after your kind, yes? People like you?" A Nord woman stood as well.

"We don't know if they're even real telepaths," she shouted angrily. An icy tension filled the silent room, as the soldiers exchanged glances.

"You are correct," I said calmly. "You don't know. I can prove it to you, though, if you would like. Please, my skeptical friend, come up here and join me." People turned and looked at her as her face fell from angry to shocked and scared. She looked around, then stepped out into the aisle and began to make her way down to the stage. The soldier, tall and lithe, climbed the stairs off to the side and mounted the stage with me. I assessed her.

She was afraid, but her face had been calmed so that her appearance did not show it. Her dark hair was smoothed back into a near-perfect braid and her clothing was perfectly in place. I looked into her mind.

"Your name is Mirabelle," I told her. Her eyes swelled with dear.

"Anyone could have told you that," she stammered.

"And you know damn well that no one did," I replied quickly. "I can feel everything, hear everything. You're from Highland, you grew up just a few blocks away, on Cartel Street. You had three pet chickens and you cried when one was roasted for dinner one night when money was tight. Your mother's name is Gunhilde, your father's Hugljótur. You were afraid of the dark until you were nine, but then when you were ten a man visited you in the night and made you afraid once more. When you were twelve, your father slapped your mother in front of you and made you even more afraid of men. You're in love with another soldier, but I won't say who, for your sake. He makes you feel not so afraid anymore, doesn't he?" I turned and began to pace the other way, then turned back over my shoulder. "Oh, and your favorite color is purple."

Mirabelle's eyes filled with tears. She fell to her knees and wailed. I turned back around and knelt beside her, hugging her to my chest.

"I'm sorry he hurt you," I whispered.

"He was my *father*," she cried. I dipped into her mind and sent her soothing feelings. She stopped crying quite so hard and quieted down.

"Do you need more proof?" I asked the horrified crowd. More silence and shock.

"Are they really back?" asked a woman in the front row timidly.

"Yes," I said. "I've killed a few."

"Are you positive that King Altren is working with them?" yelled someone from the middle of the crowd.

"Positive. I heard him with my own ears dictating a letter to their commander."

"I heard that they raped your lover," called a man from the back. I sighed and stood up, ushering Mirabelle to return to her seat. When she'd left the stage I responded.

"Aye, they did," I said. "She was in a tavern in Adaima when they slipped a drug into her drink and kidnapped her. They assaulted her, beat her, and defiled her honor. But I have killed the ones who committed those crimes, and I will kill the rest as well!"

"If she is a telepath as well, why couldn't she tell they were going to hurt her?" asked a man skeptically.

"The Blackhawks possess a psychic beacon which they are all linked to by way of enchanted tattoos on their inner left forearms. The beacon prevents telepaths from hearing their thoughts without giving them the ability to hear as we do. It is the same reason that I cannot hear my love, nor our other companion. If I broke a lodestone in half, the two new lode stones will not stick together, because they are the same, yes? It is the same principle... However," I said, looking out to the men and women staring back at me.

"If you will join me and my comrades in our quest to destroy the terror and deceit that are corrupting our government and throwing shade upon our land, then I will gain the most valuable resource I can ever hope to have; the support of the people. You will be my eyes and ears, scoping out the city, and then, the entire Empire! Together we can clear out the vile plague that is sweeping over us. Today, this moment, you must make a choice between standing up for yourselves and remaining helpless against the foes we all must face. Now is the time to stand up for what you believe is right, what is moral. Now is the time to fight against these vulgar people, who have slaughtered entire villages on circumstance and superstition, who have murdered in broad daylight because of a misplaced look! I will stand against these villains! Who will stand with me?"

The crowd roared. I pulled out my bow, pushing it up in the air.

"Raise your weapons!" I shouted. There was a clamor of metallic noises as everyone in the theater drew their swords, daggers, maces, axes, war hammers, and bows. Denne raised his sword above his head, smiling, for he knew what I was about to do.

"From this day forth," I bellowed, "your weapons are no longer simply tools for you to use! By deciding to stand for your state, you are now heralds of a *new*

Empire! One that is ruled by justice for the wronged and protection for the innocent, and not by treachery, bribery, deception, and backwards alliances! These weapons will bring in the new day, one baptized of the blood of those who dared to defy the people they rule! Raise them to the sky, and pray to your gods that we will usher in a glorious and just time to this corrupted city, this shadowed land!" The crowd let out another mighty yell. Denne was the one who spoke next, lowering his sword and stepping up beside me.

"I am Therm Audar Denne, born in the great city of Farose, Hjellmun! In thirty hours, the Blackhawk leader, Commander Dalmar Worth, will be arriving here in Highland to meet with King Altren." The crowd, having sheathed their weapons, now began to whisper anxiously. "Fear not! We will only engage if what we know from their meeting demands it! Until then, we will only watch his movements and warn the civilians about the deceit we know Altren to have committed."

"Yes, do not fear. My beloved, the Emïlan enchantress Reida, of the clan Bollaïne, will be sending a familiar into their meeting to spy on them. Therm Denne, the other telepath, Erak Birchdal, and I will watch the meeting through the eyes of her familiar. Once it has come to an end, we will address you all with the results, and any actions we plan on taking."

"It is nearly half past one now," Denne said, "so please quickly return to your barracks and tell the others of what has occurred here tonight. Tell them we stand together this day!"

The soldiers dispersed quickly. Denne turned to me tiredly as they left.

"They are on our side now, I suppose," I said. He nodded. "But only time will tell if they are to remain there."

TWENTY-ONE

The thirtieth arrived quickly. We were up before the sun rose, all in our places on the walkway on the wall, in windows of buildings, on street corners, and on the rooftops. It was a cold morning, and the first frost had fallen over the Empire the night before. Breathing sent clouds of steam rising around our faces, and our worn fingers clutched our weapons numbly. Just as the faintest bit of light was rising into the grey sky we heard the rattle and quake of carriage wheels.

From my position in the center of the bulwark, I could see straight down the road for miles. It was I who first spotted the carriage rumbling down the road. It was accompanied by eight horsemen and the driver, all dressed in black and purple, and all bearing the grim air and cloak-clasp symbol that identified them as Blackhawks. Wordlessly, I pointed out the group to the thrall sitting next to me, and he stood and walked to the interior side of the parapet. There he unfurled the flag that meant the beginning of the operation; a purple arrow on a white background. By this time, nearly quarter to seven, most of the city was awake, and all of them knew about the dangers that were riding toward the gates. I had shut everyone out of my mind, but I didn't need to hear to understand that there was fear the mixed with the haze that settled over Highland that late-fall morning.

When the carriage and horsemen reached the gate, one of the guards who was riding called up to us on the top of the wall.

"Ho, gateman!" he yelled.

"State your business," called a thrall back. A few men snickered.

"My lord has a meeting with the king, and I suggest you do not delay him!"

"The king has no meetings today," taunted another soldier.

"At least, not with anyone important," added another. I put a hand over my mouth to keep myself from laughing. The horseman ground his teeth.

"Open the damned gate, you louse!"

"Well, since you asked so nicely..." returned the original thrall. He pulled the lever and the gate went up. The carriage rolled through and we all switched to the other side of the wall to see what happened. As the wheels clacked on the cobblestones, everyone kept about their business, but with one eye on the group as it passed. As it rounded the corner, I noticed that the curtains drawn inside the windows were ominously black.

When it was out of sight, I dismounted the bulwark and gathered everyone on the streets. All the soldiers and citizens looked up at me as I climbed on top of a cart so they could hear.

"All right, everyone," I began, "one of the servants in the palace told my companions that she knows exactly which dining room is being used for the meeting tonight. It is to be held at exactly six o'clock tonight. That is eleven hours from now. Reida is preparing herself now, and will be for the remaining time. Please, if you need to get in touch with any one of us, do not come to the door of our room, but take it up with one of my companions that I will set up in the bar of the Raven's Beak. I will give an announcement tonight concerning our next move. Please, everyone, be safe and be wary."

They thanked me and then dispersed. I hurried back to the inn. Just as I'd said, Reida was meditating in her stone circle. Her aura was big and purple, humming with energy. She spent hours like that, sometimes whispering to herself. I spent the day worriedly studying materials I'd received from the soldiers. I was tense and anxious, and there was a point where I was nearly in tears, but I didn't cry because I knew Reida would hear and I didn't want to disturb her. The clock tower finally rang out the five o'clock hour. I gently slid off of the bed and tried to wake my love from her trance.

"Reida?" I called softly. "It's nearly time. Come on." Her eyes opened slowly and the glow shrunk down until it was only in her hands, then was snuffed like a candle's flame by the wind. She looked up at me and smiled tiredly.

"Can I have some bread?" she asked. I chuckled and handed her a loaf from my bags. She tore into it ravenously, absolutely famished from her hours of concentration.

"How do you feel?" I asked.

"Fine," she replied. "When will Audar arrive?"

"Soon. He's still with Lisbet. She's growing stiff and tired, and the doctors say her baby will most likely come early. He's been worried, so he's trying to spend as much time with her as he can."

"I delivered a baby once," Reida mused.

"Really?"

"Yes. When I was still with my mother, a woman came into our shop concerned that her baby had stopped moving. She was terrified that she would lose it. First time mother and all. But as soon as she came up to the counter, her waters let loose and she nearly fainted. My mother laid her down and we delivered her son. It only took about two hours, a simple and easy birth. Her husband even made it to the shop in time to see him being born. It was certainly one of the most interesting stories I have from my time there." She chuckled.

"Maybe you could help Lisbet with their daughter," I suggested. "It's her first child as well."

"I would be honored if the Dennes would allow me to. I shall have to ask Audar to inquire it of his wife." There was a knock on the door.

"Speak of the devil," I said, rising to my feet to answer the door. Denne slid inside and closed the door behind him.

"Are we ready?" he asked.

"Nearly," Reida said. "Please fill our wash basin three-quarters of the way to the top with water." Denne nodded and took it outside, then brought it back full of water a few minutes later. Reida knelt next to the basin and rifled around in her bag. She produced a vial of gold-colored powder and placed pinch into the water, then stirred it with her finger. Her aura shone in her eyes as she whispered a prayer to Drünin, then sent a small bolt of energy into the water. The surface of the water instantly seemed to harden and created a mirror-like surface, clear and smooth enough to see one's reflection in.

Reida then lit up her palms and began to circle them around each other. She was summoning her familiar now. Another prayer to Drünin was uttered. A tiny ball of light appeared in her hands and then rose up and formed itself into the shape of an average-sized fly. The familiar fly looked around, then buzzed over and landed on Reida's nose. She opened her eyes and giggled.

"Hello, friend," she said to the fly. "Now, go, be our vigilant." The purple insect rose up and then zoomed out the cracked window. Reida touched the water once more and the surface changed. The howling sound of wind filled the room, and in the basin we saw the moving images of a city flying by underneath us. Through the fly's eyes it was slightly rounded and bowed, but recognizable all the same. Denne gaped at the tub. I smiled.

"Wonderful, my love," I said to Reida. She smiled and retreated to her stone circle, where she sat and began to meditate. Her aura grew large and powerful, and it would feed her familiar as it watched the meeting.

In the basin we watched as the city passed. It took Denne and me a few minutes to adjust to the odd sensation of feeling like we were moving while sitting still. Our fly friend made it to the Grand Palace in just under ten minutes. He flew to a window and perched on the wall to observe. It was the room that we'd been told the meeting would take place in. It had a long, polished wooden table running down the center of the room, and heavy tapestries hanging on the walls. There was a small table against the wall where a crystal decanter full of dark liquid, a few goblets, and a vase of roses were set. The door opened and King Altren walked in.

We and the fly watched as he walked over to the table, poured himself a glass from the decanter, and sat at the head of the table facing the door. He sipped it thoughtfully. The fly flew down onto the side table and perched on top of a rose, providing us with an excellent view of Altren as well as the door. A few minutes later, the door opened and Commander Worth entered the room. He looked just as I remembered from the memories I'd watched in Drathis's head, only dressed differently. His hair was still frosted white, his remaining eye just as cold and calculating, his other made useless by a scar and covered by a black eye patch. Instead of his Blackhawk uniform, though, he wore fur-trimmed robes. There was a pause. Altren sipped.

"Commander," he greeted his guest.

"Sire," Worth replied.

"Won't you sit?" Worth took a place at the opposing head of the table.

"I'm sure you've received the gifts I've brought," he said.

"Yes, my wife Pernelle told me she very much enjoyed the jewels."

"I thought she would."

"Mm... Yes. Well, it appears we have business to attend to. Commander, I visited all your little hideouts, and I seems to me that your agents aren't making much progress."

"With all due respect, Your Royal Highness, you'd be a bit off the mark to think that."

"Please, by all means, correct me."

"My agents, to use your term for them, have discovered the locations of six more telepaths. And we have discovered a connection between a few of them that the others have lacked. Two of them live in the same town, and know each other. We are planning on storming the village soon, on your word."

"What happened to secrecy and learning, Commander?" Altren asked skeptically.

"We've not learned anything of value to our causes, and we doubt that these freaks will offer anything to us in the future, either. Now it is time to simply exterminate the filth." The king got a sinister little smile on his mouth. It was as if he'd been waiting for his partner to grow this emboldened.

"When will the attack occur?" he asked.

"I have men surrounding the village now. As I said, I was awaiting your approval."

"Well, you've got it. Try not to kill anyone who isn't a telepath, but rest assured that if villagers get in the way, you will not be punished for their deaths." He rose his cup to his mouth and took another gulp to drain it.

"Thank you, Sire," Worth said, satisfied. He stood and was about to turn, but then seemed to remember something important. "Oh, and one more thing... Any word on the ones who raided my den in Adaima?" Altren set down his now-empty goblet and got a funny scowl on his face.

"They've escaped for now. But my men are scouring the continent for them. They will be found."

"When you find them, my I request the privilege of killing them myself?" Worth asked, the bloodlust in his eye so intense it frightened me. He was deadly serious.

"Of course," replied the king.

"Then I shall be on my way. Goodnight, Sire." Worth turned and left the room. Altren looked into his empty cup and sighed. He stood and looked toward the table where the decanter sat. The fly, sensing its time was up, rose off of the flower on which it had perched and began to fly up toward the window. Altren saw it though, and he lunged forward toward the familiar.

Blackness clouded the fly's vision -- Altren's hand had closed around it. I gasped and Denne jumped. Then we were looking up into Altren's huge face. He swore.

"Who do you belong to, little fly?" he asked softly, voice full of a quiet rage. "If you're watching this, summoner, know that you will be dead before morning." His other fist rose, came down, and then the water's surface went blank.

From behind us, Reida screamed. I turned quickly to see that her eyes were wide and her aura was gone. She clutched her heart and then looked into her other palm. I scrambled over to her and took her face in my hands gently.

"Shh, it's all right," I told her.

"What happened?" she demanded.

"Altren and Worth are planning to storm a village where two of us live. They've moved past their dormant phase; they're willing to kill anyone who gets in the way of them killing all of us."

"What happened to my familiar?"

"Altren saw it when the meeting was over and smashed it." Reida let out a small moan of sadness and pain.

"My poor familiar," she said. "I felt it die, and it hurt inside of me."

"I'm sorry, sweetheart." I kissed her forehead and turned to Denne. "Audar, we need to stop Worth now. We can't risk that village being slaughtered."

"What should we do?" he asked.

"Before he leaves the city, we need to have everyone ready. Archers on rooftops, men stationed in the buildings along the road to the gate, in every storefront that will allow it. When he gets to the gate, we'll storm the carriage and force his surrender. Dead or alive, he cannot be allowed to complete that plan."

"Aye. I'll spread the word." He stood and quickly left the room. I held Reida, who was shaking a bit, to my chest.

"It's beginning," she murmured.

"What's beginning, *lün*?"

"A rebellion."

TWENTY-TWO

Before the sun rose, everyone was in place. Civilians had been instructed to lock themselves in their homes, archers were lurking on rooftops, and men were packed into the street-side shops. At just around four-thirty in the morning, when everything was still save for the wildly beating hearts of the soldiers, the rumble of carriage wheels and the clop of hooves on cobblestones came into earshot. Everyone tensed up.

The archers were the first to ready themselves. They'd been given orders to take out Worth's horseback guards and the driver, aiming to kill. Then, the men in the buildings would run out and surround the carriage, and I would go down from my place on a building and capture the Commander, killing him if I needed to. Something in my gut told me it would be necessary. The nature of his eye and the steel in his face told me he would not come easily. But then again, he was also calculating and highly intelligent. He might decide the odds were against him and surrender. It was so hard to read him, and since I couldn't hear his mind, I had to just take the chance.

The wheels and hooves came closer and closer. From my position I could see them coming around the bend before the stretch of road that led to the gate. I rose my hand, the signal to the archers on my rooftop to ready their bows. When every man in Worth's party had rounded the corner and gotten about halfway to the gate, I let my hand fall.

TWANG!

Several arrows were loosed at once, hurtling down at the eight men on horseback and the ninth driving the carriage. Four arrows struck their mark, hitting the driver and the three riders hard enough to knock them off of their perches. The horses all screamed with terror and threw their front hooves into the air, throwing their riders and riding off through the city. The foot soldiers began to stream out of their assigned storefronts to encircle the carriage, brandishing their weapons. When they realized that some of the riders had not been killed, they warmed them and began to hack them apart. I turned and rushed down to the street.

"Halt!" I screamed. Everyone stopped and looked down at their carnage and their gory blades, then backed up from the broken bodies of the Blackhawk riders. I gave them a sweeping look-over, then approached the carriage. They gave me a wide berth.

"What will we do with him?" asked a thrall standing near me.

"That depends on what *he* does, soldier," I replied. I pulled out my bow and opened the carriage door. There, inside, sat a calm, collected Commander Worth. He looked me over, and the way he smirked chilled my blood.

"The great Miss Talia Storm-Cloud, is it?" he said. The soldiers behind me skittered nervously.

"Come out and you won't be harmed by anyone here," I replied shortly.

"And what makes you think I will obey, hmm?"

"I deemed you smarter than to argue with a woman who controls a city full of soldiers who are just *dying* to tear you apart."

"And I deemed you smarter than to plan an ambush without checking to see if everyone was truly on your side." He laughed, and before I could react, a loud crack echoed through the air. An explosion of pain hit my lower body. Things moved slowly before my eyes as I cried out and began to fall. Everyone started to scream and shout, and faces were turned to me. I wanted to scream at them, to tell them that I could see Worth was taking a horse that was still nearby and escaping while they were worried about me, but the words didn't come, and the pain was making my vision blur. I felt myself get lifted from the ground as the blackness was creeping in around my eyes. It got darker and bigger and then it was all I knew.

I didn't know how much time had passed when I gained consciousness again. The first thing I saw was a white ceiling, and the first thing I felt was a deep, steady ache in my left thigh. I groaned dryly and looked around for someone to help me figure out where I was. A white-robed nurse, who was making a bed a long way down the row, looked up and rushed down to tend to me.

"Oh, Miss Talia," she said hurriedly, "you're awake!"

"Yeah," I croaked.

"Here, drink this," she said, pouring water from a jug on my bedside table into a cup and handing it to me. I sat up gingerly and sipped it.

"Thank you. Where is Reida?"

"Miss Bollaïne is just outside. I will go and fetch her for you," she said, standing up and scurrying off through the door, which was only about ten feet away. A few seconds later, Reida dashed in, slamming the doors open, and ran down the aisle toward me with tears in her eyes.

"Oh Talia," she cried as she fell to her knees beside me, "thank the gods, I thought you were going to die!"

"What happened?" I asked, threading her hands in between mine.

"Worth had another member of his group, a spy, in the window of a building. He shot you, but his crossbow misfired and he ended up with his bolt through your thigh instead of your heart."

"Did he get away?"

"No, we caught him. He's dead, though. I tried to make them wait until you woke up, and then let you decide what to do with him, but they were angry and they just killed him... King Altren fled the city with Worth, and is staying with him, and the Queen has gone missing. People think she's committed suicide, and she left a letter, but there has been no body found. The king's advisors have all been murdered, his military ones, too. The nobles swore they knew nothing about the plots, and they were telling the truth; Erak and I checked. But the people are still outraged, and the Duke and Duchess of Smajen got their manor raided a few days ago. The Empire is calling for a leader to direct them in completely killing off the Domaste family, and as they had no heir to the throne, it's just the king left. The Counselors tried to sneak their way into power, promising an execution of the King and a prosperous year and all that, but the people wouldn't have it. They know that the Council only looks out for itself, not them... They want Altren and Worth's heads, and..." Reida stumbled over her words, rushing to get everything out. But then she hesitated.

"What is it, *lün*?"

"They're desperate for a leader they trust, and, well... They want *you*, Talia." As if on cue, the door banged open again and more people rushed in. Erak, Denne, Chioma, and Henrik all sprinted down the corridor and huddled around me, huffing and puffing.

"We heard you were awake," Erak panted.

"Well, you heard correctly," I said, smiling.

"How do you feel, lass?" Denne asked.

"Sore," I replied.

"Hey, Talia, now we match," Chioma laughed, pointing to his own thigh. I laughed.

"Have you told her?" Denne asked Reida. She nodded.

"They're growing awfully impatient," Henrik said uneasily.

"How long was I out?" I asked.

"Nine days," Reida told me.

"The wound got infected, and your fever was very high," Erak said.

"Those damn doctors tried to say they'd done all they could," Chioma muttered.

"But last night, it finally broke. They said the infection had gone," Reida added, stroking my hair gently. I looked into her eyes and smiled.

"Thank the Divines for it," Henrik said. I squeezed Reida's hand.

"What shall we tell them?" Chioma asked everyone. "Shall we give them the news that she's alive and well?"

"No," I said. They all turned to look at me. "I will tell them myself."

The soldiers left to tell the people of Highland that there would be an informational meeting under the hospital's balcony. Reida helped me to dress in my own clothes and then acted as a crutch for me as I tested my leg's strength. I started to put weight on my left side and nearly fell over. Reida caught me as I regained the ability to breathe, looking at me worriedly.

"*Lün*," she began, lines forming nervously on her forehead.

"No, no, I'm fine, Reida," I assured her. We began to walk slowly down the aisle of the hospital wing. I was halfway around the route when Denne came in.

"Everyone's coming now," he told us. "You'd better start making your way to the balcony."

"Thank you, Audar," I said, wiping a bead of sweat from my forehead. Reida helped me down the long corridor. It still took us quite a long time to get where we needed to go, because every twenty feet or so I needed to stop and rest my leg. My thigh was searing when I finally got to the balcony. Denne was standing by the opening, looking out onto the street. I could hear the chattering and talk of the people below. It sounded like the entire city was under us. When he heard us come up behind him, Denne turned and looked at Reida and me with an odd look on his face.

"They've been talking about you," he said. "They're getting impatient, and they've started to speculate that there will be no one to lead them. There have been rumors that the Top Council has been making a bid for power. People are nervous."

"Then," I replied, "let us calm their nerves."

TWENTY-THREE

With Reida's help, I made my slow, painful way onto the balcony. When I reached the edge, a hush fell over the crowd. I looked at the faces of the people below me. The citizens of Highland had lines of worry etched into their faces. The way their shoulders slumped, the way their eyes had lost that northern fire; these people were worn, tired, and betrayed.

"I suppose," I began cautiously, "that you have all by now heard the cry to have my leadership against the king, and I also suppose that you have echoed it. I understand that much has happened in the nine days since I was injured, and since Worth and Altren escaped. I understand, as well, that you are in pain. I see it in your faces, and I hear it in the emptiness of your thoughts. It was my friends and I who opened this city to the truth, and so, I see it only fitting that we should be the ones who see that truth erased. Therefore, I will lead you."

There was no cheer, no celebration, just quiet relief. Wives laid their head on their husbands' shoulders, mothers picked up their children and whispered to them that it would be all right. Reida came up next to me, putting her hand on top of mine.

"What shall we do, ma'am?" called a voice in the crowd.

"My leg is not yet well, so we, unfortunately, must wait until I can join you on the battlefield before we may move. Until then, I need units of soldiers to clear every Blackhawk den in the North Empire. Kill all the Hawks, and rescue the captives that are able to be saved. We will post a notification throughout the Empire calling all those who possess these telepathic powers to come to Highland to be safe. Please, protect these people with all you've got." There was a bit more chattering.

"Talia," Reida murmured into my ear, "do you think that, when this is all over, they will want you to seize the throne?" Images of the smoke being from Amèni danced before my eyes.

"I do not know, *ma lün*," I whispered back.

"Miss Talia!" yelled another voice.

"Aye?" I called.

"We, the soldiers of the Imperial Army, need new uniforms! We refuse to bear the crest of a traitor on our chests!" There was a cry of agreement from all the soldiers in the crowd.

"It shall be redesigned, then!" I replied. There was another hearty yell.

"Miss Reida!" someone else cried.

"Yes?" she answered, craning her neck over the balcony to see.

"When do you think we will be ready?" Reida looked at me, thinking for just a moment before answering them.

"Within the year!" she decided. "Before the first of January, Talia will be healed and we will have made all the preparations necessary." Without thinking, I shifted weight onto my injured leg and sucked in a hurting breath.

"Now," I said, gritting my teeth, "please excuse us, as my leg is putting up a bit of a fuss." I waved to the crowd and then, for the first time, they all smiled. It wasn't a big smile, nor one of elation or joy, but one of hope. My heart swelled. I felt a strange sensation inside me. I had felt important before, on those times when people said or did things to make it so, but to have an entire city, no, and entire *nation* believing in me? It was almost unreal.

I turned back to go inside, and saw Denne standing leaning against the archway. He looked at us and smiled.

The next day, Reida and I decided to go out into town with Reida. She was nervous, because of my leg, but I convinced her to let me out, pointing out that there were benches along the main roads that I could sit on if I needed to rest. It was November tenth. The air was cold and everyone was wrapped up in wool and furs. Reida's hands were covered by mittens as she held my bare ones. My leg felt better than yesterday, but it was sore, and still bothered me every so many feet. As I walked, though, people out doing their daily errands would approach me and want to talk. They spoke of how grateful they were, and how their families felt safer now, and my leg seemed not to hurt so badly.

Reida and I were walking along the rows of homes along the marketplace when we spotted a frantic-looking man running toward us. It was Audar.

"Reida!" he called when he was about fifteen feet away.

"What is it, Therm?" she asked. He run up to us, huffing and puffing.

"It's Lisbet," he gasped. "Her water has flowed, and she told me to come get you!"

"Well, it's about time!" Reida replied. "She's overdue."

"But I thought the doctor said she was due three days from now," I said.

"Apparently you two were busy back in early February," Reida said, "because the date of conception Lisbet gave the doctors was wrong. She was due almost two weeks ago, by the look of her. When I saw her last, while you were still asleep, Talia, she was miserable. Your daughter isn't eager to meet us, Audar. This will be a hell of a delivery."

"Oh, gods," Denne whimpered. Reida patted him on the shoulder.

"Don't fret, Audar," she said. "Here, walk with Talia while I run ahead and tend to Lisbet." Denne took Reida's place, linking his arm with mine to steady me.

"Wait, are you sure it's okay for me to come?" I asked.

"Of course," Reida said. "She expressed concern to me about not having enough women there. Her mother is passed and she has only brothers, and midwives in this city are impersonal and callous. I think she'd be delighted if another woman was there to support her." Reida looked through her bags and frowned slightly, then took off running in her graceful way toward their home. Denne and I began to walk slowly down the street.

"Dear Divines, I'm so nervous," he said.

"Don't worry, Lisbet is in very capable hands."

"Oh, I know. That's not really what I'm worried about. I know my wife is strong, and that Reida is knowledgeable. To be honest, I'm worried about if I will be a good father." I patted his arm.

"You will be. You're already a good father, and you're not even technically a father yet. Just remember this: take care of her, support her, but don't hold her back. Let her follow her dreams, and raise her to *want* to follow them. Women are made of fire; you must let them burn, and in burning they will shine." Denne was silent for a long moment, pondering what I had said. Soon we got to his home, a two-story brick building that was standard issue to military officers, and walked up to the door. There was a faint cry of pain from inside. Audar shot me a frantic look.

"Go to her," I said, giving him a reassuring smile. "I'll be fine from here."

"Thank you, Talia!" he said quickly, then dashed inside, leaving the door open behind him. I chuckled and went inside. I closed the door behind me and hung up my cloak on the hooks to the right of the doorway. I looked around the bottom floor. The house was sparingly by prettily furnished with two couches covered in linen, a wooden chest in the center of the floor (which was acting as a table as well), and a second-hand padded chair. On the wall opposite the door, there was an open doorway into the kitchen, with a deep fireplace inside, set into the wall. I could see that a fire was burning, with a pot of water hanging on the spit above it -- Reida's doing. The stairs were against the wall to the right, and on the left-hand wall there were hand-drawn charcoal portraits of Audar and Lisbet. Using the walls to help me, I made my way to the stairs and slowly up to the second floor.

There were two rooms on the upper level -- Audar and Lisbet's bedroom, and one that had been turned into a nursery. I peeked into the nursery. There was a solid wooden bed for the baby, one with rails three feet high so the child couldn't roll out, and there were small wooden toys and dolls on the floor near a chest in the corner. Instead of the cold wood floor, they'd bought a new-looking rug and put it down on the floor. As this was technically government property, they couldn't paint or put any permanent decoration on the walls. But what the Dennes had done was better. Audar had put a huge piece of paper on the wall behind the bed and painted a mural on it, one with a meadow full of daisies and wildflowers under a blue sky. I realized now why everything else in their home was second-hand or cheaply made. They'd put all their money for the last nine months into making their daughter's room as beautiful as they could.

I went into their room now, smiling because of what I'd seen. Lisbet was lying in bed, wearing a shift and propped up by a stack of pillows. Reida was sitting on a stool by Lisbet's feet and Audar was on his wife's right-hand side.

"Hello," I said, hand on the doorway for support.

"Oh, you're here!" Reida exclaimed. "Won't you sit next to Lisbet?"

"Sure," I replied, limping over to her left and pulling over a stool.

"Hello, Miss Talia," Lisbet said calmly. Her voice was soft and almost melodic, even though she was in labor.

"Hello, Lisbet," I replied kindly. "I'm dreadfully sorry that the first time we meet properly is when you are in such a state."

"Oh, don't worry, Miss," she assured me, "I think that you truly get to know someone when you see them in pain."

"I quite agree with you, Lisbet. And please, just call me Talia."

"You must know me quite well, then," Reida joked with me. I laughed.

"Audar has told me lots about you, and the baby," I told Lisbet after a few moments. She laughed a little.

"You seem to tell everyone about her," she chided her husband gently, turning her face slightly to look at him. "Two weeks ago," she said to me, "we had guests over for dinner, and he spent the whole time talking to one of his military friends about the baby." Audar smiled sheepishly. I laughed. "Oh, Talia, how is your leg? My husband told me that it was giving you trouble."

"I am well," I said. "It flares up every now and then, and it is sore, but it's all right." She nodded, and opened her mouth to speak, but a contraction hit her just then and she let out a whimper and clutched Audar's hand instead. He looked worried. Reida rubbed Lisbet's calf soothingly. Her head turned toward the open door.

"Oh, I can hear the water boiling," she said, getting up. Reida took a pile of linen cloths and put them into a basket. "I'm going to clean these. Keep breathing, Lisbet. You're doing swimmingly." She hurried downstairs.

"Oh, Audar," Lisbet sighed after another spasm of pain.

"Are you all right?" he asked worriedly, stroking her arm.

"I'm fine, the pain is just coming more often now."

"Reida said that was normal, right?"

"Yes, dear. It means we'll have our little girl soon." Denne smiled and kissed his wife on the forehead, brushing back some of her honey-blonde hair away from her face. I patted Lisbet's hand comfortingly. A few minutes passed, then another contraction hit. This time, Lisbet cried out and clutched both our hands. Reida hurried in and put a wet cloth on Lisbet's forehead.

"You're doing great, Lisbet," she said. "Is there a blanket you want her to be wrapped in when she is born?"

"It's the yellow embroidered one in the baby's bed," Audar said. Reida ran and got it.

"Here," she said, giving the small blanket to Lisbet, "if you hold onto this and focus on your baby girl, you'll do just fine." Lisbet dug her hands into the fabric and squeezed. "Is there anything we can do to make you more comfortable?"

"Would it be too much to ask that someone told a story?" Lisbet suggested.

"Of course not," I said. "What do you want to hear about?"

"Tell me about Glïnéa, for I've always wanted to go there," she said.

"Well," I began, "maybe it would be more appropriate for Reida to tell you. She was born there, and she lived there for longer than you or I have been alive." I looked over to her. She smiled.

"I am not old, not in Elvish terms," she said, laughing a little. "I am sixty-two. My homeland is rich, vast, and beautiful. Almost all of our province is covered by a forest so old that it has no name, and all of our cities are built in the trees, barely separable from them. We were on the continent before the humans were, created by the gods right in the middle of all the beauty and wealth. Our goddess of nature, Kynarïn, planted for us a tree that she bore from her breast, showing us where to begin our nation. We named it the *Glïn* tree, and the city of Rodènsï sprung up around it in a circle. That was thousands of years ago."

"What does the name mean?" Lisbet asked. She had another contraction.

"It means 'the one who gives life.' It's used for addressing your mother formally, and also to address the goddesses." Lisbet smiled. "To us, appreciating and understanding the value of nature is important. We don't eat the flesh of animals, and we shape the oaks and pines into homes and shops through magick. I lived in Amèni, and you could see the mountains from the city. Behind our home was a huge patch of wildflowers."

"Wildflowers in the city?" said Audar.

"Like I said, our cities aren't like yours," Reida replied. "They are barely cities, more like settlements in the forests around us, or extensions of them. Every type of flower I can think of lived in the forests around us. My mother was an enchantress and a healer, so she taught me how to use them." Lisbet had another, more violent contraction. I replaced the rag on her head with another one.

"You know," Reida said when Lisbet was all right again, "my mother told me something fifty years ago that I think you should hear. She said to me that the way a baby is born often tells of its personality. She spent only three hours giving birth to me, and she likened it to my eagerness to go out and explore things, and how I liked to please people, and not make them hurt. And I think, if it's true, that your daughter will be steadfast, strong, and determined. She will not be afraid of anything." Lisbet looked at Audar with a happy tiredness in her eyes.

Hours passed. Lisbet cried out, screamed, and nearly broke our hands. But she never shed a tear, nor said a word of regret to her husband or to Reida and me. He comforted her as best he could, and she clung to us and the baby's blanket for support. It grew dark outside and we were forced to light candles. They gave the room a soft, warm glow that contrasted the pain it held. Around the time that the bell tower called out ten o'clock, Reida poked her studious head up from the end of the bed and smiled tiredly.

"All right, my dear," she said, "you're ready to begin to push. Don't worry, Lisbet, you'll be fine. Just told onto their hands. When I count to three, you'll push for five seconds, all right?"

"Okay," Lisbet muttered.

"One... Two... Three!" Lisbet gritted her teeth and knotted her hands so tightly in ours that I felt like screaming along with her.

"Excellent! Breathe, my girl, breathe. You're doing so well. Breathe, and I'll count again." The cycle of counting, pushing, and breathing happened seven more times, and after the eighth time, a different wail was heard through the home; the unrelenting cry of a newborn taking their first few breaths.

Reida clutched the newborn to her chest, getting blood all over her dress. But she didn't care, and she smiled and hushed the baby as she cried, and cleaned her off with a warm towel. Audar handed the blanket to Reida and she wrapped the child up in it.

"Here you go, Lisbet," Reida said gently, handing the baby to her mother. Lisbet held her daughter to her chest and looked at her with a smile on her face. The baby stopped crying and opened her eyes, revealing huge, clear blue eyes that peered with awe into her mother's brown ones. Lisbet began to weep. Audar kissed his wife on the forehead and began to cry as well. Reida stood beside my chair and I held her hand, a smile on our faces.

"Welcome to the world, Cora Eldri Denne," Lisbet whispered to her daughter. I smiled wider, and Reida chuckled.

"Talia, Reida?" Audar began, barely looking up from his daughter.

"What is it, Therm?" I asked.

"Lisbet and I are very grateful that you were here to help us, instead of someone else," he said.

"Yes," agreed Lisbet, "I don't know how I would have managed with anyone else. You two have been so helpful to us, and we don't know how to thank you."

"Please," Reida said, "there is nothing you can do that is more meaningful than allowing us to be here."

"There must be something," Audar said.

"Dear, we still haven't chosen a host," Lisbet whispered to him, motioning toward us with her head.

"Oh, gods, you're right! Talia and Reida, we'd like to formally offer you the position as hostesses of Cora's ceremony of declaration."

"Oh, Audar," I said, not sure what to say in response to being given that privilege. "We...we would be honored to host it." The Denne family smiled appreciatively.

Reida and I left an hour later, after she'd made sure Lisbet knew how to feed Cora, and had the proper medicines to recover from the delivery. The streets were empty, the city was asleep, except for the people merry-making and casting shadows through the windows of pubs onto the cobblestones. The night was bitterly cold, and clouds moving in from the north seemed to be sending a warning of snow.

"What is a 'ceremony of declaration,' *lün*?" Reida asked me as we walked.

"It's a tradition amongst those hailing from Hjellmun," I said. "No one except the parents and those present at the birth are supposed to see the baby until it is nine days old, and then there is a party to introduce the baby to family and friends. Traditionally, someone who is at the birth should be the ones who host it, but not the parents. That is why, oftentimes, aunts and uncles of the child are invited to witness the birth so they may host the party. But Lisbet, as you said, has only a brother who lives on the opposite side of the continent, and Audar is an only child. So, they picked us. When Cora is nine days old, you and I will hold the party. It's a great honor to be asked to hold the ceremony for someone."

"Oh, my, that's so lovely of them," Reida said.

"Yes," I said, chuckling, "lovely." I kissed Reida on the cheek. A spark of pain in my thigh made my leg buckle. I cried out a little, and fell forward, but Reida caught me. We sat down on a nearby bench.

"Are you all right?" she asked.

"Yes, I'm fine. Blasted leg," I grumbled.

"I can fix it, if you'd like."

"Say, why haven't you then?"

"It wasn't for lack of trying. At the hospital, they... They wouldn't let me," she admitted.

"Why ever not?"

"The doctors agreed that 'in their professional opinions' I wasn't emotionally detached enough, and that if something unexpected were to happen, I might not be able to make the correct decisions."

"Hmph. Well, I trust you," I told her firmly. She smiled and laid her head on my shoulder. We looked up into the night sky together, admiring the stars as the bell tower struck midnight.

TWENTY-FOUR

Nearly two months passed, and the year turned from 85 to 86 Post Empire. Many changes were made. The soldier's uniforms were redesigned and redistributed, much to the joy of those who wore them. The men and women in the army burned their old colors in massive bonfires in the center of the cities all over the Empire, and the pieces of armor with the old king's lion-faced crest (the 'traitor's mark,' as it was now dubbed) were melted down to fashion new, clean pieces, which were then painted with a crest that the soldier's had made in my honor. Now the soldiers wore white tunics bearing an image of a black thundercloud pouring out silver arrows.

Erak, Reida, and I were all offered the position of Hersin in the army, the highest rank, and one that is able to command over a thousand men each, but Reida did not accept. She fell that her talents were not of use in that position, and instead, chose to take control over the doctors and nurses in the army's service, taking the title of Head Matron of Medicine. She immediately began to train some of the highest-ranking doctors in advanced Elven medicine, and instructed them to take the information to the caregivers beneath them. Therm Audar Denne was promoted, and put in charge of more people. I made sure that his unit moved up with him, some rising in rank to be Drenes along with Lismari. He was to be called Jarmal Denne now, just one rank under Hersin now. It means a bigger salary for his family, something that would be helpful as Cora grew older (her ceremony went perfectly, as an aside).

As everyone else was getting excited for the march, my health wasn't progressing as fast as everyone had hoped. As soon as it would seem to be healing, it would reopen and ooze. It caused me great pain, and the doctors were doing nothing productive and were refusing to let Reida help. They talked about the possibility of amputating, but I shut them down whenever it was proposed, because I had seen enough half-wit doctors in my travels to know that amputation was essentially a death sentence. I was given pain medicines, but nothing was healing the actual wound. My leg had been bothering me until near the beginning of December, when Reida finally put her foot down. At night, when the doctors had left me, Reida set up her meditation stones in a circle around us on the floor of the hospital room I'd been placed in. She casted a few healing spells, and soon all that was left of the bolt-wound was a cherry-sized scar on the front of my thigh, and a slightly larger one on the back, a few inches farther down. The next morning, I informed the doctors that I was leaving their care, and began to live with Reida among the soldiers. I made sure to walk particularly arrogantly out of their line of sight, making a good show of how cleanly Reida had done the job.

Over the weeks, all of the Blackhawk dens were cleared and the surviving telepaths inside brought to Highland. They were nursed back to health and then given a choice: go home to their families and be guaranteed safety, or join the army, being trained, and even put into officer's positions if they were found by Jarmal Denne and Thrall Iwan (who now had the opportunity to show the military prowess he'd told of when we first met him back at Stillwater Lake) to be qualified to lead a group of warriors. People who'd come to Highland for protection were also given this choice. Of the twenty-six telepaths that came into the city (fifteen of whom were Blackhawk prisoners), most chose to return to their families, or to stay in Highland until the fighting was over. And of the eight who volunteered for service, five already had some military experience. Those who'd already served were sent to Iwan and Denne to test their mettle for officer's roles. The other three were to be paired with existing officers and fight alongside them. But before they were matched to an officer (most often a Jarmal), they had to be trained, by Erak and I, in the messy business of killing with their minds and defending themselves.

In six weeks, we were ready, and we'd kept our promise of a prepared army before the end of the year. Four squads under the command of four of the highest-skilled Jarmals were assigned to the mission, with Erak and me presiding over two squads each. In total, there were about one thousand soldiers making the move down through The Neck, as well as about five hundred and fifty doctors and nurses under Reida's guidance. We left Highland on twenty-seventh, marching down through the mountains, taking the most direct route. The way was snow-covered, but it was a safe one, with no bandits nor wolves at this time of year, and one that I'd travelled many times. In a straight line, Blackhawk Hall was only about seventy-five miles from Highland, but with the curves in the trail, and sometimes the lack of trail, made the total distance something more like ninety. We arrived at our destination in the middle of the day on January third.

Blackhawk Hall was a huge stone fortress that sat with its back wall up against a mountainside. It sat at the back of a long, narrow valley, with the east and west sides of said valley framed by mountains. The northern side of the rectangle-like space was sparsely dotted with trees, but mostly open, and so we advanced through this open space and made our camp with our backs up against the western mountain, staring at the fortress. The valley was about a mile and a half in length from the bases of the two mountains, and the line of catapults we set up drew the lines to be about one mile away from their front door.

We did not fire the first night, but at sundown on January fourth I ordered the preliminary attack. Our projectiles were mainly piles of tightly wrapped wood, but also large boulders from the base of the mountain and the surrounding area. The boulders put dents and holes in their fifty-foot parapet, which the men inside scrambled to patch. Their cannons could barely reach us, their projectiles hitting the ground ten or so feet before they reached the catapults. A few lucky shots took out one of them, but it was quickly repaired with a beam made from a nearby tree.

At about seven on the night of January fourth, I was sitting outside of my personal tent (one I shared with

Reida), watching the fireballs shoot across the sky, and observing the only real obstacle that stood in the way of our conquering the fort. The Blackhawks were at a severe disadvantage; they were outnumbered, outgunned, and their forces were depleted and mismanaged, as most of their officers had been killed off by the raiding of their dens. They were also lacking heavily in morale, as they were, in the basest sense, cornered rats, as opposed to my armies, who were deeply and nobly driven by the thought of purging their nation of the long-dreaded organization. Such was their desire, there were times during the weeks that we spent training and preparing that the soldiers had made mannequins of Worth and Altren and paraded them around the city, lighting them ablaze in the squares and toasting their demise. But the damn Hawks still had one thing left. Their damn drawbridge.

Around their fortress, the Blackhawks had dug a trench ten feet wide and seven feet deep, and lined it with pikes and sharpened poles pointing up and out at us, making it completely impossible to get in and out without using the drawbridge. The Blackhawks had pulled the bridge in, sealing us out, but also sealing them in. We could, in theory, starve them out, as we had direct supply lines to Highland, and they were stuck with whatever they had inside their Hall. But my soldiers would not stand for that. They wanted action, they wanted to see Blackhawk blood and have Blackhawk gore on their weapons. Who was I to deny them that? No, we needed an active way to get into the fortress.

I looked closer. The drawbridge had a three or four foot gap between it and the wall, through which the mechanism that control the opening and closing could be seen. It was a flaw in the design, and if the Hawks had wanted to fix it, they would have needed to take off the huge fifteen-feet-high door and completely reset the mechanisms that controlled it -- a massive and expensive endeavor. The Hawks had been so cocky and sure of themselves until now that they'd most likely never saw a reason to fix it. If the door was held in place by ropes, I would have sent out a group of archers under one of my sorcerer's magick shields to burn through the ropes and make the bridge fall, but it wasn't on ropes, it was suspended by thick, iron chains. I couldn't send flaming things too close to the door as it were, anyway, because it was made of wood, and if it was destroyed then we would probably never breech their walls. Maybe, I thought as I sat there alone, I could use the magick-shield idea to send out sorcerers to use their magick to cut through the chains. And then, once the bridge fell, perhaps Erak could lead a charge into the fortress...

A hand on my shoulder woke me from my trance. I jumped and turned to see the owner of the arm, and relaxed when I saw Reida's gentle face looking down at me.

"Sorry *lün*," she said, laughing to herself.

"Ah, it's all right," I said, smiling. "I was just thinking about how to lower that damn bridge of theirs."

"Don't worry about it, my dear, something will come to you," she assured me. "Look, you've forgotten what day it is because you've been thinking too much." I chuckled.

"No, I haven't. It just seemed like an improper time for a party."

"Oh, come on, it's your birthday. Please, let me take your mind off of things. Just for tonight?" she whined. I sighed, then laughed and extended my hand for her to help me up. She pulled me up and then held my hand, giggling and beginning to lead me off somewhere.

"Where are we going?" I asked.

"You'll see," she replied. She pulled me through row after row of encamped soldiers, past campfires where men and women scrambled to salute to us as we passed them eating their dinner, past the bathing houses where people were preparing for the battle by relaxing in the warmth of magick-heated water, and through the already-quieted sections where only dim candles gave light from the insides of tents. Finally, Reida stopped in front of the large headquarter tent, where we did strategies during the day. She pulled back the flap to reveal only darkness inside, then motioned for me to go inside. I stepped inside, and Reida followed me, closing the tent. A giant ball of warm light filled the room and blinded me for a moment.

"Surprise!" came the exaltations of my friends. Denne, his unit, and Erak were all standing there, around and in front of a table. They each held parcels wrapped in colorful paper and tied with silk ribbons.

"Oh, gods," I cried, clutching my hand to my heart.

"Happy birthday, *lün*," Reida said, kissing me on the cheek.

"This is all for me?" I asked, looking around at everyone smiling at me. Erak and Akua were holding hands, and Henrik had a huge grin on his face as he laid his head on Rudo's shoulder. Lismari and Chioma were laughing.

"Of course!" Denne said. "I'm of a firm belief that everyone should have a party on their birthday."

"How old are you, dear?" Lismari asked.

"Twenty-eight," I said.

"Here, I made this," Akua said, stepping forward and turning so I could see what was on the table. It was a cake, covered in soft-looking purple frosting, with a knife and a stack of wooden plates next to it. On the top, white frosting was laid down in letters reading, 'HAPPY BIRTHDAY TALIA.'

"Oh, Akua," I tried to protest.

"No, no," she cut me off, "I won't have it. It's your birthday, so you must eat cake. It's my mother's recipe." She picked up the slicing knife and everyone took a plate. I relented and decided to have a good time. After we ate, everyone gave their gifts.

From Lismari, I received a letter opening with the handle engraved with silver. Vrold, Iwan, and Bergliever knew how much I loved Rosemary, so they pitched in their money and bought me a new blanket for her, to put under her saddle. Uduak, showing as much care as I'd ever seen him show, gave me a vial of carefully brewed poison, with a note attached saying he "wished me luck" in leading the attack tomorrow, and that I should use this if I was ever in a tight spot. Audar gave me a beautiful brooch with a tiny, painted portrait of him, Lisbet, and Cora mounted in it.

"With some the money I received as a bonus for being promoted, Lisbet and I had our portraits properly painted," he explained. "When the artist told us we could get brooches with the image on them, I thought maybe you'd like one." I looked into their faces, seeing the life in tiny Cora's eyes, and smiled.

"Thank you, Jarmal," I said.

Akua and Erak presented me with a new clasp for my cloak, one with tiny green gems on the edges. Henrik and Rudo have me a palm-sized porcelain horse wrapped in a thick handkerchief, and Chioma and Eru presented me with a new quiver, complete with a dozen newly-fashioned goose-feathered arrows. Eliza gave me a pair of hair pins, long silver ones, encrusted at the end with a single pearl. They looked delicate and old.

"They were my grandmother's," she told me. "My hair isn't thick enough to hold them, but yours is so long, I figured that they would look good on you." I smiled, looking down at the two pearl-tipped pins.

"Let's see about that," I told her. I pulled up my braid on top of my head, piling it up and around itself, and slid the pin into the base of the coil. The braid-bun was held in place. "Huh, I guess you're right. But I still have one pin..." I looked at her and smiled, then walked over to where she was sitting and stood behind her. I pulled her hair up with a hand and put it into a bun at the crown of her head, sliding in the pin when it was finished. Her hair slipped a little, but then it found its place. Eliza blushed and beamed.

"Why don't you keep that one?" I suggested. She laughed a bit, the first time I had heard her laugh by itself. It was dainty and light, just like the woman it belonged to.

"And now," Reida said, "my gift." She pulled a small box tied with twine from a pocket in her cloak.

"Please," I protested, "you've all spoiled me too much already tonight."

"You can't escape this one, dear," she laughed.

"No, you certainly cannot," Denne agreed. "You've done far too much for all of us. Cora's ceremony was wonderful."

"Rudo and I have never been happier," Henrik said, a content love in his voice. His quiet lover smiled and squeezed Henrik's hand.

"You've got a quick wit, and it's gotten us out of more than a few sinkholes," Iwan added, thinking of the scuffle at Kimball's Landing.

"You saved my life back at the Blackhawk den in Adaima," Erak said. "If you hadn't killed those bastards when you did... I don't know if I would be alive right now." Akua patted the back of his hand.

"And you saved mine a few times as well, so let me give you a gift on your birthday," Reida concluded.

"You've already given me so much," I pleaded.

"Then what's one more thing?"

"Oh, fine. You're a stubborn little thing."

"Oh, you love me," she laughed cheekily, kissing me on the side of the head. She slipped the box into my hands. I slid a finger under the twine and untied the knot, then popped off the lid. Inside, nestled between folds of velvet, was a silver ring crowned with a glittering green stone.

"Oh, Reida," I said, not knowing what else to say.

"Look on the inside of the band," she said. I pulled the ring from the fabric and looked. In neat, curling writing the word *trïnas* was engraved into the silver. "It means 'always,' in Elvish."

"It's so lovely, goodness... Thank you. Everyone. This is the happiest birthday I've had in many years."

"You're so very welcome, Talia," Akua said.

"Yes, it was nothing, lass," Denne agreed. "And... I hate to break up a good party, but it's nearly a quarter to midnight, and the sun is set to rise at about seven in the morning."

"Right," I said. "Back to business. Have a wonderful night, everyone. Get enough sleep if you can. I'll see you first thing tomorrow." Everyone said their goodbyes and took their leaves. Reida and I went, arm-in-arm, back to our tent. The camp was deserted by this time, and only a few low-burning fires remained, and the only voices spoke in low, hushed tones about secret things. As we made it back to our quarters, I looked lovingly at Reida as she lit the lamp and began to change.

I watched as the folds of her dress fell off of her body, revealing a soft, cocoa-brown complexion riddled with goose bumps, though the hearth burned on. I pulled on her dark hand with my cream-white one and she smiled and half-tumbled down onto my lap. She kissed me and I pressed my mouth back into hers. Reida pulled back to unbutton my cloak, and I looked into her eyes as she did so. The hazel of her irises was closer to brown than green tonight, and sparkled like diamonds in the lamp-light. Her slim fingers dug into my tunic and made me shudder. I wrapped my arms around Reida and pushed her under me, running my hands over her beautiful, unruly curls that splashed out behind her head. She poured her body all over mine, rushing over me like an addictive sort of flood.

During the night, when our bodies weren't separate, we exchanged quiet words while the lamp flickered and died.

"I love you," Reida whispered quietly. *"Ai lüne mé, trinas."* Her words slipped into Elvish, as they did sometimes when she was close to sleep. I smiled and tilted her chin up so I could kiss her. She gave a small moan when I pulled her closer. I sighed and looked into her weary eyes.

"What is it, *ma lün?*" she asked.

"Just looking at you," I replied.

"You've been 'just looking' at me a lot lately. Is there something on your mind?"

"There's just... There is a question that I feel that I must ask you, but I haven't found a good time to ask it yet." Reida smiled.

"Well, now is as fine a time as any, I suppose," she said.

"I... I don't know."

"Come on," she urged, sleepily propping herself up on an elbow, "go on and ask."

"Well, all right." I sat up and pulled my cloak up from the ground where it had been discarded. I slipped a hand into the interior pocket and felt the cold metal chain hiding inside. My stomach leaped.

"Reida," I began, "it's been just four and a half months since we first laid eyes on each other, and yet, would you not agree that it feels like so much longer?"

"Yes, I would," she replied.

"For me, it feels like I have spent an entire lifetime at your side. I have poured nearly all my love into you, and I hope beyond all hopes that you think I am worth any morsel of yours. I've been with many, but you, Reida, are the only woman who I feel like spending an actual lifetime with." I began to slide the chain out from the pocket. "I guess, what I am trying to say is:

"Reida, will you marry me?"

I don't know what I expected. Happiness, maybe? Perhaps I'd even ventured to imagine a scream of joy or two. But that's not what I got. Reida's face twisted into one of apprehension, even doubt.

"Talia, I..." she said, stumbling over her words in a manner that was exceedingly rare for her.

"What is wrong?" I asked.

"I... I am sorry, but I cannot help thinking that you are only asking now because of the battle tomorrow."

"No, no... I, it's... I would have asked at another time, but it felt so right... I really do want this, I really do love you." Reida looked uneasy. She slipped out of bed and started to pull on her clothes hurriedly. Her breathing was becoming irregular.

"I do not think that your love is feigned, it is just... I do not think your sense of the time is correct! I am sorry," she repeated, her voice breaking, "but... I cannot accept like this!" She pulled on her cloak and ran from the tent, tears brimming in her eyes. I shoved the chain back into my cloak pocket and wrapped the cape around me.

"Reida!" I called after her. I ran out into the night and looked around. "Reida, please!" Maybe it was the darkness of the pre-morning sky, or maybe she had gone, but either way, my love was nowhere to be seen.

TWENTY-FIVE

T he dawn was met by cannon fire. The plan was more of the same from the preliminary attacks: we were to bombard the walls with cannon balls, knocking holes in their defenses, but avoid the wooden bridge at all costs. Breaking it, as everyone already knew, could mean the end of the siege. Nearly none of our archers could shoot far enough to reach the fortress, so we could not use them to send volleys of arrows over the wall. Instead, we sent rocks lit ablaze with magick fire over the walls. Some of our people were skeptical, thinking that the fire would extinguish in the air, but it wasn't like normal fire, and the screaming of Blackhawk soldiers was confirmation to their utility. As soon as they were weakened enough, I would put my plan for lowering the bridge into action.

I was patrolling through the line of catapults when a thrall approached me about that very plan.

"Hersin Storm-Cloud!" he called, running up behind me. I turned around to look at him. He pressed his fist to his chest in salute.

"Be at ease. What is your message, thrall?" I asked him.

"The enchanters who volunteered to bring down the gate have assembled, and are ready for the operation to begin."

"Good. Take me to them, please."

"Aye, ma'am!" He turned and hurried off. I followed him closely as we weaved between lines and masses of people. We passed the medical tent and my eyes wandered to the opening. Looking in, I caught a very quick glimpse of Reida. She was standing giving orders to a young nurse, one who looked pale and had blood on her hands. As if she knew I was there, Reida looked up, and our eyes met, if for only a split second before she turned away again. I felt my stomach get heavier. We kept moving.

At the very head of our camp, directly across the field from the drawbridge, we met up with the witches, wizards, and enchanters who had volunteered to help me. There were five of them, and when I came into view they all saluted at me. There two Emïlan, two Nords and one Valian.

"Be at ease, I beg of you. We've little time for formalities," I told them. I turned to the thrall who led me to the enchanters. "Thank you, Thrall. You are dismissed." He turned and quickly went back to his position. I looked around at the group. Eru was among them, as I'd specially requested him to be there. The other Emïlan was a half-Nord woman with red hair and an indifferent face. The Nord men and the Valian woman looked newer to the art than the others. As I scanned their faces, I met Eru's gaze. He smiled at me. I gave the grin back.

"All right, everyone. Look around, introduce yourselves to people you don't know. As of now, we are not six different people, we are one big cooperative being. Got that?" They nodded. "Has the plan been explained to you?" They shook their heads. "Well here it is: Thrall Eru Søndervik is the tall Emïlan in the back there. He's good with defensive magick and that's why he's here. Eru, tell me you can produce a shield around us all that will protect us from arrows, cannonballs, rocks, and people, but let all those things out."

"Just say when" he said, grinning.

"Good. Now... Eru will produce the shield and all six of us will walk across the field toward the drawbridge. I've looked long and hard at that damn bridge, and I know that there is a gap between the door and the walls where the chains holding it up can be seen. How far away can we be from the chains?"

"I need twenty feet," confessed one Nordic man, one with sandy hair and worried eyes. His brunette companion gave him a sympathetic look.

"Then we will go to twenty feet," I replied. "If there are enemies on the ground, though the gods could say how that would happen, I will protect you from them, and I will pick off the archers on top of the Blackhawk wall. When we get within range, you four will use your magick to break the chains. Pair up, decide on your strategy. Does everyone understand?"

"Yes, ma'am!" they said. I nodded.

"Eru, if you would?" He nodded and stepped out of the group. We made a cluster around him. He took a breath and closed his eyes, and his palms began to glow with the bright, vibrant green of his aura. Eru twisted and pulled the energy in his palms and a small orb began to form, and then started to grow. It encircled Eru but did not stop, expanding until the light had ensnared us all in a huge dome over our heads. The enchanters marveled at his exceptional level of control over his aura. Eru's eyes opened to reveal that they, too, were glowing, and he smiled at me.

"How does it look, Talia?" he asked, beaming. His enthusiasm made me laugh.

"Like a dream. Now let's go!" We turned toward the fortress and began to scurry across the field. It was torn up and cratered by the boulders and cannonballs that both sides had been tossing back and forth, like a pockmarked cheek. Our side had stopped firing, as per my instructions, but the opposite side had no such restriction. For the first twenty or so feet, there was nothing. It was eerily silent on the battlefield. The Blackhawks seemed stunned by the giant green dome moving toward them. But then the storm of projectiles began.

The first thing to hit us was a volley of arrows. Everyone tensed except for Eru and me. The Valian woman cried out, but the arrows bounced off of our shield and fell onto the ground. Everyone relaxed and we moved faster. The enchanters looked at Eru with new respect. The next thing to fall on us was the cannonballs. As the *boom* of the Hawks' cannons echoed over the field, their ammunition flew at us. The women screamed, but, as if made of gelatin, the shield around us allowed the cannonballs to stretch the wall inwards, but then bounced them back and shot them towards the fortress. They travelled nearly as fast as they had the first time they'd been shot, and ended up breaking holes in some places of the wall. Needless to say, there were no more heavy objects shot at us.

"All right," I began as we went, "have you all decided which spells to use on the chain? I don't care what you choose, just make sure it works."

"Aye," came the four replies.

"Listen, now, I can hear your anxiety and your doubt. Calm your minds, don't let the environment deter you from what our goal is. Right now, we *exist* to destroy those chains."

"Yes, ma'am!" I looked up. We were only about two hundred feet away from the wall now. The angry-looking Blackhawk archers, even having been shown that our dome was impregnable, were in the midst of preparing another volley. I nocked an arrow and sent it hurtling up at the wall. One of the archers was struck in the arm and, in his chaotic reaction, fell backwards off of the rampart. I sent two more, killing two more archers in the process. When we reached the edge of the moat, in a place to the side of the drawbridge where we could see both chains through the gap, I turned to look at the volunteers. They were less shaken than before, but were still uneasy. I was about to give an instruction when a rock bounced off of our shield. The Valian woman jumped in fright. I looked up, annoyed. On the top of the bulwark were men holding rocks in their arms, poised to pelt us with them.

"Do they honestly think pebbles are going to break this?" I asked no one in particular. I nocked an arrow and aimed upward. I shot and it struck one of the men in the center of his neck. He gargled his blood and then fell forward into the moat. I saw it slower than it occurred: he toppled off of the wall and soared downward without turning in the air, then was impaled on one of the pikes, not three feet from us. We heard the crack of his ribs and spine, and saw the monumental splash of blood that came from his mouth. The Valian woman screamed and fell to her knees.

I quickly threw down my bow and knelt before her, placing my palms on her shoulders.

"Thrall! Thrall, look at me, not at the body. Come on, look at me." I put my hands on her face and gently pulled it to look at my face.

"He... He..." she stammered quietly, her eyes wide and full of terror.

"What's your name?" I already knew, of course, but I needed her to focus.

"Oni."

"How long have you been in this army, Oni?"

"F-Five months."

"Where did you learn magick?"

"My m-mother... Oh gods!"

"Easy, now. Have you ever seen someone die, Oni?"

"Not... Not like *that*, dammit!"

"Why did you volunteer for this assignment? You're about three seconds away from seeing all of these Blackhawks go up in smoke."

"I-I wanted to... to help. There are so few magick users in this army..."

"Well lying on the ground isn't going to solve the problem we have here. Oni, I need you to get up and focus on our task." I turned to look at the others, all of whom had paled and begun to feel sick. "And that goes for you all, as well! I will not stand for any sudden cases of weak knees or hearts! Now, group back up and get to work."

"Yes, ma'am!" I helped Oni up and she and the other woman stood together. The men did the same. I picked up my bow and observed. The male pair chose the chain closest to us, while the women chose the one further away. I was intrigued to see what they'd do. Their hands and eyes lit up: bright orange, pale red, sky blue, and an almost-grey slate color.

The two Nordic men began sending bolts of sharp-edged energy at the bit of chain at eye-level with us. After a few shots, they'd mastered the aiming and began to nick away bits of a chain link. The door creaked, and the people inside the fort began to panic when they realized what we were doing. Bits of rock and arrows began to fall down onto Eru's magick wall, only to be bounced away time and time again. I looked over at the women. They'd chosen a different method, one that focused on the weakness of metal: the elements.

First, they worked together to heat up a single chain link. I watched as it glowed red, then orange, yellow, and finally got to the verge of being white. But then, the women switched tactics. They began to rapidly cool the metal, using gusts of freezing air and pulling ice from the ground and wrapped it around the chain link. I understood what they were doing. It was the same premise as cooking with a pot and then dunking it in very cold water. If you do it enough times, the pot will shatter from the stress of being heated and cooled so many times in a row. The women repeated this process until, finally, one side of the chain snapped. The bridge lurched as though it was going to be ill. My eyes snapped over to the other chain. The men sent one last energy bolt shooting at the chain, and, to my joy, it sliced the remaining bit of link straight in half. The other link was slipping, holding on to the rest of the chain by just a tiny fraction of its width.

"Quick," I shouted to them, "cushion the bridge! If it breaks, this will have been for naught!" As the last word left my mouth, the chain link slipped, and the bridge began to fall. The Emïlan woman and the brunette Nordic man responded, her sending a huge gust of wind to keep the drawbridge from falling too fast, and he sending a huge ball of his condensed aura at it. The red blob morphed into a hand and caught the bridge in its three-foot palm. I nearly laughed at the genius behind the move. The hand lowered the bridge delicately and placed it onto the ground on the other side of the moat, then dissipated and was gone.

The hailstorm on our bubble stopped abruptly, and I knew why. I looked back at our line, and, perfectly according to the plan, saw Erak mounted on his horse riding at the head of a large charge of people. He had a ferocious look on his face, and he was letting out a bloodthirsty war cry, but I could not hear it over the chorus of screaming voices and clamoring feet. With his sword in the air he rode ever forward. I laughed.

"Eru," I called, "I'm going out! Take these four back to the camp and make sure to remind me that they are to be rewarded for their service." I nocked an arrow and ran outside of the bubble. It felt like a sheet of silk opening around me as I passed through it. I ran into the fortress about fifty feet before Erak's group reached the bridge. The Blackhawk soldiers were scrambling now, having been stunned by their perimeter being breached. Thirty or so of them were running down the steps inside the fortress walls to get to the huge courtyard inside.

"Protect the doors!" screamed one of the officers. At the back of the courtyard was a huge wooden entryway with double doors, and the Blackhawks obediently formed themselves into clumsy rows in front of it. I fired arrows into the people in the first lines, aiming at throats and hearts. Erak rushed into the yard as I did so.

"Erak!" I cheered happily, sending one soaring into a man's chest. People rushed at us.

"Talia, your plans worked like a dream!" he called back, pulling his sword through a person's ribcage. The air filled with the fresh smell of death.

"Thank you, friend! I must say, you looked quite ferocious on the way up here!" Our conversation was held jauntily, as we were slicing and cleaving our way through Blackhawks as we exchanged words. Men and women rushed past us, weapons blazing in the cold, mid-morning sun. The slaughter continued, until a terrible scream caught my attention and I turned to look towards the back of the courtyard. Most of the Blackhawks had been killed, and a deathblow was about to be struck down on the skull of one of the surviving men.

"STOP!" I shrieked at my soldier. Her gory halberd was halfway through the swing when she heard me. Quickly she realized she could not stop the blade already so full of force, so she turned to the side and plunged the momentous swing into the chest of a dead Hawk instead. I ran over, Erak following behind me.

"What are we sparing this scum for?" the soldier asked, a bit confused.

"We need a bit of information before we go inside," I replied.

"Yes, ma'am," saluted the woman. She stepped aside and I knelt beside the dying Blackhawk.

"What is your name, Thrall?" I asked him. He looked me over.

"So you're the blonde freak, then?" he mused gruffly. "The one who sent her dogs into our dens."

"I am Hersin Talia Storm-Cloud, and I could have cleared out all of your dens by myself if I needed to," I spat.

"Ha! Well, Hersin, I am Wickern, and you shoulda let your lady there kill me, because I ain't going to tell you shit."

"Oh, trust me, Wickern, you will. You don't know the lengths to which I will go to get what I want out of you, Thrall." He tried to chuckle, but he coughed up blood instead. I looked down to see that he had an arrow -- one of mine -- stuck in his gut. "Damn it, you'd better talk to me before I have one of my sorcerers keep you alive to suffer this wound."

"Of what should I talk, Hersin?" he asked weakly.

"Tell me what's behind these doors. If you went to such lengths to protect them, Worth must have laid a trap behind them as well."

"You might be a freak, but you're not a stupid one, I'll grant ye that... You know, I really always hated that damn Commander. Maybe I'll indulge myself and tell you some things to help get rid of him... Yeah, I'll do that. There's a wire trap behind the doors. Break it, and a volley of arrows flies out and kills everyone in front. But that's not all." He coughed again, spraying a bit of blood onto his cheek.

"Yeah, Worth laid down pressure plates and hung swinging logs and axes... Oh, and bear traps, too. He started to get paranoid near the end... Really locked up the place." He chuckled bitterly.

"Where is the beacon?"

"You know about that too? Hmm. It's in the main assembly hall. It's up on a pedestal near the back of the room. The beacon's a huge crystal, pink-ish and soft. Watch your asses, though, because Worth put the rest of us down in there to guard it."

"Do you have a map of the place on you?"

"No, but I'm sure some of us did..." He coughed up a bloody chunk of something and blanched. I wiped his mouth with the corner of my cloak.

"Thank you, Thrall. Just one more thing."

"How can I be of service?"

"You seem like you could be a truly decent person if you thought about it. Why did you join up with such awful people?" Wickern got a sick kind of smile on his face.

"Truth is, Hersin," he said, "I didn't have a choice."

TWENTY-SIX

The thrall spat up a bit of his organs and then died before my eyes. I sighed and got to my feet heavily.

"Search the bodies for a map of the Hall. Get as many as you can," I ordered. A few older soldiers began rifling through the Blackhawks' pockets.

"Lass!" a voice called to me. I looked up to see Jarmal Denne running toward me. He hadn't been in the initial charge, having stayed behind to direct the movements of the catapults and cannons, and was only arriving now.

"Ho, Jarmal," I called in reply. He came closer.

"What is the plan to get inside?" he asked.

"I was just about to announce it," I told him. "Everyone! Come closer, listen up! The way into the main hall is lined with traps, and we must find a way to get rid of them before we all go in. The first of said traps is this door. Behind it is a wire that will send arrows at us when it's broken. Here is the plan: One of you will run back to camp and fetch the enchanter called Eru Søndervik. Bring him to me and he will put up a shield in front of the door, break the wire, and catch the arrows in the magick wall. Then we may pass without becoming mincemeat. I will allow the archers to fill their quivers with the arrows if they seem to be in good enough shape. Do be careful not to cut yourselves, though, as we don't know if they are poisoned or not. All right?"

"Yes, ma'am!" they yelled. I pointed at a random man in the mass.

"You! Go and fetch the enchanter!" He hastily saluted and then ran in the opposite direction. I turned to Denne and Erak.

"Do you think this will work?" Erak asked me.

"It damn well better. You saw what he did on the way over here. If he can't do it again, I might have a few words for him." Denne chuckled. Eru and the messenger returned twenty-five minutes later.

"Another shield, I'm guessing, Storm-Cloud?" he said when he arrived.

"Aye. Arrows will fly out of the door when the trip wire is cut, and we don't want anyone caught in the firestorm. This time, please make it so the things hitting it get stuck in it, not bounce off, because they might hit another trap, and that would just be a bad time for all of us." Eru nodded.

"I expect a bonus from all this," he joked.

"Didn't your mother ever teach you respect, kid?" I replied. Eru was, in fact, only a few months younger than I, with a birthday on April seventh. He laughed and walked out in front of the doors. He took a breath and braced his legs. His eyes and hands began to glow again. Two of my soldiers pulled the doors open and ran to the sides. We all hid behind the open doors and along the wall in which they were set. A great ball of energy began to form between Eru's hands. He shot it at the vast entryway and it became a sheet of green magick covering the doorway about a foot inside the doors. He walked up to the opening and looked down. There, about six inches off the stone floor, was a silver wire barely thicker than a hair. Eru smirked and stomped on it.

There was a loud snapping noise, and then a tremendous *whoosh* as arrows were launched from their places inside the walls. Everyone cowered or snapped their eyes closed, but Eru didn't move. He stood solid as the arrows' tips were caught in the wall he'd made, buried to the end of their metal heads. Half a second passed, and everyone looked up. Eru grinned and let the magick dissipate. About a hundred and fifty arrows fell and clattered onto the floor. There was a collective sigh of relief. I got up and walked over to where Eru stood.

"Lovely work, dear Eru," I said dramatically. He laughed.

"Anything for you, dear Talia," he replied. I punched him in the arm and turned to my soldiers.

"All right, everyone, here's the plan. Where are those maps?" Some of my men held up handfuls of papers. "Hand me one, please. Thank you. Now, the beacon is located in the main hall, on a pedestal. However, there are traps that must be disabled first. Jarmal Denne, Hersin Birchdal, and I will go in and disable as many as we can on the way here. Once we reach the place marked on this map where the paths split, Birchdal will return and lead you all to the Hall. Be wary, as there may be traps we do not find on the first go, and also because a large number of Hawks will be stationed there. Denne and I will proceed to where the traitor-king and Worth are hiding. When you've destroyed the beacon, come aid us. And remember! Altren is *not* to be harmed! He is to be taken back to Highland in one piece so he may be tried and executed. Do I make myself clear?"

"Yes, ma'am!" came the reply. I turned to Denne and Erak, smiling.

"Are you ready, boys?" I asked, whipping out my bow.

"Hell yeah!" cried Erak, pulling out his sword.

"As I'll ever be," replied Denne.

"Farewell, everyone! I'll see you on the other side!" I yelled to the soldiers. I saluted them and then looked at the men beside me. Together, we passed the boundary and stepped into relative darkness. The first twenty feet of the hall were unlit, but then we began to see low-burning torches scattered along the walls. I handed the map I'd been given to Erak.

"Please tell us where to turn, Erak," I said quietly.

"All right," he said.

"I'll watch the floor for traps. Audar, will you please watch the walls and ceiling?" He nodded. "We move as silently as we can, all right? Watch your footing." There was silence for a moment.

"We're coming up on a hallway. We need to make a left," Erak whispered, pointing ahead of us. I could see the path in the flickering light of a torch placed just before the turn. As the fire jumped, something on the floor caught my eye.

"Wait," I said, holding up my hand, "there's a tripwire here." No one moved. Lightly I tiptoed over to the corner and poked my head around to look. To my surprise, there was no guard standing around the corner. There was no axe waiting to take off my head or gore me. But from the ceiling was suspended a very solid-looking log, enough to knock a person off their feet and fling them a good ten feet, breaking a few ribs at the same time. I followed the line of the tripwire up the wall and into the mechanism that held the log in place. If the wire was broken, it would dislodge a wedge of wood that stopped the log from swinging. I turned back to the men.

"Swinging log," I told them. "I'm going to break the wire and let it swing."

"Won't that be too loud?" Erak asked.

"It doesn't seem that alone is close enough to hear," I said.

"Yes, doesn't it seem odd to you that no one has been walking the halls?" Denne observed.

"That Thrall said they were concentrated down in the assembly hall," I replied.

"Yes, that's true. Still, you'd think they would have more people posted in the hallways..."

"Well, at least it's beneficial to us," Erak grinned. I smiled.

"Here goes nothing," I said, unsheathing the dagger strapped to my thigh. In one quick motion I cut through the wire and pressed myself to the wall. There was a snapping noise, and then the creak of metal, and then a log when rushing past my head. It swung backwards, and then began to slow down. When it stopped, I looked at my friends.

"We should get going," Erak said. I nodded and we kept moving forward through the dim hallways. At every intersection, Erak would whisper a direction and I would peek around the corners. Time and time again, there was no one to be seen. It began to eat at all of us.

I frowned. There was something wrong in this fortress, something more ghastly than traps or people. The air was heavy and the whole place smelled stagnant, as though no one had moved through these halls for a while. Something close to the ground moved suddenly. I gasped and jumped back, pulling my bowstring. But when the form skittered into the light, I saw it was only a plump little mouse. I sighed and lowered my weapon.

"This place is making me nervous," Erak whispered. I nodded in agreement.

"There is definitely something wrong," I replied quietly. We kept moving, our palms beginning to sweat. I fought to keep my breath from shaking. We dismantled three more traps; cutting down a flying axe, ripping up a pressure plate, and disarming another log. Finally, we came to the place where he had to split up.

"You two will need to go to the right," Erak told Denne and I. "Go about three hundred feet, and there will be a small hallway on your left. That's the door to Worth's chambers, and it's right above the assembly hall.

The door should be guarded by two men, but I don't know if they will be there."

"Worth knows we are coming for him. He will have those men there," I said.

"Either way, it is nothing you two cannot handle. Now, I'll go get the others."

"Be safe, Erak," I implored him.

"I will be careful," he assured me. He turned and disappeared around the corner.

"Let's not dally, Talia," Denne murmured.

"Of course."

TWENTY-SEVEN

Denne and I crept down the hall, encountering no more traps and still no people. It made no sense to me; the outside of the fortress had been crawling with them. So where was everyone in here? There was not even a whisper or a clank of metal in the darkness to suggest an ambush somewhere. The jarmal and I grew more worried as we got closer to the hallway Erak had told us about. There was a light being cast on the walls where it was, as the main corridor was dark but the small one fully lit. By the time we reached the glow, I was nearly hoping that someone would pop up behind us and try to kill me. Maybe then I wouldn't be so scared of this place. Living enemies I could kill, but this silence was immortal.

When we reached the corner, I slowly slid my head around to look. As I had predicted, there were two guards standing there at the end of the short hallway, one on either side of the double doors that led to Worth's chambers. They were leaning against the walls silently, arms crossed, as if examining the floor. They had weapons strapped to their belts. Quickly I snapped my head back. I nodded at Denne. He flexed his fingers on the grip of his sword. I sucked in a breath, then launched myself outward. I rolled across the ground on my shoulder, planted one knee and one foot on the ground, and took the shot. Denne rushed out behind me, taking long steps toward the men. But before he got too far, he stopped quickly.

Our faces twisted in horror. The guard I'd shot had my arrow lodged in his ribcage. But he had not moved, nor made a sound. His body had slid with the impact, so now he was in the corner by the doors, arms hanging limply. Denne lowered his sword and took a step backward, and I slid down onto both of my knees.

"By the Five," he stammered, "they... They're dead!"

"Oh, shit," I swore quietly. "Audar. Do you know what this means?"

"W-What?"

"This is the reason that no one has been in these halls."

"You don't mean -"

"I do. All of the Blackhawks inside the Hall... They're all dead." I felt sick, but angry at the same time, like I was going to vomit and scream and swear all at the same time. I got to my feet and stormed forward, passing the corpses, my throat getting tighter.

"Talia, wait!" Denne called after me. "You could be walking into a trap."

"Audar, you should know that I am incredibly pissed," I snarled, turning back to look at him, "and it will take more than Commander Worth to kill me right now." I paused for a moment, my eyes drifting over to the soldier I had shot. A slow ooze of stale blood was dripping from the wound. I shuddered.

"Should we put away our weapons?" Denne asked me quietly.

"You might. I need it in my hand. It calms me." He nodded and slid his sword into its sheath. I turned back toward Audar.

"Worth is dangerous," I said. "He was dangerous before this, and I fear he may have lost himself. Be careful."

"Only as careful as you are," he replied. I gave a small smile, and turned back toward the doors. I laid my hand on the polished-brass handle and pushed. They swung open lightly, on well-oiled hinges, barely making a sound.

Before us was a long, narrow room with polished floors and dark, broody tapestries on the walls. Parallel to the walls ran a thin carpet, red, and led my eyes in a straight line to the small platform on which two thrones were placed. The thrones were identical, but the men who sat in them were not. On the throne on my right side sat Commander Worth, who bore a sick sort of smile and had calamity in his eyes, like he had found some great madness since I had seen him last. Worth was a man with white hair and an eye patch on his left side covering a torn-out eye with scars peeking out from under it, and still he looked more alive than ever. But on my left, Altren Domaste sat quiet, broken. He was pale, thin, with sallow skin and an unkempt beard. His eyes frightened me, not because they held fire, but because they held none. Worth's eyes were alive and full of danger, but Altren's were cold and unaware. The Commander's voice boomed out.

"Ah!" he exclaimed, scaring me just a little. "So here we are. Miss Storm-Cloud, who is your friend?" Denne took a step forward, trying not to let the man know how his mind was racing, picturing Lisbet and Cora and me, Reida and Erak and his unit, how lost his family and his soldiers would be without him. He spoke with steel in his voice despite his thoughts.

"I am Jarmal Audar Denne," he said firmly.

"I'm sure you both know Altren here," Worth said, gesturing absently at the pale monarch.

"Where are the rest of your men, Worth?" I demanded. "And why does Altren look like he's seen a specter?" He grinned.

"I silenced them. Poor King Altren couldn't seem to comprehend it. He's been like this for a few hours now."

"Bullshit!" I screamed. "He's much thinner than he was two months ago, his hair is unwashed and his beard untrimmed. If all that happened in the last few hours, he must be a medical marvel. When did you kill those men?"

"You're clever. Well, if clever means 'good at stating the obvious.' I got rid of them last night."

"Then what did you do to him for the past two months, Commander? Why does *my* prisoner look like he's been put through a mill?"

"He didn't take to life here very well," Worth summarized. I could tell I would have to pry that answer out of him later. Or, an option easier for me, I could search Altren's head once I had time.

"I see. So, another question. Why would you kill your own soldiers?"

"They were becoming insubordinate. They were begging to be let out to fight, to leave the fortress and fight on the field. They began to question my wisdom, my word, my authority. So... I flipped a switch, and they all dropped dead." He laughed, a terrible sound that chilled my bones and made Audar grit his teeth.

"Why didn't the men outside the walls die as well?"

"My switches are perfect. I am able to choose as many people as I want and infiltrate their heads. They are all my puppets, nothing more."

"So what makes you any different from me, then? What separates you from me, or Reida, or any one of the people you tortured and killed?" I demanded, my heart pounding with rage. "You've turned yourself into a telepath. You go into minds, you change things, but instead of leaving again, you wipe them clean, turn them into full-grown infants! You can't escape the fact that when it comes down to it, you are *just* like me!" Worth pounded his fist on the arm of his throne.

"I am willing to make myself into a monster if it means that all the rest of them will die!" he roared. I smiled.

"Indeed, a monster you've become. Because even though I can easily kill people like you can, I have the bare humanity to refrain!" I pulled out an arrow out and nocked it, drawing my bowstring back. I aimed for his skull.

"Only one monster can leave this room today, Commander," I said, "and I plan on seeing my lover tonight." I fired, waiting for the crunch of bone and the splash of blood.

But it didn't come.

Worth was quicker than I knew a person to be, and he dived to the side to dodge my arrow. When I'd readied another shot, he was on his feet with his sword drawn. The black blade flashed in the torch light.

"Come now, Talia," he purred, "don't you want to fight me like a warrior?" He was taunting me. I thought for a moment. He was lighter on his feet than I'd expected, and I knew I was going to waste more of my arrows trying to hit him than I wanted to risk. What if I shot my whole quiver and didn't hit him? I didn't want to be left in combat with him with only my two daggers to protect me. And I couldn't allow Denne to get hurt. What about Cora, and Lisbet? He had a family, and this was my fight more than anyone's. I sighed and lowered my bow.

"Jarmal, please lend me your sword," I said gently. He took my bow and my quiver and handed his blade to me. I looked it over. Denne's sword was a beautiful weapon, one-handed and slim, and perfectly balanced. I turned its grip over in my palm and looked up at Worth.

"Very well," I allowed. "I will fight you blade on blade."

"To the death?" Worth implored, seeming excited.

"To the death," I agreed. "No tricks, no one but you and I, got it?"

"I wouldn't dream of it," he said, still holding that terrible smile. We raised our weapons and bowed, then he ran at me. I parried his attack and ducked under his next swing. I jabbed my loaned sword at his gut, but his block was already there.

I bit back an oath. He was quick, too quick to surprise. I needed to focus and watch the way he moved, the way he held his sword, anything to help me find a weakness. I glanced at his feet. They were fast, and almost too deliberate. He calculated each step. And where there are calculations, there is always the potential for miscalculations. Worth always seemed to know my next move. But maybe he was too sure of them. If I did something other than I would normally do, perhaps it would throw him off guard long enough for me to strike. It was a risk, but it was the only way I could see to disadvantage him.

He swung at me once more, and I ducked under the blow. But instead of standing back up, and popping up behind him, I stayed down. Worth fumbled, stepping forward and tripping over me. I raised my sword as his body tumbled past me, slicing through one of his shin guards and cutting a precise line deep into his skin. He cried out and fell into the ground, slamming his shoulder into the marble flooring. I jumped to my feet and held up my sword, pinning him to the ground with my knee. I pressed the blade to the back of his neck.

"Didn't you say no tricks?" he growled.

"There's nothing tricky about observing your weaknesses, Commander." He bucked back at me with surprising force and I was tossed onto the ground. I heard Audar shift uncomfortably and take a step forward.

"No!" I shouted at him. "You can't interfere." I got to my feet just in time to block a slash. The sounds of metal clashing filled the stone room and echoed off of the walls eerily. Denne grew tenser and Altren didn't seem to notice that anyone had moved at all. I parried a crushing swing, then ducked and swung at Worth's left side. I caught his armor in a tiny weak spot below the heart, leaving a deep gash in his side. Worth swore and clutched his side with his left hand, keeping a shaky grip on his weapon. Splashes of his blood dripped down onto the floor, leaving dark red puddles as memorials.

"Oh, Commander," I said, "it's nearly admirable how you delude yourself into thinking that you can win. I killed off all the men in one of your dens by myself, as I'm sure you would like to forget. You are a worthy opponent, but you mustn't kid yourself." I must have struck a nerve in him, for he seemed to erupt before my eyes.

"I am over twenty-five years your senior, girl!" he bellowed. "I have fought scarier things than you and walked away with less than a scratch!"

"And yet, my blade has twice tasted your blood in this fight. Are you quite sure that you've seen more frightening things than me?"

Worth let out a cry in lieu of an answer and launched himself at me, catching me just the slightest bit off guard. He swept a leg behind mine and I fell backward, my heart falling down to the bottom of my stomach. I slammed into the floor and all the wind was knocked out of my lungs. I gasped for air as Worth's boot came down on my chest. I looked up at Commander Worth's hate-filled eyes, trying desperately not to let my fear show on my face.

"You will pay for what you've done to my organization," he snarled. "We are proud, we are ancient, and I will be damned if I let some blonde freak defile all my work!" Images of the bodies of the Blackhawks outside the door flashed through my head. He was truly delusional, to think that he could rebuild the Blackhawks after murdering them all. And there would be others to fight him if I died. There was Denne, just a few dozen feet away, there was Erak and Reida and everyone we'd rescued, there were ordinary people who hated this man more than they thought they could hate anyone. They would take my place before my corpse could grow cold, and Worth would die. His eyes and his horrible smile did not know this, though. Or, maybe they did, but they did not choose to understand it.

"First," I said, my voice shaking, "I must ask you, Commander, for it has burdened my mind since I first heard of your organization. How did you manage to move everyone from the old Hall into this one? All of those people, how did you get them to leave so abruptly?" He sneered.

"What concern is it of yours? You will not have long to know it. You are no threat to me anymore. So, goodbye, Talia Storm-Cloud." Worth raised his sword. I closed my eyes. Faces swam behind my eyelids. Azark, Majka, Eorlund, Mirabelle, Erak, Akua, Eru, Henrik, Rudo, Reida... Reida! My love, my life, my everything. How could I die with her upset with me? I imagined her finding me here, with a sword through my neck. How she would cry, how she would wail and mourn and fret. I felt my eyes fill with tears, my throat close up. I waited for the blade to fall.

TWANG!

My eyes shot open and a tear fell. I saw Worth's mouth fall open, but no sound came out. In fact, I couldn't hear anything, only see. He was looking up, looking away from me. Before I could think, I pulled my thigh-dagger from its sheath and took hold of the foot on my chest. In one quick motion, I sliced through Worth's ankle. Blood showered over my chest, splashing onto my neck, and Worth fell to the side, his mouth open in a terrible, silent scream. I saw Denne flash by and then they were both out of sight. It felt like everything was moving slowly, like I was a fish trying to swim through honey instead of water. I sat up and suddenly everything snapped back.

Denne had tackled Worth after I'd cut through his tendon and pinned him to the floor about ten feet away from me. Worth was writhing in pain under him, and Audar had a grimace on his face as he slammed the Commander flat. Slowly, I got to my feet, my hands shaking, still gripping the dagger in my right hand.

"Be still, Worth," I said, my voice less steady than I was used to it being. I wiped my eyes with the back of my hand, seeing the blood and the tears mixing. I opened my mouth to speak once more, but something shifted very suddenly in the air. We all felt it. The oppressive tension that had settled down on us was now gone, like we had been covered in a heavy blanket that had been lifted. Everyone felt it, even Altren, who had still been engrossed by the floor. He looked up for a moment before returning his stare to its place. My head began to spin, filled with thoughts and emotions that weren't mine. They were Worth's. Suddenly I understood.

"What have you done?" Worth shrieked at me. "What have you done?"

"Oh," I groaned, "oh, dear Commander. Your beacon is gone. My men have smashed it."

"NO! No, you've ruined everything!" he screamed, thrashing under Audar's weight.

"Oh, gods," I murmured, falling to my knees. "I can hear... *Everything.*" Worth was horrified. "Perhaps... Perhaps I should show you how monstrous I can be, Commander."

"Keep out of my mind, you bitch!" Denne bared his teeth and smashed Worth's shoulder into the marble.

"I cannot. I'm too curious, Commander. I need to know your secrets." Ignoring his threats, I closed my eyes, took a deep breath, and dived in.

TWENTY-EIGHT

It was dark at first, dark and warm. My eyes cracked open, and I saw lights shimmering down from between the leaves of an oak tree. I realized that I was not myself. I was inside Worth, seeing everything from his perspective, from his eyes. He was laying under a tree, hand in hand with a beautiful dark-haired woman. Her stomach was swollen with child, her other hand resting on top of it protectively. She turned her head and opened her eyes.

"Are you staring at me, dear?" she asked gently, her voice clear and sweet.

"No, my love, I was just wondering how I got such a beautiful wife," I heard myself say. But the voice wasn't mine, either, it was a younger, happier version of Worth's.

"You flatterer, you," she chided, laughing. He laughed too, not in the terrible way of his later years, but in a more genuine, *saner* way.

"How many months is it now?" he asked, moving closer to lay a hand on his wife's stomach.

"Two. The doctor told me it would be near the twenty-eighth of August."

"I can't wait to meet our little girl," Worth murmured. I felt my own body go cold. Audar's face flashed in my head before the memory returned.

"Neither can I," the woman laughed, giddy like a small girl. A name came to me. Augusta Worth.

The scene changed, stretched into another one. Through Worth's eyes I saw the couple's bedroom, sparse and plain, and lit by sunlight streaming in through a window. Augusta was laid up in their bed, her face contorted with pain and shining with a thin layer of sweat. A midwife sat beside the woman, a damp cloth in her hand. A date came to me. It was now the fifth of September, in the year 51 P.E. Over thirty-four years ago.

"Madame, you told us she would be here eight days ago," Worth said to the midwife, spitting the words out angrily. "Why is she so late?"

"Well it's not very exact," the woman replied, crossing her arms in front of her. "Babies come when they feel, not when we'd like." Worth swore under his breath and looked down at his crying wife.

"Dalmar," she moaned.

"It's all right, Augusta," he comforted her, holding her hand.

The scene changed again, jumping ahead to a time later that day, when the sky was dark and the bed chamber dimly lit by low-burning candles. Augusta was ghostly pale, her face still damp in the dancing light. In her arms she tightly held a small bundle, and she looked at it lovingly. But Worth was not filled with that love, and he sat in a chair far away from his wife. Horror pulsed through his body, and he felt sick. Something was terribly wrong.

"Augusta -" he began quietly.

"Don't you want to hold her, Dalmar?" she interrupted. He paled.

"Augusta, please," Worth begged.

"My love, hold your daughter."

"I don't want to hold it!"

"But why, love? She's beautiful."

"Augusta, please, let the priest take it. We'll give her a lovely goodbye, and everything will be all right." As he spoke, Worth stood and came nearer to her, and she clutched the bundle tighter to her chest. His hands came down and tried to take it away from her, but she screamed and pleaded for him to stop, turning away from him so he couldn't touch her. I caught sight of the child; blue, unmoving, silent. Stillborn. My mind recoiled.

Time passed. It took two days to pry the dead child away from Augusta. When it was buried, she wailed and cried, and shut herself away in their bedroom. She refused to eat, barely slept, and wouldn't let her husband touch her. Worth tried as best he could to give her space. He did not force her to see him, and slept in the front room near the fireplace. During the night, when Augusta thought she had only the stars to keep her company, he could hear her sobbing through the walls. Worth thought at the beginning that if he allowed his wife to grieve, she would eventually come out and they could live like before. But the days passed, and then became weeks, and his hope dwindled.

It was early October when he decided to see if she would come out. He had spent the day debating his chances of convincing her, but now the dusk was approaching and he knew he had little choice. Worth knocked on her door.

"Augusta," he called to her. "Augusta, please. It has been nearly a month. I know you are hurting, but please, let me share your pain. Please, please do not lock yourself away anymore." No matter what he said, she did not answer. He was about to give up when he heard the noise of a chair falling over. Worth reached his hand down and tried to open the door. It was locked. Fear shot through his veins like a lightning strike. He put his shoulder into the door.

"Augusta!" he screamed, pounding at the door. Finally, the lock gave way and the door swung open. Worth froze.

Augusta, with eyes closed and cheeks tear-stained, was hanging from the rafters, a rope about her neck. Worth was stuck, glued to the floor by terror for what seemed like a very long time. When he could move again, everything seemed to rush before my eyes. He cut her down and held her to his chest, wailing and screaming for someone, anyone to help. Worth howled when he looked at her, for behind the sleeves of her nightgown there were long, thin slices where her grief had made itself visible on her skin. The time blurred and it seemed to last forever. He sat there on the floor cradling her body until a neighbor came to help.

Augusta Worth was buried the following morning, quickly and without much ceremony, and next to the child that she loved so much.

Six days following her death, a man in purple and black knocked on Worth's front door. This memory, unlike the death of his wife, was strong and sharp in the Commander's mind.

"Who are you?" Worth demanded when the man arrived. He smiled.

"Therm Wuld, of the Blackhawks. I've come to offer you a position." All the blood in Worth's body suddenly ran cold.

"W-Why would you want me?" he stammered. It was odd, I thought to myself, to see the man who would become Commander so frightened on his first encounter with the Blackhawks. But he was still just a civilian, a farmer, and the Blackhawks were still very active at this time.

"We should talk inside," the therm said.

"You'll not step foot in my house until you tell me why you're here!" Wuld smiled.

"I already said, Mr. Worth. We want you in our organization."

"And I already asked, why would you want me? I am... I am just a farmer."

"Hm, well. Truth be told, it involves your late wife." A feeling of melancholy laid itself over Worth at the mention of his wife.

"Augusta?" he murmured.

"Am I wrong in saying that you want to know more about her death, Mr. Worth?"

"What else is there to know? She took her own life, and that's all there is to it!" Worth tried to close the door, but Therm Wuld placed his boot in its way.

"Is it?" he asked. "You'd like to believe that, Mr. Worth, but you know that's only part of the story. Let me in, and I will tell you the rest."

"How could you possibly know if there was any more?"

"We are the Blackhawks, Mr. Worth. We know everything. You want to know the truth about Augusta?" Worth flinched at Wuld speaking her name. "If you let me it, you can know. You can find the truth, and... You can get even." He thought of her, thought of his beautiful wife falling so deeply into the darkness inside her head, thought of how quickly his life had fallen apart. The idea that there was more to Augusta's death than what he had seen didn't seem too far-fetched as he stood in that doorway. The image of her slashed skin and dark eyes danced in Worth's head. He opened the door.

The two men sat by the hearth.

"Mr. Worth, what do you know of witches?" Wuld asked.

"Not much," Worth replied. "You suspect black magick to be the cause of all this?"

"It is a very real possibility. Witches are a vengeful sort, jealous and quick to anger. Perhaps someone was envious of your wife's youth, her beauty, and cursed her. The child..."

"Stillborn," Worth finished the man's thought. He saw the blue, silent thing all over again and went pale.

"Common," Wuld mused. "Your wife was cursed to lose the child. It's impossible to know right now if the witch meant for her to die, but her grief was undoubtedly strengthened by the hex."

"It wasn't just grief, Therm. She would wail and cry during the night, and there were... Wounds. Ones that she inflicted."

"A witch's torment. Augusta was driven to such lengths by the curse."

"Please, Therm, you must help me discover who would do such a terrible thing," Worth pleaded.

"Join us, Mr. Worth, and you will find out. You'll learn all that you need to hunt the beast who took your wife from you."

Months passed. Through Worth I saw the old Blackhawk Hall, felt the drills, the weapons training, the lectures on werewolves, vampires, witches, soul eaters, the undead, hags, witches, brewers of illicit things, faeries, nymphs, and all forms of monsters that parents threaten their children with when they misbehave. Worth soaked it all in like a rag. The image of Augusta and their stillborn child was always burning behind his eyes, pressing him forward. He rose through the ranks quickly. Within one year, he'd gone from a thrall to a drene, and was now one rank under Wuld.

Eighteen months passed, and finally Wuld, who had become his mentor, told Worth that he was ready to track the witch who had allegedly killed his wife. The memory was bloody.

The woman lived one village over from the one that the Worths had made their home in. She was, by all forms of the word, not a witch. She grew a few strange herbs in her garden, but it wasn't to curse people, do spells, or brew potions. But of course, Worth did not know the true reason. He knew in that moment only that the woman was secretive, acted like a witch was supposedly said to act, and that he was angry.

Worth slaughtered the poor woman, beating her nearly to death and then slitting her throat to the bone. Her collarbone was broken, her ribs shattered, her face bloody and torn. She'd screamed, begged and pleaded, and insisted many times that she was not a witch, that she used the herbs to make medicine, but Worth knew that a witch would say those things, and so he did not stop. In the moment that Worth had turned from her bloody corpse, he saw a dark shape in the corner, where no light could fall. The shape had eyes, wide with fear, and thin appendages that shook with each shuddering breath. It was a small boy, weak and frail, crying silent tears and staring into the eyes of the man who killed his mother.

Worth saw the boy and pondered. Maybe the woman was telling the truth about not being a witch. This tiny child obviously needed medication, and she said she was making some. If the boy was a bastard, it would explain why she kept him hidden. But it was possible to make medicine and still be a witch, he decided. And it was very witch-like to have illegitimate children, according to the many lectures he'd attended about them. Worth turned away from the sobbing child, deciding that the woman was, indeed, a witch, and walked out of the home, feeling nothing.

Years passed, and ranks were replaced with higher ones, ones with more honor and more blood attached to them. Worth began to develop quite a reputation in the Hall, one as a ruthless and effective killer. Newly-recruited thralls were fascinated by him, and by the stories that circulated every time he returned from a hunt. Soon, nearly everyone was calling him "the mercenary."

When Worth was thirty-three, nine years after he had been recruited into the Blackhawks, he was promoted to Hersin, the youngest person to ever hold the title. The Hersins of the Blackhawks sat on a council to the Commander, who called them to talk about serious matters that arose and needed to be dealt with quickly. On one February morning, in the year 60 P.E., just such a matter arose.

The council had been called to speak with the Commander, who would not say what the issue was, only that it was urgent. All six people, three male Hersins, two female Hersins, and the aging Commander, sat around their oval table to discuss the mysterious problem.

"Well, everyone," said the Commander, his voice reedy and thin, "I'm sure you know what this meeting means. Something has come up, and it requires immediate action."

"Is it another target?" Worth asked.

"It could be," the Commander replied. "Recently, one of our scouts discovered an enormous gemstone buried in the side of a mountain in The Neck."

"A gemstone? Are we treasure hunters now?" asked one of the men incredulously.

"Peace, Hersin. It's not a regular gem. Some of our men tried to excavate it, thinking it could be used to fill our coffers. But they could not get it out. Strange vibrations and energy radiate off of it, making it nearly impossible to approach. Our researchers believe it to have some sort of psychic power."

"Based on what?" asked a female counselor.

"People who come close to the stone have reported visions, memories playing back, headaches, and brief episodes of telepathic powers. We're in the process of getting it out of the mountain, and we need to decide what to do with it once we have it in our possession."

"We should destroy it," said one man.

"The scientists should deal with it. Let them do their research, and let us take care of any physical threats that may arise," reasoned the second woman.

"Aye," agreed Worth. The others agreed as well. So, the gemstone was excavated, and the researchers and scientists continued on their quest to unlock the secrets of the gem, while the soldiers of Blackhawk Hall remained unaware.

Half a year later, the gem was as near to understood as it could be. The stone was a light pink color, and quite large. It was three feet in diameter, and neatly cut into an eight-sided shape by human or humanoid hands. It was obvious that someone had handled the stone before, but this only opened up more questions for the Blackhawks. If it belonged to some group or civilization, why was it abandoned in a mountainside cliff? That was what the tiny research group was meant to find out. The massive thing was now housed in a chamber beneath the Hall, with only a selected few allowed to know it existed. Worth was one of the handful.

The scientists had explained what they found to the council as the group came down to the chamber. The gem, they said, had the power to bring up memories in the minds of those who got too close, and when it locked onto a certain person, it emitted a faint pink glow from the inside. But it could also protect a person's mind. They explained that if the stone was touched, the one whose hand was laid on it would feel a sort of shell appear around their subconscious, like an eggshell of energy.

"Marvelous," Worth muttered after he'd tried it.

"This could be something," the Commander said. "If this stone has psychic powers, is it not possible that a person could have the same ability?"

"It is very possible," said one man. "I propose, Commander, that we begin searching for rumors of those who can do such things."

"I agree," said one of the women. "We should not kill them yet, only observe, and see if the rumors about them are true. Then, we may decide what to do."

"See to it," said the Commander.

After putting their ears to the ground, the Blackhawks began to dig up stories about people with strange abilities. A messenger from one of their outposts came with a stack of papers as tall as man's knee, full of reports and stories of telepaths. They worked for months tracking down every lead. Most turned out to be false, but every once in a while, an unsettling truth came to light. There were psychics roaming the North Empire. In late October, another report came into the council's meeting room. The Commander sighed as he read the official copy.

"Another one," he announced to the worried Hersins. "A little girl, from a tiny village in The Basin."

"A little girl?" someone repeated.

"Aye. Barely old enough to talk."

"So they're not just magick users," said one man, disproving a theory that had been passed around a few weeks prior.

"No, they're being born this way," replied an aghast member.

"It appears so. And it is entirely possible that they know we are aware that they exist," the Commander reminded the group. "We must prepare ourselves, for I fear we are woefully weak against a group of people with that kind of power."

"And all of the continent knows our location," added someone anxiously. "No one has attacked because everyone fears us. But these people, they have no right to fear us. We don't know the full capacity of their minds. They could kill us before we take a step, for all we know."

"Aye," agreed the Commander solemnly.

"What if we were to move?" Worth suggested. Everyone turned to look at him.

"What do you mean, Hersin?" asked the Commander.

"Well, sir, if we leave this well-known place and move to a more secluded location -- somewhere in The Neck, for instance -- we could prepare ourselves and continue working on the stone in relative secrecy. And then, when we are ready to face this threat, we may do so quietly."

"That would require moving nearly two thousand men nearly five hundred miles, Hersin," said one of the other counselors.

"Plus, we would need to tell everyone about the stone!" exclaimed another. "Are we sure they are ready to know?"

"They are loyal," said Worth. "They trust us, and they trust you, Commander. They will follow. And for any that refuse... They know the consequence."

And so, the idea was passed between them, argued over, and finally agreed upon. I watched through Worth's eyes how the soldiers heard the news and abandoned nearly everything in the Hall. It was eerie, how mindlessly and numbly they obeyed. They gathered their personal effects, formed into their traveling arrangements, and left. I saw the construction of the new Hall, which took five years to completely finish, and I saw the old Commander die. He was replaced by the next eldest Hersins, but his position was soon vacant, due to a mysterious poisoning incident. Through strategic murder and a series of threats, Worth took the position of Commander and did away with the council, becoming the sole seat of power in the entirety of the Blackhawks. The men and women serving him didn't seem to care. They needed nothing more than a target to hate and a way to kill them.

The time until the present passed in a flash, and I didn't see the details, for I already knew most of the story. My vision faded, and then everything was black.

TWENTY-NINE

I was snapped back into the present. I gasped, my head spinning. I put my palm to my forehead and tried to make my skull stop pounding. Worth was still pressed under Audar's weight, but his face was no longer filled with anger. He had seen it all with me, and he looked incredibly sad. I looked up at Denne.

"How long was I gone?" I asked him weakly.

"Just over a minute, lass." I nodded.

"I understand," I said to them both. "I saw everything, and now I understand. You were so angry, Commander. You were too full of hate, and it ruined you. You're hollow now. You're empty, and the only reason your heart is still beating is because the fire you lit inside yourself still burns. But I sense that it's waning. You burned too hot, and now you're barely an ember. I understand, too, that you cannot be left alive. You cannot change, Commander, because fires only burn once, and then they are gone." There was a moment where no one moved. "If it means anything at all, Commander, I am truly sorry about her." Worth's face seemed to break.

"If you could do me just one dignity," he said, his voice crumbling, "and let me be buried next to her, I would consider you an honorable woman, Miss Storm-Cloud."

"So it shall be done." I looked deep into his eyes and dipped inside his mind once more. I found the connection between his heart and his mind, and I looked at it sadly. Here was a man who did so much wrong, and yet, my heart hurt for him. His past did not condone his actions, far from it. But still Augusta Worth was branded into my head.

"Goodbye, Worth," I said. I took the connection and snapped it in half. The breath left his body, and I felt the spark inside him die. Audar slid off of him and sat on the floor for a moment. He put his hand on his side and pulled it away. His fingers were bloody.

"Dammit," he sighed.

"Jarmal!" I exclaimed.

"No, don't fret, lass. He got me when I tackled him off of you."

"You saved my life, at least allow me to worry about your health." I helped him to his feet. He leaned against the wall for support. "The others should be here soon, we'll get you out to see Reida, and you'll be fine." A few moments later, the door opened and Erak rushed in. With him were a handful of our soldiers.

"Talia! Jarmal! What the hell is going on here? They were dead, all of the Hawks down in the hall."

"Worth killed them. I'll explain everything later, but Audar is hurt, and he needs to be taken to Reida." Erak looked behind him.

"Two of you, take Jarmal Denne out to the Matron, now!" Two men rushed over and had Audar put his arms about their shoulders. They hurried him out of the room.

"And Altren seems to be... gone. His body is here but his mind seems to have left him," I told Erak. He looked over at the man, who was still staring intensely at the floor.

"Has he been like this the whole time?"

"Yes. It's like he hasn't noticed that anything has changed. The only time he looked up was when you shattered the beacon."

"What should we do with him?"

"No matter what state he's in, we need to get him to Highland. I'm going to try and talk to him."

"Be careful," Erak said. I nodded and approached the throne.

"Altren?" I said softly. "Altren, may I please speak to you."

"Dead," he replied, his voice strained and hoarse.

"Who, Altren? Who is dead? Who did he kill?"

"All... All of them. Dead. He killed them."

"I know. Why don't you come with us, and we can take you away from all the bodies, all right?" He looked up. His eyes were vacant, but at the same time swimming with confusion.

"Oh, it's you," he said simply.

"Yes, it's me. Will you come with us?" Altren stood without replying, walking as if he didn't quite know why he was going away. The remaining soldiers escorted him out. Erak looked at me.

"Poor sod," he said quietly.

"Don't pity him, Erak," I said. "Broken or not, he was a terrible, heartless person."

"I suppose you're right. Come, let's go. This place is making me uneasy."

"Aye... Where is my bow?" Erak pointed back toward the door. It was laying on the floor, having been tossed aside by Denne after he fired it, grazing Worth's arm. I retrieved it and began to walk out of the door.

"Oh, Erak," I said.

"What is it?" he answered.

"Please make sure that the Commander is buried in the village where he was born, next to his wife."

"He had a wife?" I grew sad once more.

"Aye. He... He asked me to make sure that he was buried next to her."

"I will see to it," he replied.

"Thank you, Erak," I said. I added, to myself, "An honorable woman. How far I've come."

When we got outside, the scene had changed. There was a temporary medical tent set up in the courtyard of the fortress, to treat the soldiers who had been injured in the fighting here, and also to calm those who had fallen ill at the sight of all the dead Blackhawks. Reida had come along with the temporary station. She was overseeing the treatment of a man who had caught a crossbow bolt in the shoulder. I shuddered at the sight, and decided that I really hated crossbows. When she looked up and caught sight of me, I lost my composure. She set down the tray she was holding and ran at me. I felt my throat swell up. Her eyes welled up with tears as well. Reida ran into my arms, and I started to sob.

"I'm so sorry," I cried. "He almost killed me, and I thought of you and how terrible it would be if you had to see me dead."

"It's okay," she sniffed, "it's all right."

"Do you forgive me?"

"Of course." She pulled away and looked at all the blood covering me, her face turning worried.

"It's all Worth's," I said feebly. She pulled me back towards her. I started to cry harder.

"Shh, it's all right."

"He had a wife," I told her, "and she lost her baby. She grieved so hard, she took her own life because of how much she loved the baby. And the Blackhawks," I sobbed, "they took advantage of it, and they made him think that it was a witch who cursed his wife... He killed her, Reida! He killed her when she wasn't a witch, and she had a son, and he watched her die. I watched the whole thing, and I just -" my sentence finished with another bout of crying.

"It's over now," she said. "It's okay, I promise. I love you, and everything will be okay."

"It's over now," I repeated. "It's over now."

THIRTY

By the middle of January, Blackhawk Hall had been burned to the ground and my soldiers had been placed back into their peacetime posts. Altren was shipped back to Highland, still glazed and unaware. He was placed in a comfortable cell in the Imperial jail, awaiting his trial, which had been set for January thirty-first. There was an issue, though, and that was the fact that he needed to be proclaimed fit to stand trial. We brought in doctors from the Physician's College to try and get him out of the state he was in, but it seemed they had few results. They only got him to speak twice in the eighteen days he was held in his cell.

Meanwhile, the people of the Empire had been anxiously awaiting the rise of an Imperial ruler. The

Council had been jockeying for position even as the fighting in The Neck was raging, but the citizens were vehement in their opinion that there should be a ruler above them. A threat of forced removal from their offices was enough to quiet the Counselors down. Then, the Imperial people looked at me. Since the battle, Reida, Erak, and I had all taken up residence in the Grand Palace, as none of us had homes anywhere in Highland. Letters from all over the Empire began to pour into our chambers. People wrote to all three of us, trying to convince us that we were the ones who needed to take over. They referenced our skills in combat, the victory in The Neck, strategic knowledge... Before too long, we were receiving over a hundred letters every day.

On the morning of January twenty-ninth, two days before the trial, the three of us were sitting in our common parlor. Reida was reading a book in Elvish, while Erak and I were reading letters. I was halfway through my third when Reida set down her reading and looked over at us.

"Who is that one from?" she asked me.

"A housewife in Farose," I replied. "She seems to have taken our victory quite personally. Oh, because her son was part of the advance, and has apparently told her very nice things about me."

"What's his name?" Erak asked.

330

"Thrall Thaddeus Onik," I replied, reading it off of the letter.

"I think I remember a face for that name," he mused.

"They really love you," Reida said.

"Hmph," I huffed back.

"I sense that you have doubts. Tell me, what is holding you back from taking the role?"

"I am not sure. Maybe I am afraid to be inadequate," I said. "Or, perhaps I am worried that the power will go to my head." All of the sudden I remembered the festival in Amèni. Or, more specifically, the being made of smoke. I remembered its voice, its words. And, as if it had hit my across the mouth, I realized what it meant. I felt the breath in my lungs leave me.

"What is wrong?" Reida asked nervously.

"Reida, do you remember the smoke-person that you conjured at the festival?"

"Of course," she replied. "What has it got to do with this?"

"Did you know that it could speak?" She very quickly looked frightened.

"What did it say?" she demanded. "Who did it talk to?"

"Me. It said 'You will rule,' and then it sang its little song and disappeared. At the time, it sort of struck me as odd, but everyone was drunk and no one else heard it, so I just thought nothing of it. I reasoned that it was possible that you'd just given it a bit of psychic power by accident. But now... Now people are urging me to become the Empress of the damn Empire!"

"Sometimes," Reida began slowly, "the deities reveal themselves to mortals, ones that have potential for higher things, and only when they deem it necessary. My lady Drünin sometimes does this through the conjuring of her followers. It was not her festival, but it was still a time when we are closer to their realm... It must have been her."

"How can you be sure?" I asked, beginning to feel overwhelmed.

"Conjured things do not have characteristics that their summoners do not give them. We decided as a group to make the thing dance around and sing at the end of her performance. No one made it talk. It is the only way that it could have spoken. But Talia, you're a non-believer! The gods don't speak without reason, but especially not to those who do not follow them. Do you know what this means? You *have* to take the throne. It's her will!"

"Gods above," mumbled Erak, leaning forward in his seat. "She's right, Talia. If you don't do this, things are going to go very wrong around here. The people know you're the best one for the job, and apparently so do the gods."

"Ah, shit," I sighed, putting my forehead in my palm. I thought for a moment. As much as I didn't want to believe the divine had told me to take the crown, it was the only way I could see to make sense of the smoke being talking to me those months ago. I knew what I had to do. It wasn't just for my benefit, nor that of Reida or Erak. They would live comfortably, of course, and Reida would rule by my side for as long as I could manage to have her. The Empire would be managed well, and I could manage to see a peaceful reign. But this was now a matter of a much higher importance. Now it came down to following the will of a being that could bring the entire Empire to its knees if she saw fit.

"There's just one thing I don't understand," I said. "The thing's voice when it sand was so clear, so lovely, but when it spoke it sounded so dry, like it had been screaming for hours before it spoke to me."

"How odd," Reida said.

"Maybe Drünin had a chest cold that day," Erak suggested, a lopsided smile on his face. I covered my mouth with the back of my hand.

"Erak!" Reida giggled.

"What?"

"She's an almighty being," she scolded, fighting back her laughter.

"I hope she's got an almighty sense of humor, too."

The day between us and the trial came and went, and suddenly it was the morning of January thirty-first. Reida and I rose solemnly that morning. I dressed in my freshly-polished army uniform, with the ceremonial cape draped around me. Reida wore a new purple gown that a kind seamstress had given her as a gift, a sign of faith in the city and its inhabitants. It was unusually balmy that day, so much that you could not see your breath cloud in front of you. While comfortable, the weather made me uneasy. How odd that on such a tense day, the sky would be so calm.

The trial was to take place in the public square underneath one of the palace's low balconies. Two sides of the courtyard touched the castle, and on the wall that did not hold our balcony had a large stone platform nearly pressed up against to it, about fifteen feet on each side, and the top about seven feet above the ground. Running through the middle was a pole to which the prisoner was chained, and on the side facing the castle was a long covered table where the Counselors sat. Five steps lead up to the top of the stone block. Crowds had gathered, hoards of people all wanting to get a glimpse of the traitor they were going to try. It wasn't the first time in the history of the province of Ealemoore that a ruler had been tried and executed, but the last time had been nearly one hundred and fifty years ago, and no such thing had happened since the creation of the Empire. Thus, it was a spectacle.

The bell tower struck the time to be nine in the morning. Reida and I took our seats near the edge of the balcony, with Erak to my left and Audar to Reida's right. We sat next to one another, hands clasped. I stroked the back of her hand with my thumb to reassure her. We had been told the night before that we would be testifying, and ever since then, Reida had felt rather nervous and unsettled. As the final bell rang out, the crowd began to part around the entrance to the square. The civilians were giving a huge berth to something, and we all looked down. Between the people walked five men and women in long purple robes wearing my crest. I smirked at the gesture. These were the Counselors of the North Empire.

It took them a few minutes to ascend the steps and fully take their places at the table on the platform. From left to right I scanned their faces, and names came to me. First was Palmina Bergman from Hjellmun, then Magnus Stone-Heart from The Basin, Lesedi Masego of Middle Vale, Joacim Almhelm from Adaima, and Marwin Friholm of Ealemoore. I leaned forward a bit closer. They looked uneasy, as if they knew I was watching them. After the bit of time where they'd been trying to sneak into power, they knew no one was happy with them. A minute or so passed, then a different sound began to echo through the hushed courtyard. The rattle of wheels on the cobblestones.

I sighed. The dungeon Altren had been kept in was on the other side of the castle, two levels beneath the surface. He could have come here through an underground tunnel, as civilian prisoners were. But we had been petitioned by many people to allow Altren to be paraded around in the prison cart. I knew the people would be even more hysterical if we refused, and so I reluctantly gave the word a few days prior to this. Slowly, the murmuring of the crowd became talking, and then speech turned into shouts of anger and taunting. As the carriage came closer, more people started to join the frenzy, and finally the cart came through the entrance of the courtyard. Altren was sitting in the very middle of the cart, his feet tucked under him to make his body look smaller. His beard had grown wildly and his hair was untamed, and on his body was the ragged uniform of a common criminal. There were only thin wooden bars to protect him from the crowd. A few people tossed eggs and rotten fruit in his direction, but most just hurled insults. I saw Altren flinch away from the abuse, but he did not lose his composure.

When the cart reached the platform, a dozen city guards moved the civilians back from the cart, while two others escorted Altren to the pole and re-shackled his handcuffs around it. He was shoved down onto his knees and was left to face the crowd and the Counselors alone. Counselor Lesedi Masego was to lead the proceedings. She produced a gavel from inside her robes and slammed it down hard onto the table, once, twice, and a third time. Before the final blow, the courtyard was silent.

"This trial," she began firmly, "is thusly begun. Counselor Magnus Stone-Heart will now read the charges placed upon the accused." The man to her right stood and took a wide scroll from inside his cloak. He unrolled it and read aloud in a rich baritone.

"Altren Domaste, former King of the North Empire, you are hereby accused of the following crimes: high treason, unlawful conspiracy, and the infliction of unnecessary suffering on the highest scale. Do you understand the charges brought against you?" Everyone's eyes flicked over to him. No one was sure if he would respond, or if he would be silent and still like he had been in the Hall those weeks ago. The doctors had told me that he would "probably" answer them, and that, to them, it was enough to clear him for trial, but there was no way to know until the moment came. I heard the breath catch in Erak's throat, and Reida's hand tightened around mine. But his mouth opened in a half-smile, and he spoke.

"Aye." I felt a wave of uneasiness sweep over me. He sounded *hollow*.

"Let it be known to all that the accused has stated his understanding," proclaimed Masego. "The Council will now call their first witness. We call upon Matron Reida Bollaïne to testify against the accused. All the eyes shifted up to the balcony. Reida shot me a nervous glance. I patted her arm and let go of her hand as she stood and made her way to the edge of the balcony, where the railing began.

"State your name," instructed Counselor Masego.

"I am Reida, the last member of the clan Bollaïne." Her hands were shaking as they took hold of the banister.

"What is your line of work?"

"I am the Head Matron of Medicine in the service of the North Empire, but I was an enchantress of personal items and a brewer of potions when I lived in the city of Amèni."

"What is your involvement with the accused?"

"I was kidnapped and... dishonored by the Blackhawks, the group of men and women that the accused was working with." The crowd gave cries of sympathy but were silenced by the scowl on Masego's face.

"How long were you held captive by the Blackhawks?"

"Thirty-two days."

"Who rescued you?"

"No one. I broke out and was found in the woods by Talia Storm-Cloud." There were shouts of joy beneath us.

"Is it true that you overheard your captors plotting to kidnap more people?"

"Yes, I heard them planning to kidnap Erak Birchdal."

"After his rescue, the three of you went looking for the Blackhawk headquarters. Is that correct?"

"Yes."

"How did you and your companions discover that the accused was working with the Blackhawks?"

"We were buying supplies in a trading post close to the Adaima-Valian border, and we spotted the royal carriage outside. Talia and I thought it was suspicious, and so she listened to one of the soldier's thoughts as he was inside the shop as well. We discovered that the King was off doing something in secret, and that the carriage was a decoy. Erak remembered a conversation he'd heard the Blackhawks having about 'inspections.' We put the pieces of the puzzle together, and Talia listened to a conversation between Altren and one of his advisors. They were composing a letter to the Blackhawk Commander." The crowd booed and cried out so ferociously that Counselor Masego was forced to pound her gavel a few more times.

"Only one more question, Matron Bollaïne," she said. "Do you believe that the accused should be executed if found guilty?" A ripple of surprise went through the crowd, inciting whispers and anxious looks up to Reida. Her face was solemn and unchanged, but her hand clung to the railing harder, her knuckles going pale.

"I was raised," Reida began, "among people who believe that each living thing deserves the same amount of mercy and compassion as every other being. The belief we hold is called *zül*." The crowd exchanged looks and small murmurs. "However," she continued, "there are, as in nearly every rule, exceptions. One of these is in warfare, when enemies must be destroyed. Another is self-defense, when someone else will kill you if you do not strike first, and also in mercy, when something is suffering and the quality of their life would be abysmal if they were left alive. But there is another exception, one that applies here, and that is the need to kill a person who has committed egregious crimes for which there is no space for compassion. The accused is charged with crimes of such an atrocious nature that no human, Elf, or Divine can forgive him of. So the answer to your question, Counselor, is this: Altren Domaste should die for what he has done."

There was barely a pause between the time of her statement and that when the square erupted into tumultuous cries and screams of approval. Over the clamor, Counselor Masego slammed her gavel and screamed for Reida to be dismissed. She turned around with a blank expression on her face and sat back down next to me. The crowd eventually settled down and the Council called the next witness.

"We call Jarmal Audar Denne to testify against the accused." Dene stood calmly, looking around at us as he walked to the edge. "State your name."

"I am Jarmal Audar Denne, from the city of Farose, Hjellmun," he replied, only the faintest trace of worry on his lips.

"What is your line of work?"

"I am a soldier fighting for the Imperial army."

"And what is your involvement with the accused?"

"When he led the Empire, I served him."

"Could you please explain to us how you became associated with Hersin Storm-Cloud, Hersin Birchdal, and Matron Bollaïne?"

"The former king was alerted that an entire den of Blackhawks had been cleared out, and its prisoners rescued and escaped. He was also aware that these two prisoners and, presumably, whomever rescued them, had been seen in a trading post near Adaima's border with Middle Vale. Of course, he didn't tell us this. He assigned my unit and me to track down the three without any knowledge of their real crime. All we were told was that they were traitors and that they needed to be arrested.

"So, we tracked them down and found their campsite on the shoreline of Stillwater Lake. We attempted to take them into custody, but Talia bade us listen to their story before we made any decisions. I decided that they posed no real threat to us, as there were three of them and twelve of us, and so we listened to them. Talia, Reida, and Erak told us about what the king was really up to, and how he was working with the Blackhawks. We were... Horrified. The cruelty that our commander was perpetuating was unbelievable. Collectively, we decided that we did not want to serve under such a man. Some of my soldiers and I went and cleared out another den in the south of Middle Vale, which is where the three had been headed. The rest of my people went with the three to Glïnéa."

"I understand that the fifteen of you met in Rodènsï in order to make your way to Highland," Masego said.

"Aye, we did."

"What was your goal in coming back here?"

"We planned on spreading the news of Altren's treachery to the people and soldiers of the city."

"What kind of a response were you hoping for?"

"We knew that the Blackhawk Commander was coming to the city for a meeting with the king. Reida was to use her magick to spy on them, and we needed the city on our side in case something happened and we needed to respond immediately."

"Who spread the information?"

"My unit and I did most of it. Reida, Talia, and Erak were wanted criminals, but news of our deserting had not reached the city, so we knew that us as soldiers would blend into the woodwork and be able to spread the news faster. And most of us had contacts and friends, even family, in the ranks stationed here."

"I see. I think everyone here remembers the events of the night of the meeting between Altren and Worth," Counselor Masego finished, looking over the crowds of people. They nodded and murmured agreements. "Just one more before our final question, then, Jarmal. During your service with your unit, prior to learning anything about the accused's involvement with the Blackhawks, did you or any of your soldiers ever show signs of treasonous behavior?"

I looked up at Audar. He knew what this question was really asking as well as anyone did. It was a plain, unabashed trick. The Council was trying to suggest that he or his unit had personal reasons to oust the monarch. I listened in on his thoughts, and he knew the reason why, as well. The Head Counselors had flourished under Altren, free to do as they please on a heavy salary, with almost unlimited free time. With no heir to the throne, they were on unsteady ground. They knew that if they could reveal a vendetta against Altren, they had a slim chance at showing people that we were not to be trusted. They wanted control, and they were grasping at straws trying to get it.

I exhaled heavily, twisting Reida's birthday gift around my finger. Audar looked Masego dead in the eye.

"I have an honorable, patriotic unit, Counselor," he said steadily. "My soldiers love this Empire as they love their families. None of us, and especially not myself, would let a thought of treason pass through our heads. Upending the government thusly has not been a matter of personal gain, nor of politics, as it seems you would have it. This ordeal is, and always has been, for the good of the people."

The crowd exploded into heated shouts at the Counselors. Audar's face was troubled. No one on the balcony was happy with their line of questioning, but especially not him. After all the service he had done the Empire, and thus the Council, they dared to suggest that he'd been unfaithful. It hurt worse knowing that they'd accused his soldiers of the same. In all the time Audar had known them, nothing but good had come from his unit. They were like his family. It *hurt* like they were his family.

"Jarmal, do you believe that the accused should be executed if found guilty?" The question came after Masego was forced to pound her gavel a few times to quiet the crowd. Audar snarled and spat his answer.

"I have a daughter, Counselor, and I don't want to raise her in a world where this man lives. Altren Domaste deserves nothing more than to die a shameful death." Before he was dismissed, Audar turned around and stormed back to his seat. The people below us were shouting and screaming at the Council, calling them power hungry, gold hoarders, fickle. The gavel-pounding didn't seem to have much effect. Masego screamed over the crowd.

"We will now call out last witness! We call Hersin Talia Storm-Cloud to testify against the accused."

THIRTY-ONE

The crowd buzzed like a hive as I took my place behind the railing. I knew I would be called, and so did most of those below me, but it was not comforting to be prepared. The Counselors were not happy with me, and everyone could see it. My stomach did a flip.

"State your name," commanded Masego.

"I am Hersin Talia Storm-Cloud, born of The Basin."

"What is your line of work?"

"I am a commanding officer in the Imperial army, and before this, I was a woman of many trades."

"Can you tell us some of these trades, Hersin?"

"I was an adventurer, foremost. I travelled, solving problems and making money doing odd jobs for people all around the continent. I was a barmaid a few times, a combat tutor for two separate wealthy families, an assistant of a librarian, and amongst many a job one could hardly call a trade."

"I see... What is your involvement with the accused?"

"The accused was working with the Blackhawks, and the Blackhawks killed my friend."

"What was your friend's name, and their occupation?"

"His name was Eorlund Winter-Born. He owned the Riverdell Inn in the village of Wittman's Creek, Adaima."

"How was he killed?"

"A Blackhawk agent stabbed him with a dagger meant for me."

"Did you leave Wittman's Creek seeking revenge for Mr. Winter-Born's death?"

"Yes."

"Have you found it?" All of the sudden, it felt like a hand had curled its fingers around my heart and squeezed. I didn't know whether to be angry or not. The question was a personal jibe, trying to take away from the impact of my testimony. But it made my brain race. In my mind, since the day I decided to leave the inn, the image of Eorlund had been floating around, resurfacing in my nightmares and times of mortal danger. But was this all for him? Was it supposed to be? It has wrestled for position with Reida, and with the good of the Empire, and now I believed that maybe it had lost. My lover and my nation had taken priority. Keeping them safe became my goal.

Yet, Eorlund haunted me. His face, the blood, the knife, all of these things were burned into my head. I had been branded by them, and sometimes that wound smarted. Had I really gotten what I left for? Did I get revenge for him, or for Reida? For Erak? The other telepaths? The Empire? Or, maybe, it had all been for myself. The Blackhawks were gone, every single one of them. They would never hurt an innocent person again, and they would never touch my friends. They would never touch me. I looked down, directly into Masego's eyes.

"Yes," I decided. She was shaken, and fumbled with the papers in her hands.

"How did you and the soldiers in your charge infiltrate the Blackhawk headquarters those weeks ago?" she asked after a moment of shuffling paper and tense silence.

"I lead a group of magick-users who had volunteered to help lower their drawbridge. They used magick to cut through the chains supporting the bridge, and then Hersin Birchdal lead a charge into the courtyard inside the fortress. Jarmal Denne, Hersin Birchdal, and I went into the Hall and dismantled traps to allow for the soldiers to reach our objective, a large crystals possessing telepathic powers in the center of the Hall."

"I understand that you and your soldiers discovered rather odd and, I dare say, *disturbing* things inside of the Hall. Would you elaborate on that statement, Hersin?"

"Upon entering the fortress and disarming the traps along the way, Jarmal Denne and I went to the chamber where Commander Worth was waiting for us. We saw no one inside. There were no guards. We thought this was odd, and when we reached the chamber, outside of the door, we discovered that... Well, we found that Commander Worth had murdered his own men." The crowd stirred uncomfortably. The news had reached their ears already, but it was still enough to make their skin crawl.

"Would you please explain how he killed them?" Images of the guard falling limply to the side appeared in my head.

"One must first understand how the crystal worked, before my men smashed it. The crystal had the ability to conjure memories in those who got too close, and even induced psychic episodes in some. When touched, though, it sort of... Wrapped a sheet around the brain. It was an immediate way of accomplishing what many magicians and witches have long strived for -- a way of cutting the brain off from those who wish to access it. Being telepathic, I could break through the barriers of most amateur attempts at such a feat. But this crystal gave an instant shield, one so powerful that it could not be pierced. The same thing occurs when two psychics come into contact, but for a slightly different reason.

"What the Commander did was crush up bits of the crystal, grinding it into dust and mixing it with ink. He then tattooed himself, and then all of his soldiers. These people, then, were always connected to the crystal, and therefore were always protected. The Commander was the first one to be tattooed, as an experiment. He learned to manipulate the power, control it to do his bidding. Almost... Becoming one with the crystal. He could, thusly, control aspects of his soldier's minds.

"As insurance that he would never be caught, Worth laid a sort of trap inside his soldiers' minds. He knew of the existence of telepaths, and he knew that if his organization was found to be active, we would try to find out more about them... Last fall, when I raided the first den, we interrogated one of the soldiers. Reida removed his tattoo by magick and I discovered the location of Blackhawk Hall. It appears that his "trap" was not triggered by this, perhaps because I was delicate in my searching. Perhaps it was supposed to, and malfunctioned. We cannot be sure. But when Erak tried to wipe some of his memories away, it was triggered.

"The Hawk, he... He was reduced to a shell of a person. Like a baby in the body of a grown man. He wept, and it seemed that there was nothing left inside his head except for the basest things. We decided to... To put him out of his misery. He's buried in that clearing, under a tree.

"This is how the Commander was able to kill his men inside the Hall. He perfected the trap, and was able to murder hundreds of them with a single thought. There was no thought, no mercy. They simply dropped dead where they stood."

For a long moment, the Council was changed. They looked at each other with horror, instead of the smug indifference they'd possessed minutes ago. Women in the crowd sobbed and children hid teary, confused faces in their mothers' skirts.

"Do... Do you know why the Commander would do this?" Masego spoke as if she was out of breath.

"He was starting to become paranoid, and suspected some sort of mutiny from his soldiers. I think, honestly, that no such thing was being planned, and that it was simply his mental state declining. He sought no resolution other than their deaths. He wasn't all together anymore."

"Did the accused know about this?"

"Yes. He watched it happen." There were disgusted mutterings from the crowd. "His despondent state was brought upon by abuses laid upon him by Commander Worth, and also by witnessing the deaths of so many people at once."

"One final question, Hersin Storm-Cloud. Do you believe that the accused should be executed if found guilty?" I let a long breath leave my nose and drew in another with my mouth closed.

"Altren Domaste," I began, "is responsible, both directly and indirectly, for more deaths than I believe he knows of. Negligence and deceit on such a scale cannot be ignored, nor forgiven, and must be met with blood. Yes, Altren Domaste should die." The masses let out one large wail, a sound that made my stomach twist up. It was a mixture of elations, sobs, mourning wails, and manic laughter. I turned without being dismissed, feeling my throat close up around the air I tried to breathe. Reida was crying, her face buried in her palms, and Audar was trying to comfort her as best as he could. I sat beside her and pulled her close to me.

"Now the accused may make a case for his innocence," proclaimed Masego. The crowd turned to booing her and shouting more abuses at Altren, who merely perked up his ears to listen. She slammed down her gavel, and they were reduced to discontented grumbling.

"What say you, Altren Domaste?" demanded Counselor Bergman, breaking her silence. Altren, who had, until now, only been looking forlornly down at his knees, rose his head. The people closest to the platform skittered backward. His eyes scanned the faces of his judges, and some of those in the crowd. But his gaze was not malicious, only curious. He seemed to be pondering something about his current situation. He swallowed and opened his mouth.

"I am not innocent," he croaked. A chorus of whispers arose. "I saw many horrors. So many of them, that I am not sure I *can* be innocent." He looked around at the crowd again. "I am... sorry." There was a pause, and then shouting.

"Murderer!" someone shrieked. "Defiler!" All eyes turned to a woman near the platform, only a few feet from where Altren sat. She was being held back from climbing the stairs by a man and another woman, and fighting hard against their grasp. "Your damn Hawks killed my son! My only child, my boy! Execute him!" The crowd roared with her.

"Your grandfather would be disgusted!"

"Burn him alive!"

"Draw and quarter the bastard!"

"My son, my son!"

City guards rushed in and pushed the crowd back away from the platform. Fists were thrown, blood spilled onto the pavement, and Masego was furiously pounding down on her gavel, but nothing seemed to change. Several people were dragged out of the square in handcuffs, and many more had to be restrained before they calmed down.

Ten minutes passed before the trial could continue, and the tension in the air had become suffocating. It appeared that Altren had started to cry.

"Altren Domaste," Counselor Masego said, "do you wish to say any more in your defense?"

"No," he whimpered.

"Then this court, presided over by the Top Council of the North Empire, shall now announce its verdict." The Counselors looked at one another and nodded. Counselor Friholm stood and looked into the crowd.

"We, the Honorable Head Counselors of the North Empire, hereby find the defendant, Altren Domaste, former king of the Empire, guilty of all charges, and sentence him to death by beheading."

The roar that rose from the crowd was deafening. People threw their hats into the air, fell over weeping, fainted, and smashed open bottles of alcohol, even kissed back other. Guards tossed Altren onto another prison cart and drove him away from the square. The Council made their way back into the castle, away from the people, who were intoxicated with the news, and so to be with drink. But on the balcony, things were solemn. Reida broke down again, sobbing into my chest. Denne put his hands together and pressed the sides to his mouth, closing his eyes. Erak flinched at the noise of the people and looked down at the floor. I just held Reida and decided to put off my feeling.

"It's over," Reida whimpered between ragged breaths. "It's really over." I pressed my lips to her forehead.

"I suppose they'll be awaiting your announcement, lass," Audar murmured to me, pointing with his eyes to the people huddled below the balcony, looking up at us. I gave a sigh and released Reida, standing to address them. I stood by the balcony and waited for quiet. I didn't trust my voice to yell over them. A few moments later, I spoke.

"I know that this past season was full of uncertainty," I said. "I know that you need a leader, someone who you trust will not have the same egregious faults as the man who you called King. All that anyone needs now is to move on with their lives and to feel safe once more. I understand, and I hope to put your minds at ease when I tell you I am here to reveal that a decision has been made.

"Over the past few weeks, many of you have written letters to us, and especially to me. They were full of wonderful things about us, and I am truly touched that you all think so highly of what we have done, and I am also truly honored that so many people believe that I can take this position as ruler of the empire. At first, I was doubtful of myself. The traitor-king has left bad airs about the palace, about the monarchy, and about the title. Those airs made me question the wisdom of taking the place. But when I read your letters, when my dearest and my bravest friends told me the same, I figured that so many people could not all be wrong.

"People of Highland, of Ealemoore, of the Empire... I am hereby decreeing that I, Talia Storm-Cloud, will be taking the Imperial Throne."

I saw the people react, but I tuned it out. I was tired of the noise. I bowed my head to the crowd, turned, and walked away. In my head, the vision of the smoke-being danced before me, and instead of the cheers and happiness, I heard her gravely words.

"You will rule."

THIRTY-TWO

The execution of Altren Domaste was set for the next day, February first. On Reida's request, we did not attend, and were instead given details by Erak, Denne, and the unit. My coronation was scheduled for the third, a rushed affair because the country was eager for a ruler. It was quite fine, as it turns out, that I stayed inside with Reida on the first, because I was constantly bombarded with questions from mousy palace servants, event coordinators, directors of feasts, florists, professional cooks, and tailors asking me my preferences on every detail there was to be had at a coronation. I was up to my neck in requests for most of the first and second of February.

On the night before my ceremony, Reida and I were undressing quietly, getting ready to go to sleep. Since the trial, she had been unusually somber, but I had been busy for nearly two days straight. Perhaps it was my fault. As I sat on the edge of the mattress, watching as she tied up her hair in silk ribbon, I decided that it probably was. Reida finished tying the last ribbon, and set her dainty hands down on the vanity where she sat. I saw her eyes meet themselves in the mirror, and she sighed.

"Talia?" she began.

"Yes?"

"I've been thinking quite a bit about what happened in those mountains."

"The battle, dear?"

"No, I mean... between us."

"Ah." Yes, this was my fault.

"I feel that, maybe, I was wrong to leave you like that, and on your birthday, too." I was surprised, and leaned back against one of the four posts that supported the canopy of our bed. "I was upset because of the timing, and I acted rashly."

"Don't feel bad," I told her. "Honestly, the timing was pretty shit. It was stupid of me to ask such a big question in that situation." She turned around in the seat to face me.

"I can't help but feel bad. When the men came out of the fortress, talking about piles of bodies and the smell of death, I thought the worst. I began to wonder, what if you had died, and were gone without... Without knowing that I really *do* want to marry you?"

I smiled, and then I laughed. Reida tried to hide her grin, pressing her chin to her chest and looking away.

"Reida," I said, sliding off of the edge of our bed, "you... You really want to marry me?" My cloak was lying across a chair. I reached inside and found a pocket.

"Yes, of course I do," she said, her voice catching in her throat. "Do... Do you still want to marry *me*?" I felt around in the pocket of my cloak and found what I was looking for. I pulled out the necklace I'd been keeping there, an ivory amulet in the shape of a circle. In the center was a piece of crystal, colored pink. I pulled Reida to her feet and stood in front of her.

"It would be the greatest honor to marry you," I told her. She choked out a laugh, and a tear fell from her eye. I held the necklace in my palm and showed it to her.

"It's beautiful," she whispered.

"It's for you," I replied, slipping the chain over her head and around her neck. She looked down at the amulet, then up at me, and then flung her arms around my neck.

"I love you," she said into my ear.

"I love you, too," I said. She pulled back to look at me, and then pressed her lips to mine. I put one hand on the back of her head and used the other to pull her close to me. She gave a tiny groan, one that sent a shiver down my legs. I bent at the knees and scooped her up into my arms. Reida wrapped her legs around my waist and I walked the few feet to the edge of our bed with her in my grasp. I laid her beneath me and pressed my mouth to her neck. With one hand, I untied her dressing gown and slipped it off of her chest.

I felt Reida's hands in my hair as my mouth moved down her torso, to her navel and below. She writhed against my mouth, biting her lips and getting caught up in the linens. Her slim, powerful thighs tightened around my head, her hands moved, and I smiled. I grazed my teeth against her soft flesh and she let out a small cry. I felt her stomach grow taut, and I looked up at her. One hand was over her mouth, the other caught up in the bedcovers. Around her neck were two chains, and the betrothal amulet rested off center between her small breasts. I just smiled.

The time passed between us like velvet over skin, and we slowly melted together.

THIRTY-THREE

Reida and I were roused by servants, two women who had come in every morning since we began using the room. Annastina was a cheerful, stout Nord woman who chirped her words and sometimes lost control of her tongue. Katya, on the other hand, was a slim, serious young Nord-raised Emïlan who always seemed to be worried about something. Together, they made a wonderful pair of ladies, quick to help and slow to anger, and ready with a joke or a handkerchief.

"Wakey, wakey, Miss Talia," Annastina chimed, drawing open the curtains.

"Yes, a very big day ahead of us," Katya said, coming over and patting Reida's shoulder. Reida groaned and rolled onto her back, shielding her eyes with the back of her hand. The morning sunlight made her necklaces sparkle. Annastina caught sight of the engagement chain and grinned widely.

"What's that I spy hanging from your neck, Miss Reida?" she teased. Reida giggled sleepily and covered her face with her palms.

"Last night I asked my dearest to marry me," I laughed, sitting up, legs hanging from the edge of the mattress. I yawned, then smiled.

"Oh, My Lady!" Katya exclaimed, clapping her hands together. She giggled and handed me my linen underthings. "A coronation *and* a wedding! How utterly wonderful." Reida sat up and patted her hair to see if the ribbons were still in it. They weren't having been scattered over the bed covers. She frowned and looked around the room groggily.

"Would you like a corset, ma'am?" Annastina asked me.

"No, thank you, Anna. I can't stand those wretched things."

"Aye," Katya added, "I heard they can squish your innards so hard that they'll come out your mouth!"

"I don't know," Reida said. "I think they make my hips look nice." Katya furrowed her brow.

"You don't need a corset to make them look nice," I teased her. She rolled her eyes, but she laughed, and stood to get dressed. After she'd put her linen shift on, Katya began to lace her up. Meanwhile, Annastina helped me into my dress. I was wrapped in a midnight-blue silk gown, one with buttons down the back to let me in and out. The sleeves were edged with white lace at the cuffs, and the bodice was embroidered with silver thread in a swirling pattern, dotted with crystals every so often. The fabric was a bit heavy, but it wasn't so cumbersome that I could not move. I sat in front of the vanity while Annastina ran some combs through my hair. The length of it was now nearing the small of my back.

"I can never seem to get past how lovely your hair is, My Lady," Anna said, looking at it. She'd finished running the finest comb through the tresses, and my hair looked smoother than the silk of my dress.

"Thank you, Anna," I said sincerely. "It's a shame that all I ever do is braid it."

"A good braid works when you're running through the woods shooting arrows," she said, "but an Empress should do something more elegant with her hair, don't you think."

"Oh, come now. I am not a very elegant person."

"You speak well enough that people can be filled with hope just by listening to how sure you are, My Lady. You might not be vain, but you know how to wear a dress, which is more than I can say for some of the people in this court."

"Anna!" Katya giggled. I laughed too, and Reida covered her mouth.

"Oh, please, Kat. You know it's true!" Katya just laughed.

"You two," Reida chided, though she found it just as funny.

"Hmm," Anna hummed. "I'll tell you this: I will keep some braids in your hair, but still have you looking like royalty."

"Thank you, Annastina." She nodded and ran her fingers through my hair. She began to braid the hair framing my face, pulling it back so the braids were made of the pieces on the sides of my head. She met the two braids back near the back of my head, and took two long pins from the vanity's drawer. She pinned the braids into my hair, leaving all the rest of it flowing down my back. I used a mirror to see the back.

"What do you think, My Lady?" Anna asked, smiling.

"It's lovely," I said, running a fingertip lightly over the sides of my head, feeling the soft bumpiness of my hair. "Where did you learn to do this?"

"My mother was a handmaid to Empress Malena, the traitor-king's mother. When she was the Princess, before she married, that's how my mother would braid her hair. Sometimes, when it was late at night and she didn't need to be with Malena, she would braid my hair like that before I went to bed, saying that I was a princess too." I laid my hand on top of Anna's.

"It's perfect," I told her.

"And... Done!" Katya said, stepping back from Reida. I turned and looked.

Reida stood glowing in a dress of light pink material, floaty and soft-looking. It was tight around her corseted bodice, but full in the skirt and the sleeves, making her look like some sort of flower bud, ready to burst open. She had pulled her hair up into a high, voluminous up do, and above her left temple, set into the hair, was a beautiful clip carved out of ivory, and painted to look like a lily. Around her neck hung her two necklaces, the one from her mother tucked into the bodice, but mine in full view. Annastina sucked in a breath.

"You look... Stunning," I said, thinking about my words longer than I meant to.

"As do you," Reida replied, a bit more color filling her cheeks.

"No," I said, standing. "You're absolutely gorgeous." I reached out my hand to her, and she took it. I was about to pull her in, to kiss her and tell her that I loved her, but outside the bell tower struck eight in the morning.

"Oh!" exclaimed Katya. "Come on, My Ladies! The coronation begins in *one hour*!" She and Annastina grabbed out elbows and ushered us out of our chambers.

We hurried through corridors and halls as quickly as our skirts would allow us to, and, twenty minutes later, entered the temple attached to the palace.

By eight-forty-five, I had been instructed by the High Priest of Highland exactly what to say and do. I was to swear the Oath of Forbearance, stating my good intent for the Empire, and let him place the crown onto my head. Then, I would stand holding the ceremonial Sword of Conquest, the blade that belonged to the first Emperor, forged over a hundred years ago, while the High Priest read the traditional words to make my rule legitimate and indisputable. The only way to remove me was to prove to the Top Council that I had broken my Oath, a formality that was not needed in the removal of Altren Domaste. He had vacated the throne on his own free will, instead of being kicked out on his ass.

After all this tradition and unnecessary pomp, I would walk out into the public square outside the temple, and address the crowd. And after that, the long, arduous, terrible hours of greeting the court and citizens of the Empire. It was not the civilians I was dreading, though. It was the royals with purchased titles who thought that, because they had money, they could "rule" a section of the Empire and collect taxes. Of course, most of the money came to highland to fill the Imperial coffers. But the premise of money equating right made me angry.

As the last ten minutes passed, I tried to clear my head of the nobles, and think about my duties in the coronation. My nerves were at a steady, if high, plateau. My left hand was shaking a bit, and my right one kept itself busy by becoming twirled in a lock of hair. The doors in front of me led into the temple, and the ones behind me into the public square. There was commotion and chatter coming from both ends, but more so from behind me. It seemed as if a hoard of people were watching me and walking about me, even though I was alone.

Finally, the bell tower struck nine times. The doors in front of me were pulled open, and suddenly I had five dozen pairs of eyes staring at me. I held my chin high and began my walk down the center aisle, toward the noble-looking High Priest. His face was rigid, but his eyes and his thoughts were encouraging. He'd done this twice already, for Altren, and then his wife Pernelle. Why, he thought, should this feel any different to him?

Aye, I thought, he might have done this before, but I certainly haven't.

As I came closer to the altar, I felt a little more at ease. I tried to remember all the times I had had more eyes on me than this. All the speeches I'd given to soldiers and townsfolk. This was very unlike those things, I knew, but putting it in perspective calmed me a little. I tried, also, not to hear the thoughts of those I passed. They thought about my hair, my dress, my composure, and my shoes. They thought about Reida and how proudly she was showing off what everyone knew to *obviously* be an engagement necklace. It made me feel happy, but at the same time, oddly afraid, to know that everyone knew that we were to be married.

It felt like I was walking for an hour. When I reached the altar, the High Priest smiled.

"Talia Storm-Cloud," he began, his voice echoing off the walls, "by what right do you claim the throne of the North Empire?"

"By right of merit," I answered, trying to make my voice heard.

"Then, by your merit, do you swear to protect and serve the citizens of the Empire?"

"On my honor, I do."

"And do you, by your merit, swear to enforce the laws brought upon by the Treat of The Wall, which ended the White War?"

"On my honor, I do."

"And do you, by your merit, swear as well to keep peace over the Empire as oft as you may have it?"

"On my honor, I do."

"Bow your head." I obeyed. The High Priest turned and picked up my crown. It was gold, with five prongs in the front. Each point had a jewel encrusted into it.

From left to right, they went ruby, sapphire, diamond, emerald, and amethyst. Each prong and each jewel represented one province in the Empire; Adaima, The Basin, Ealemoore, Hjellmun, and Middle Vale, in the same order as the jewels. It had been forged eighty-six years ago, when the White War ended and the Empire was born, and every ruler since had worn it. Looking at it gave me chills.

The high Priest slipped the crown onto my head. The cool metal touched my skin and I shuddered. The voice of Drünin pounded in my ears. I pulled myself up to my full height and was handed the Sword of Conquest. I turned slowly to face the people sitting in the temple. They stood to greet me. Reida and Audar sat in the first row on the left. I caught their eyes. From behind me, the Priest began to speak once more.

"On this, the fourth day of the second month, in the eighty-sixth year Post Empire, a new head bears the crown. By all the Divines' hands, and by the power they have given me, and that which the Empire has bestowed, I now invest in you the title and power of Empress Talia Storm-Cloud, Ruler of the North Empire."

The nobles in the rows clapped politely, but Audar and his gang erupted into cheering. Akua flung her arms around Erak and Henrik and Rudo kissed each other. Audar beamed. Reida looked like she was going to cry.

Her hand was clutched around her pendant. I turned and handed the sword to a servant.

"Place this in my quarters," I told him. He nodded and ran through a side door, cradling the sword like a newborn. I stepped down from the altar and took Reida by the hand. I looked around at my friends, and then all fifteen of us ran outside to greet the crowd. As I pushed open the doors, a roar went up through the people. I felt my throat close up and my eyes grow teary. I held my hand up for them to let me speak.

"Oh, my friends," I began, dabbing away my tears, "I am so very touched by everything you have done, and everything you have believed in, all the support you've given us over these months. I swore an Oath this day, one to protect you, and to rule with a peaceful and kind hand. I swore to serve you with respect, and with sympathy. You all know where I come from, what I believe in, and what I stand for. I do not wish to have so much power that I forget who I am; for I am just like you. My father was a farmer, my mother a seamstress when we needed money. I have not been coddled my whole life, and I certainly have not been blinded from the nature of the people who live in this Empire. I see you all not as subjects, not as a work force, nor as tools.

"You are people, just as I am a person, with your own wants, your own needs. I understand this. Beginning

370

today is a leadership which will take care of its people, and will never make them feel as though they have been used, deceived, or abandoned. It is because of you all that I have this power, and so I swear, on all the honor I have, that I will use it to do right by you!" There was a thunderous cheer. I held up my hand once more.

"Just one more thing," I said, "and then you may all come and celebrate. Last night, I asked Miss Reida Bollaïne, Head Matron, if she would do me an unprecedented honor. So now, I am officially telling you all for the first time -- Reida and I are engaged to be married. Erak laughed and nearly tackled us. The unit and Denne piled all around us and began to scream. The crowd went berserk, throwing up their hats. I pulled Reida closer and kissed her hard on the mouth. The roar grew louder.

THIRTY-FOUR

The coronation party was full of surprises. Traditionally, the nobility were the first to come and give their congratulations. Out of the eight noble houses, those of the Duke of Hjellmun, the Duke and Duchess of Ealemoore, the Count of Smajen, and the Baroness of Mount Ilien were the most flattering. Since the white War, those titles meant nothing in terms of power. The nobility who owned land could tax those who used it or lived on it, but eighty percent of the money went to Highland. Often, the nobles had nothing more than a tiny fortune and a lot of unfortunate breeding. Many of the titled families had lost their wealth over the years, and the few clans that remained clung to the ruler's coattails for favors, regardless of who the ruler actually was. I found the lot of them exceedingly dull. Those who came after were much more interesting.

Erak and Akua were the first couple to see Reida and I. Akua was beaming, clutching Erak's arm.

"Oh, Talia, Reida," she cried, "I'm so happy for you both! You two will make such fine rulers."

"Thank you, Akua," I said, reaching out to lay a hand on her shoulder. She smiled.

"And congrats on getting engaged," Erak said. He offered me his hand. I clasped mine around his wrist and he took hold of mine; a sign of respect between warriors.

"Yes, congratulations on that as well," Akua, kissing Reida on both her cheeks. Reida mirrored the gesture. A servant in a good suit began to look at the couple, and at the line forming behind them.

"We'll have to have a party soon," Erak said as they were being ushered away.

"Of course," I called, waving after them.

"Oh dear, we certainly *are* on a tight schedule tonight, aren't we?" Reida observed quietly. I nodded. Reida squealed as she saw who was next in line. The Denne family was approaching. Cora was being held by Audar, a proud father, and was dressed in in a red frock that matched her mother's. Lisbet looked slightly tired, but she was a beautiful thing to see, wrapped in crimson satin.

"Congrats, lasses," Audar exclaimed when he was close enough for us to hear him.

"Yes, it's so wonderful. People are feeling hopeful again, and patriotic," Lisbet said.

"Thank you, both of you," I said. "I'm so happy to hear that people are feeling good about our situation once more."

"Lisbet," Reida said, "may I please hold Cora later?"

"What kind of woman would I be, if I didn't let the woman who delivered my baby hold her?" Lisbet joked. Reida smiled down at the child. Cora looked up and saw her standing there. Her lips curled up into a smirk. Reida cooed at her. Audar laughed.

"Isn't she gorgeous?" he said, reaching out his finger for the baby to clutch. They were about to be shooed away.

"Come find us, Miss Reida," Lisbet told her, walking away with her husband. Cora peered back at us as she was carried off.

Henrik and Rudo came next, arm-in-arm. Henrik was teary-eyed, and when they were hinted at to move along, he hugged me so hard that he nearly had to be pried off of me. Rudo was his usual, quiet self, only looking out for his lover and making sure to hold his hand as they were leaving. The rest of Denne's unit came in pairs and trios, except for Eru. He was last in the line of our friends, alone and dressed in a polished uniform.

"Hello, ladies," he said, grinning.

"Eru!" Reida said, opening her arms to him. They embraced.

"How are you feeling?" I asked him. He shrugged and gave a half-smile.

"Meh. I'm all right most of the time. I might try to swing by and get someone on my arm to come home with me," he joked. I laughed.

"Just try and remember to get their name, all right?"

"Anything you say, Talia." Reida kissed him on the cheek before he left.

"Enjoy yourself," she told him. "Promise you'll try."

"I promise, Reida," Eru laughed. He sauntered off and picked up a glass of wine from a servant's tray.

"He's so lonely," Reida said sadly. I squeezed her hand.

"He'll find somebody," I told her. "Maybe more than one somebody." Reida smiled.

"I just want Eru to be happy. He's such a sweetheart, and his skill with magick is... incredible. It makes you wonder how he hasn't found his soul mate yet."

"Some people wait almost their whole lives before they do. You and I, we're lucky."

"I suppose you're right." I looked up to see our next visitor and nearly fell over. Walking up the center carpet was Hjond Raskun, doctor from Wittman's Creek. He had tears in his eyes.

"Hjond," I breathed. He smiled.

"How are you, Talia?" he asked, laughing because of how absurd he felt standing there, bleary-eyed.

"By the Five..." I looked to Reida. "Hjond, this is Reida. Reida, this is one of the people from Wittman's Creek. He's a physician, he helped me a lot when I left." I turned back to Hjond. "Reida and I are engaged."

"That's what I've heard around the punch bowls," he joked. "My, quite a bit has happened since you left. You're sort of a legend back in the village. The inn has been sold, it's doing quite well. Leila is pregnant now, it'll be her third."

"Oh my. Tell her to send me a letter some time. In fact, tell everyone to send me letters." I laughed.

"Has my dagger served you well, lass? Or, I mean, Your Majesty?"

"Excellently. And, please, just call me Talia, Hjond." He nodded, bearing a look that was almost melancholic. A servant tried to step in and tell Hjond he had to go, but Reida flashed him a severe look.

"One moment," she hissed. His eyes widened and he stepped back.

"No, no, I don't want to cause trouble," Hjond insisted. "We have much to talk about, Talia. I'll be here, just come find me." He looked at Reida. "It was an honor to meet you." She nodded gracefully, smiling. Hjond stepped out of the line, looking for a drink. A few minutes later, there was another surprise.

"Hello, songbird," someone familiar cooed at me. I snapped my head to the side. There, standing beside the line of people, was Majka and Azark, arms linked.

"I swear, you all just want to make me cry, don't you?" I demanded, pushing a tear from the corner of my eye. "Reida, love, this is Majka and Azark-El Manot, my friends from Silmen."

"We heard about what has happened since we last saw you," Azark said, looking more content than I had seen him in a while. "And we have heard of your deeds as well, Miss Reida Bollaïne."

"And we are proud of you both," Majka said. "We heard what sort of shape you were in, and what those brutes did to you, Miss Bollaïne. You are so strong, and so brave. And you made my songbird happy. Or, perhaps, she's *your* songbird, now."

"Thank you, Miss Majka, and Mr. Manot," Reida said. "You are both very kind. Thank you for being friends with my *lün*."

"Oh dear, it seems we're being moved along," Majka observed sadly, watching a servant boy approach them. "Do you think if I offer to sit on his face, he'll leave us be?" Reida covered her mouth with the back of her hand while I nearly choked on my own saliva. Majka gave us a sly smile.

"Majka, behave," Azark chided her.

"Oh, well. We'll be here!" The pair walked off. Reida looked at me, and we started laughing again.

Thirty minutes passed, and everyone cleared out of the line. The music was playing, alcohol was being passed around, and people were dancing. It was inviting. I looked at Reida.

"Do you want to dance with me?" I asked her. She smiled.

"Of course I do." I took her hand and stepped down onto the dance floor. Just then, a fanfare rang out. It wasn't brassy, though, it was high pitched and sweet-sounding. I looked over my shoulder, hesitantly stepping back onto the small platform.

"Are there more noblemen coming?" I asked Reida quietly. She shook her head.

"The Lady Night-Moore was the last on the list, and she came through an hour ago. There is no one else. But that fanfare. That wasn't a trumpet. That was..."

The doors at the end of the ballroom swung open, and a group of people entered the hall. A group of *Elves*.

There were two pin-straight lines of elves, three in each row. These Elven men were all blonde, pale-faced and serious looking, with drab, dark-grey robes draped over their thin bodies. They each held a banner, and on every banner was a different symbol. I recognized the symbols, but I couldn't recall where they were from. Not at the moment. But these six Elves were obviously not the ones I was concerned about. They were obviously the entourage for the seventh, a tall Elven man walking between and behind the two lines, making a pointed shape. The last man, their leader, was well over six feet tall, and looked to be everything that the entourage was not. He wore robes of winter-white, had silver hair, and wore a smug smirk on his face, instead of the stolid expression of his companions. As the procession made its way to Reida and I, people were stopped dead in their tracks, shock painted on their faces and in their blood. The music had stopped, and all was silent, save for the synchronized footsteps.

"Oh gods," Reida breathed. She looked like she was going to faint.

When the elves reached our platform, the two rows parted and the man in white walked between them. Around his neck he wore a pendant made of silver, bearing a symbol that resembled the ones on his servants' banners. Now I realized what was going on. I hadn't recognized the symbols because the set was incomplete. I knew it from the palace of the Elven Council; it was the symbols of the clans that made up the Council. This one was always pictured in the center, and as the largest of the group. This man was the head of the Elvish government. Never in the eighty-six years since the Empire was founded, had any member of the Elven Council visited the ruler, and especially not the head of it. And yet, here he was, come to my coronation party *with no invitation*.

He bowed graciously.

"Your Majesty," he began, his tone honey-sweet and cold, "would it be forward of me to assume that you know who I am?" I opened my mouth to respond, but Reida spoke first.

"You are Patron Alarch Dépren," she said, her voice uneven, "head of the *eal* of Dépren, and of the Elven Council." Everyone in the room seemed to have inhaled.

"Ahh, Miss Reida Bollaïne, I presume?" he replied.

"Yes, that is I."

"And Her Imperial Majesty, the Empress Talia Storm-Cloud. No doubt you are wondering why I have chosen now to come and make such a historic visit to your Empire. The truth of the matter is this: I have made the journey here to extend to you and your people a hand of opportunity and friendship. We would like to open up more trading routes, and more materials, to you, the Empress. Our nation is known for making fine goods of all sorts and necessities, yet we have surprisingly little resources to work with at this time. Meanwhile, your great Empire is teeming with lumber, mines, rivers, lakes, and natural resources of all sorts. It is of the Council's opinion that both our nations could benefit from such an alliance."

Every pair of eyes in the room switched from Alarch's face to mine. I took a long breath.

"On behalf of myself, and of the North Empire, I formally accept your kind and generous proposition," I said, pulling out one side of my skirt and bowing. Alarch smiled.

"Wonderful," he said, chuckling. "Please, do not allow me to interrupt the celebration any further. My companions and I will be seeing our way out." The Elves turned to leave, and made their way slowly out of the ballroom. I turned to a servant.

"Make sure they find their way out of the city," I told him. "Send mounted guards to keep the roads clear for them." He nodded and ran. I looked at Reida.

"I believe," she said, "we need a little something to get back into a festive mood." She inhaled and let her palms glow purple. The crowd watched as a ball of energy formed in her hands. When it got to be the size of a melon, she tossed it up into the air. The orb flew up, nearly touched the ceiling, and then exploded. There was a flash of purple light, and then thumb-nail sized pieces of energy began to fall down onto the crowd like snow. Children screamed with laughed, and the adults began to laugh with them. Music started to play again. I heard Cora squealing in the distant, and Audar Denne's booming laugh. I turned to my fiancée.

"What do you think of that visit?" I asked her quietly.

"I cannot say what drives him," she replied honestly. "I have only conjecture. I sense, though, that we should be wary."

"I didn't try to read him. Did you?"

"I reached out, but his mind was sealed off. Not like the Blackhawks, it was a different sort of energy. One built up from years of practice, instead of a bit of quick magick. There were holes, I could feel them. But I didn't want to risk searching, and having him know that I was prying."

"Aye, if someone has that much training, they would surely be aware when they're being searched. I am assuming he is a magick-user, then."

"One of the best there is. A loyal devotee of Drünin, and has been for three hundred and seventy years. He fought in the last war that the Elves had, and gained quite a reputation for his magick abilities. Alarch was not a Counselor then, only an officer in the Elvish army. But by the end of the war, he'd found his way to the Elvish equivalent of a Hersin. In only six years, he jumped three ranks. And it was all because of his skill with offensive magick. There were... Rumors. People whispered about how he could incinerate people with a glance, snap his fingers and turn them to dust. My mother used to tell me stories, ones that her mother told her..." I got closer to her and brought my voice down even lower.

"How could he have fought in the last Elvish war? You said five hundred was old for full-blooded Elves, and yet the last war between your people and ours was six hundred years ago, before your mother was even born,"

"There were rumors that he used magick to increase his lifespan, as well."

"Isn't that considered to be against nature?"

"Of course. But who is going to stop him? He has had all of Glïnéa in his pocket for nearly a hundred and fifty years. He can execute people, Talia. Killing someone in that circumstance is one of the biggest offenses of all in the eyes of Méllék and his Divines. But they are not here on this plane, and last year there were three executions in Rodènsï, all in the months before I left home. Gods only know how many more there were after I crossed the border."

"You are correct, then, my love. We must be extremely wary with him."

"Your Majesty!" called a woman from the crowd. I looked over toward her voice.

"Yes?" I answered.

"Won't you come join us?" She held up a glass of wine and smiled. I chuckled.

"What do you say, *lün*?" I asked Reida. She took my hand.

"I *do* want to go hold Cora..." she said, laughing. "Oh, come on. Let's go be carefree for a little while."

"For as long as you'll allow me," I replied. She pulled me into the party.

The End